JESSICA SORENSEN

FRACTURED SOULS

A SHATTERED PROMISES NOVEL

For information:
jessicasorensen.com

Cover Design and Photography:
Mae I Design
www.maeidesign.com

Interior Design and Formatting:
Christine Borgford, Perfectly Publishable
www.perfectlypublishable.com

Fractured Souls (Shattered Promises, Book 2)
ISBN : 9781490409573

PROLOGUE

L ET ME DIE. Please. I don't want to wake up hollow and numb, a ghost of myself. I want to remember what it felt like to be touched all over by someone, be kissed like I meant something; if only for a moment. I want to remember what I went through, both the good and the bad. If I can't, then I want to die. Please, please, let me die.

"Gemma Lucas," a welcoming voice graces my ears. "Can you hear me?"

I blink my eyes open to wispy clouds lazily floating across a crystal blue sky. The sight is breathtaking and makes me feel calm and serene. Yet something about it is off. The clouds look almost too wispy, like a smeared watercolor painting, and the sky has jagged edges that slope in distinct directions as if it's one gigantic, glistening crystal.

I roll to my side and through the gemstone grass. Where am I? "The City of Crystal," I murmur. "What the hell?"

I quickly push to my feet. The land is paved with a winding path of shattered teal porcelain that leads to a silver throne perched on a podium. To my right is a crystal wall that fences through the grass, flashing vibrant images of people and landscapes like a television screen.

"Why am I here?" I turn in a circle, searching for life,

a Foreseer, even Dyvinius.

"Gemma." Suddenly a figure of a woman flickers across the screen then rapidly fades, lines covering the glass. "Gemma, can your hear me?" Her voice is glitched, but it's still clear enough that I recognize the sound and pitch of it.

I race through the grass and up to the screen, panting as I tip my head back. "Mom, can you hear me?"

A woman with flowing brown hair and bright blue irises appears clearly on the screen. In the background, a circular light forms, glowing brighter and brighter until a lake forms, I've seen it before. The entrance to The Underworld.

"I need you," my mom whispers, pressing her hand to the glass. Drops of water drip from her hand and down the screen. "Gemma, please help me . . . save me . . . I can help . . . I know about the star, you just need to save me. Please."

I press my hand to the glass, lining our fingers up. "Mom, I don't think I can . . . I think I might be gone . . . I think my body's somewhere and my mind's dying."

She shakes her head, her hair blowing in the wind as the water starts to vibrate and ripple. "You'll be okay . . . now please come help me."

Tears burn at the corners of my eyes as I push my hand harder to the glass, as if I can go into it, however there's resistance as the screen begins to splinter and crack. "How can I?"

"Look around you. Gemma," she says as the water rolls closer to her, the cracks spreading and spider-webbing the glass. "You have so much power. The possibilities of what you can do are endless."

"Is that how?" I panic as she falls back with the waves, her hand leaving the glass. "Mom, can my power *save you?"*

She reaches out as she's hauled back into the lake. Seconds later, thousands of boney arms emerge from the water and pull her down beneath it. I scream, backing away as the image fades and the glass wall bursts. Sharp fragments sail through the air and claw at my skin as water rushes through the ruined screen and into the land around me. The force knocks my feet out from under me and I fall to the ground on my back. The rapids nearly slice me in half as they roll over me and I'm pulled away with the violent movement. I sink and then submerge, fighting against the water, flailing my arms and kicking my legs while trying to figure out how to swim. It's a powerful force, though, one that I have no control over. And finally, I lose the willpower to fight and just let myself drown.

CHAPTER ONE

BETRAYAL.
Betrayal.
Betrayal.

It's an echo in my head.

How could this happen? How could Alex do what he did? How could he hurt me . . . there's so much pain inside. I hate it. Hate him. Hate myself for being so stupid and trusting him. There's so much loathing and anger inside me that I feel like I'm rotting, spoiled, decaying on the inside and turning into something morbid that no one wants. The vile feeling spreads and the weight of it crushes me. I open my mouth to scream, but my lungs burst and bleed out; at least that's what it feels like. At least I want them to because it will take away the agonizing pain inside my heart.

Never again.

Never.

I'll never trust anyone in this world again. I'll never get crushed. I'll protect myself at all costs; that is, if I ever get out of this darkness.

Then suddenly my head starts to buzz like a Goddamn bug trapped in a light, over and over again. It just about drives me crazy; it's to the point where I feel like I'm going to gouge my ears out. I seriously consider it, too, but I can't see past the darkness—I can't see light.

My skin swelters with invigorating warmth, my body peacefully relaxing as the ground below me becomes soft and inviting. I feel content, blissfully and almost alarmingly content. *Feel?* What the hell . . . I'm supposed to be dead, or at least locked in a coffin within my own head.

My eyes shoot open as I bolt upright, but as the blood rushes from my head, I collapse back onto the mattress. I swiftly glance around and my jaw drops. After the dream I was having, I had expected to be buried in water, however I'm dry and breathing. Alive. Unlike my mom.

I try not to choke on the image of her drowning in the water, the Water Fey dragging her down, and I take in where I am. I'm lying in a bed in a room with pale purple walls and a small window that lets in minimal sunlight. The view outside is painted with colorful lights and flamboyant buildings that stretch toward the skyline.

"I know this place . . ." I gradually sit up, clutching my throbbing head. "Vegas . . . I'm in Vegas."

"It was the safest place I could think of." The sound of Alex's voice sends a chill down my spine, but then electricity counteracts it and my body erupts with heat, awakening my heart from a very deep slumber.

He ambles through the doorway, taking tentative steps as he inches toward the bed. Emotions of hate mixed with lust amplify and every image of the last time we were in bed together flashes through my mind; the way he'd made me finally feel like I was breathing. Then he stole it all away, betraying me, ripping my heart out of my chest and shredding it to pieces; he probably still has my blood on his hands.

"Are you okay?" He comes to a stop at the foot of the

metal-framed bed. He's wearing a black t-shirt and a pair of loose-fitting, dark blue jeans and his brown hair is disheveled and damp. He also has a black smudge on the center of his forehead, like ash or charcoal. He almost looks like a normal guy, completely harmless, yet his welcoming demeanor is just an illusion. I know this—I've learned better.

I throw the blanket off me and swing my legs over the side of the bed. I'm not wearing the same clothes; a pair of boxer shorts and a t-shirt that don't belong to me have replaced them. I don't even want to think about how I got changed while I was blacked out. One of my wrists is bandaged up . . . the one I had slit myself when my emotions had gotten the best of me . . . I can remember. *I can remember?* "Stay away from me you asshole."

"Gemma, I'm not going to hurt you." His voice is as smooth as silk as he winds around the bed, his radiant, green eyes fixed on me. "I promise I won't hurt you. Everything's okay."

I laugh sharply as I put weight on my weak legs. "That's the biggest lie I've ever heard come out of your mouth, which says a lot since you're the biggest liar I've ever met."

Alex stops dead in his tracks, his skin tinting red with his anger. "What the hell is that supposed to mean?"

My knees shake as I square my shoulders and find my stability. "It means your promises are bullshit. At least, the ones you make to me." I fling my arms out to my sides. "You told me once that you made me a promise that you would never to hurt me, but I'm finding that hard to believe since you keep hurting me over and over again."

A condescending look appears in his eyes. "My promises got you to Adessa's, *safe* and *sound*."

"Safe and sound doesn't exist." I step back toward the

wall, dropping my hands to my sides. "And I'm not stupid enough to believe otherwise."

"But it does . . . right now it does." He matches my step and instantly reduces the space I put between us. "And you'll understand why, if you just let me explain what happened."

I dare to move forward, needing to get out of the room and away from him. "I'm leaving. I don't know why I'm even able to walk around . . . why I'm alive and normal, but I'm not going to waste my time listening to your lies."

"You're walking around normal because of me—because of how I feel about you." He's coursing with infuriation as he inches to the side, obstructing my path to the doorway. "Just let me explain."

I dodge to the right and skitter around him, however I'm like a newborn deer and my knees give out. I collapse to the floor, but before I hit, his arms encircle my waist and he catches me. Then he swiftly picks me up, slipping his arms underneath my knees, and carries me over to the bed, setting me back down before I can even conjure up a protest. I start to sit back up, but he puts his hands down on the mattress, one on each side of me, and lowers his face toward mine.

"I just need five minutes to explain," he almost begs, and it sounds strange coming from his lips; almost as if he's never begged for anything before. I bet he's been begged to a lot, though. "Five minutes for me to tell you what happened, and then, if you don't like it, I'll leave."

I search his eyes for the person that lay with me in the bed, but I'm not sure who that is exactly—who he really is. I find myself hoping that I can find out. I hope he doesn't crush me again. What I really want to do is run away, yet he's has me trapped and I know how strong he is—how easily he could chase me down and hurt me if he wanted to.

"Five minutes." I push him back a little, his chest searing hot beneath my palm. "That's all you have, and if one single thing sounds like a lie, then you leave, not just the house, but my life."

He nods without hesitation and leans back, allowing me to sit up.

"Where are we?" I finally ask when he doesn't say anything right away.

He sits close to me on the bed, his hands near his lap as he keeps flexing his fingers, channeling his tension there. "We're at Adessa's, the Witch we went to see in Vegas to get the crystal. This is her house which is attached to her store."

"Is it safe here?" I scoot to the edge of the bed and put my feet onto the hardwood floor.

He nods. "For now. Aislin and Adessa covered the house with charms."

I raise my eyebrows, overwhelmed already. I'm still getting used to the supernatural stuff that's invaded my life over the last couple of weeks. "How did we get here?" I wonder. "Because the last thing I can remember . . ." I trail off, aiming him a dirty look. "Well, I think you can remember what happened."

"Don't blame me until you hear the whole story," he says. "And we got here because Aislin transported us here. It's a simple as that."

"Oh, yes, super simple," I respond in a derisive tone. He's already getting under my skin, not just because he's pissing me off, but because of the damn electricity. He's sitting close to me, too close to me on a *bed*. It's driving me mad because my mind is begging me to let him do things to me; touch me, kiss me, fill the void within me. "Where are Laylen and Aislin?"

"It is that super simple," he retorts. "Aislin and Laylen are downstairs and if you want the whole story then keep quiet and listen." He watches me with challenge in his eyes and I know he's doing it on purpose, attempting to get under my skin.

Needing to get the last word in—needing to prove that I still have some say in this—I say, "Fine, continue."

The corners of his lips quirk, as though he's enjoying the bantering. "After Aislin went back to get Laylen in Nevada, there was a huge ambush of Death Walkers. I guess their cold ruined Aislin's transporting crystal so they had to bail out and come here to get another one. Then they transported to Colorado and ended up saving all of us."

I fold my arms across my chest. "But how? I mean, if I remember correctly, which I'm pretty sure I do since I was the target of everything that was going on, there was an ambush of Death Walkers there also, along with your father who was trying to kill me with that smoking rock."

"It's called a *memoria extracto,*" he says flatly.

"Thanks," I mumble. "Now if I ever have to take a test on strange crazy things that shouldn't exist, I know I'll pass."

He covers his mouth with his balled fist, either pissed off or trying to hide a smile. "Well, I'm glad to see that you still have your twisted sense of humor."

"Barely," I retort, holding his gaze while he holds mine. "But I can already feel it fading, just like everything else inside me." All I can feel at them moment is rage. It's like a fire, ready to burn me to pieces. I wish I could turn it off, but I can't seem to figure out how. Shit. What if something's wrong with me? What if whatever did happen broke my emotions instead of getting rid of them.

He lowers his hand onto his lap and sighs. "When

Aislin and Laylen showed up at the cabin," he continues. "Stephan and the Death Walkers were gone. They just upped and left while I was—"

"*What?*" I interrupt. "That doesn't make any sense, since Stephan was pretty much dead set on breaking my soul and mind apart." I pause, eyeing him over, closely watching his reaction. "Something you were pretty dead set on helping him do."

He swiftly shakes his head. "No, I wasn't."

"Yeah, you were. At first I thought you were going to save me, which felt . . ." I trail off, trying to figure out exactly how it felt, but I can't quite piece what I'm feeling together. "And then I guess you changed your mind and decided to side with the devil."

"I didn't decide to side with my father," he insists. "I did what I had to do because it was the only way to keep you safe."

I tap my foot anxiously on the floor. Do I want to sit here and listen to more of his story? Or try to run? I feel like I'm in a maze where almost every end is a dead end or a trap and it's hard to figure out which path will get me to wherever I need to go. Also, my emotions are confusing, combine them with the electricity; I feel like I'm being pushed toward Alex and then pulled back. Pushed and pulled. Pretty soon I'm going to tear in half.

"I know what I saw." I place a hand on my bandaged wrist. "You stood by while your father tried to erase my mind and I bled all over the floor; I could have died."

"I would have never let you die." He reaches for me, however I hover back, shaking my head, not ready to be touched by him yet. He sighs and withdraws his hands to his lap, clenching his fist so tightly his knuckles turn white. "Do you remember that necklace I gave you?"

I grab the hollow of my neck and then panic at the

bare space. "Wait. Where is it?"

He sets a hand on my knee before I have time to react and a burst of passion swells through me. "Relax. I have it."

That doesn't make me relax at all. I keep remembering how Laylen and I talked about Alex being brainwashed. What if he's right? What if he has to be here because the *memoria extracto* didn't work and Alex is helping his father hold me hostage until they can figure something else out?

"Why do you have it?" I ask warily.

He takes a deep breath and gradually frees it, his fingertips massaging my kneecap. "When I gave you the necklace, I wasn't just giving it to you because it belonged to you. I gave it to you because it has sugilite in it," he says. I'm about to ask him what sugilite is when he adds, "That's the purple stone in the center of the locket. It protects whoever's wearing it from certain kinds of magic." He pauses. "Like the mind erasing kind of magic."

"I thought you said my mother gave me the necklace when I was little?" I ask. "Did she give it to me to protect me from something, too?"

He sweeps my hair back off my shoulder and I tense, unsure why he is so persistent about touching me. "She gave it to you because you have the star's energy in you. It was her way of trying to protect you from anyone who tried to use magic on you to get to the star's power."

"So why didn't it work when I was little?" My voice is sharp and bitter. "When Sophia detached my soul from my emotions? Why didn't it protect me then?"

Alex shuts his eyes, his face contorted in pain. "Stephan knew what it was and he took it off you before Sophia detached your soul." He opens his eyes and they're glossed over. "That's why I tucked it into your shirt in the

Jeep. So he wouldn't see it and take it off."

I remember when Alex was about to climb out of the Jeep back at the cabin in Colorado. The Death Walkers and Stephan had just shown up and stopped us from running away. Alex had reached over and tucked the locket under the collar of my shirt, whispering, *whatever you do, keep that hidden. Don't let anyone know you have it.*

"So you were planning all along to save me." I'm doubtful because none of this makes sense. There are so many questions without answers, like why Stephan and the Death Walkers would just walk away.

He shrugs. "Pretty much."

"But that goes against everything you said . . . how my soul had to be detached or else the star's power would die and then the portal would open and the world would end." I frown, thinking of my dooming fate. That I might die, or live and be hollow, neither of which were options that I wanted. I want normalcy, plain and simple.

His hand slides up my thigh and halts at the top of my shorts and the rage burning inside me fizzles. My heart and body want one thing and my mind another. *What do I want?*

"Things changed between us . . . you know that. When we . . . after we . . ." He drifts off.

"Had sex." I strive to sound blasé, but my cheeks heat.

His eyes are secured on mine and he displays no emotions at all. "It was more than that, wasn't it?"

My cheeks flame even hotter, though I refuse to look away. "I have no idea . . . I have nothing else to compare it to. Besides, that was my fault . . . I pretty much begged you to do it."

He keeps one hand on my thigh and reaches his free hand up to cup my face. Being touched intimately always throws me off guard since I didn't experience any human

connection for about fourteen years. Something as simple as being touched both frightens and enthralls me to
the point where I do irrational things, solely based on my
hormones.

"You asked me to kiss you. I'm the one that took it
that far because I . . ." he grapples for words he never does
find. "And I meant what I said when I woke you up. If my
father wouldn't have shown up, I would have gotten you
out of there and hid until we figured something out."

"But we didn't make it that far, did we?" I scoot away
from him. "And then you held that rock up in front of
me . . ."

He rubs his hand across his face, letting his fingers
linger on the smudged black spot on the middle of his
forehead.

"What happened to your head?" I reach out to touch
him, but then retreat. The last thing I want to do is trust
him again and end up in a situation like back at the cabin
in Colorado.

"It's from the *memoria extracto*," he whispers, rubbing the spot with his fingertips. I'm surprised when it
stays and doesn't smudge.

"Why did it do that to you?"

"Because the magic bounced back on me."

I scan him over; long lean arms, solid shoulders, a
firm, stubbly jawline. "But then how could you . . . do
you . . . huh?'

"That's what the sugilite does," he explains. "Those
who try to use harmful magic on someone who has sugilite on them, automatically gets magical harm done on
them instead. So when I used it on you it bounced back
on me."

"And you knew that was going to happen?" I gape at
him.

"Better me than you." He shrugs, acting nonchalant, the exact opposite from the meaning his words convey.

"When you say the magic bounced back on you, does that mean your memory was erased?" I inquire. "Because you seem fine now."

"I am fine now," he assures me. "But for a while there . . ." he blinks and then his face contorts like he's remembering an excruciating memory.

"But you weren't fine?"

"No. I blacked out. When I woke up Stephan and the Death Walkers were gone."

"And you have no idea where they went?" I question. "Or why they just left?"

He shakes his head. "By the time I came to, Aislin and Laylen had shown up to a torn up cabin and you were still passed out."

Pushing past my confliction, I extend my hand forward to rub the black spot on his head. The contact brings a euphoric tingle to my body that I secretly bask in. "Is this permanent?"

He watches me intently. "It'll go away eventually."

I withdraw my hand to my lap, fighting the impulse to touch him some more. "What about your head?"

The corners of his mouth tug upward. "What about it?"

"Is it okay?"

"Do you want it to be okay?"

I tuck my hand under my leg to keep from touching him again. "I'm sure it probably has its benefits."

"Like what?" he wonders, looking amused.

"You tell me," I say. "I'm sure you have answers. More than you're probably sharing."

Frowning, he retrieves something from the pocket of his jeans. "Put this back on." He holds his hand in front of me and in his palm is a silver, heart-shaped locket with a small, violet stone in the center.

I don't take the locket right away. Can I trust Alex to help me instead of harm me? Is he finally telling the truth? Considering his track record, my initial instinct is to scream *no!* However, there's something else inside me that's conflicting. My emotions. Those Goddamn tingling and fluttering sensations in my heart that are fucking with my head.

"You can have it back." He urges his hand at me. "I want you to wear it again, so you'll be protected."

I still don't take the necklace. "I don't understand why you took it off me to begin with."

"Because Aislin had to use magic to get us out of the cabin," he explains, slipping his hand under mine and forcing me to open my palm. "And if you would have had it on it would have hurt her."

He lifts the necklace above my hand and releases it from his fingers, allowing it to fall into my palm. The metal is cold, yet his touch brings warmth. He chews on his bottom lip as he studies me while I put the necklace around my neck and secure the clasp. I feel weirdly better now that it's back on, so I release a stressed breath, shutting my eyes for a moment, taking everything in. I don't know what to do. What to believe. I know what I want to do and that's pretend that Alex is a trustworthy person, but things aren't that simple.

I open my eyes. "Alex?"

"Hmm . . . ?" He looks distracted in his thoughts.

"What happened to the *memoria extracto?*" I ask.

He snaps back to reality and shifts uncomfortably on the bed. "Aislin and Adessa destroyed it with a spell."

"And what about your father?"

"What about him?" he asks, his tone clipped. "I

already told you I don't know where he is."

I observe his reaction closely. He's upset about something. "But you said he's immortal, and that even the sword won't kill him."

He presses his lips together. "Yeah."

"That's all you have to say?" I'm baffled. "Is yeah?"

He shrugs. "What else do you want me to say besides the fact that he is?"

"How about explaining why you never mentioned this and how we're supposed to get rid of him if he can't die." I clutch onto the locket, wishing it could make me feel safe, too, rather than so vulnerable.

His expression hardens as he inclines back, putting space between us. "Even though it seems like he's working for the bad side, he's still my father and I don't want to kill him."

"*Seems* like he's working for the bad side?" I fume. "Try *is* working for them. In fact, I'm pretty sure he might be the leader."

"Of who exactly?" he counters heatedly. "The Death Walkers? Demetrius?"

"How the hell should I know? I never know half the shit that's going on."

"Exactly." He stands to his feet, towering over me. "Which is why you have no right to make accusations."

"I have the right to do whatever I want." I rise to my feet very unsteadily and brace my hand on the bedpost to keep my balance. "Besides, the reason why I don't know what's going on is because you keep half the shit to yourself."

"And now we're back to where we started," he snaps hotly, stepping closer. Even though I'm tall, he's much taller and I have to tip my chin up to meet his beautiful, yet heated eyes. "No matter what I say, you never trust me."

I point my finger at the door, ignoring the electric current boiling in my blood and dampening my skin with sweat. "Which means you can leave. That was the deal, right?"

His gaze darkens as he slants closer to me, stopping only inches from my face. I can feel my heart thrashing in my chest and I'm almost certain I can hear his as well, erratic and pounding. At first I think he's going to kiss me and I wonder how I'll react if he does. The need spiraling inside my body makes me speculate if I'll make a dumb choice, one based solely on my hormones.

But then he steps back and raises his hands in front of him, surrendering. "Fine, you want me gone, then I'll leave." He storms to the door, pausing just in front of it to call over his shoulder, "Aislin put some clothes in the dresser if you want to get dressed." He jerks open the door and steps out in the hallway.

"Where are you going?" I ask, but he slams the door shut, cutting me off and leaving me alone in an unfamiliar room with my thoughts and confusion.

I stare at the door for an eternity, trying to decide what to do. There's no way he would really leave, is there? I doubt it, though I'm still not simply going to sit around and wonder.

I stumble over to the window, dizzy and kind of nauseous. How long have I been out? I glance outside at the city and the sun setting. Hours? Days? Weeks? I have no idea. The last thing I can remember is Alex holding the rock in front of me and then seeing images of what I'd be missing out on, or what I thought I'd be missing out on. Then I blacked out and saw my mom begging me to help her. The question is: was that a dream or something more?

Moving away from the window, I open the top dresser drawer and find a few clothes folded up inside. I take out a pair of very small, black shorts and a tight, maroon tank top that has a black ribbon lacing the front. Definitely not my style, but everything else in the drawer resembles the slutty gothic look so I slip them on anyway. There's some sort of elastic in the shirt that pushes my breasts up and I feel fully exposed as I pull my tangled, long, brown hair up into a ponytail and secure it with an elastic that I find on top of the nightstand next to the bed. I carefully peel back the bandage on my wrist, wincing as the tender wound hits the air. It's still fairly fresh, which means too much time couldn't have gone by since I'd cut it open.

Sighing, I wrap it back up and search the room for my shoes. I find a pair of black combat boots next to the foot of the bed and quickly put them on.

I feel almost naked with the way my ass hangs out of the shorts and I wonder why on earth Aislin would put this outfit in there for me. It's definitely not her style, either.

I go out into the hall, wondering where I'm supposed to be going. There's a line of doors on my one side and a spiral stairway to my other. I turn for the stairway, when arms slip around my waist. I open my mouth to scream when a hand clamps down over my mouth. There's no electricity, no sign that it's Alex and all I can think is that I'm in deep shit.

CHAPTER
TWO

"GEMMA," SOMEONE WHISPERS in my ear. "Relax. It's just me."

I try to twist my arms free as I squirm against the stranger. Yet they easily haul me back into the room as if I weigh nothing.

"Jesus Christ, Gemma. Calm down," Laylen says in a sultry voice as he loosens his grip on me. "It's me. It's Laylen." He lets me go and I reel around, panting with my hand over my heart as he shuts the bedroom door.

"*What* the fuck are you doing?" I pant profusely as I work to slow down my rapid heartbeat. "You scared the shit out of me."

"Shhh . . ." Laylen puts his finger up to his deep red lips that are ornamented with a silver loop. He glances around the room and then at the window. "Keep your voice down."

I take in the sight of him, insanely tall, at least a few inches taller than Alex with striking blue eyes and skin as pale as snow. Wisps of his blonde hair hang down his forehead, the tips dyed blue. He's dressed head to toe in black, very gothic, very sexy, in a way that sends me yearning for things it really shouldn't. I remember how

I used to dream about Laylen, back before I met him, or re-met him anyway. The dreams were erotic and would alternate between Alex and Laylen. I wonder if they mean anything. If down the road, I could end up doing something with Laylen. The idea is exciting and unsettling at the same time, considering I have feelings for Alex and Aislin has feelings for Laylen, yet I also have feelings for Laylen, too; I merely can't quite decipher what kind yet.

"Why do I have to be quiet?" I hiss, standing up straight and stepping toward him. "What's going on?"

He glances nervously around the room again and then locks the door. "So what do you think about what Alex told you?" He rests back against the door, his gaze flickering to the top of the shirt that I'm pretty much bulging out of.

"I'm not sure." I fold my arms over my chest self-consciously. "Some of it seems plausible, but it seems like he's still keeping a lot from me. Like the fact that his father just disappeared along with the Death Walkers and just left us all behind."

He rakes his fingers through his hair, leaving his hand on the back of his neck, his elbow bent upward. "I'm unsure about that part, too . . . I'm hesitant about a lot of things."

I sink down on the foot of the bed. "When you guys came back from Nevada, how did everything seem? Was it only Alex and me inside that mess of a cabin?"

He takes a seat beside me, sitting near enough that our legs press together. I can't help thinking about how he can manipulate emotions and, for a second, I contemplate telling him to give me a moment of solace, anything to make the pain go away.

"Pretty much," he says. "Alex was just sitting there, holding you. He looked like he was freaking out, but then when he saw us, he went completely calm."

It's so confusing, a tangled mess of wires that need to be unwound. I ask him a few more questions about what Alex has told him so we can compare stories. For the most part, everything adds up, nearly matching. Maybe a little too much, as if Alex's story was rehearsed. I think about all the times he lied to me; how he pretended he didn't know me when he did, how he knew my memories had been erased, yet only divulged the information when I asked him. He's extremely good at keeping secrets, what's not to say he doesn't have more locked away inside him?

"So do you believe him?" I ask. "When he says he has no clue where the Death Walkers and Stephan went or why they ran off?"

He stretches out his legs in front of him and crosses them at the ankles. "I have no idea what the hell to believe." He leans in, his shoulder brushing against mine as he lowers his voice. "What I do know is that there's a slim to none chance that the Death Walkers are just going to leave when they know you have the star's energy in you. Plus, if Stephan's in on it with Demetrius and the Death Walkers, which I'm sure he is, then he's the kind of person that'll do anything to get what he wants. So walking away from you is pretty much impossible if what he wants is the star."

"From what I saw that's what he wants," I tell him. "I mean, he showed up with a herd of Death Walkers."

"I wonder why, though. I wonder if it's for the same reason as Demetrius . . . if he wants to open the portal . . . or he has other plans for you and the star."

"Laylen did you . . . do you know that Stephan is Immortal?"

With a clenched jaw, Laylen nods. "Not until yesterday, though . . . when we got you here. Alex explained

23

some things that apparently he's been keeping from everyone—even Aislin. Like the fact that his asshole of a father pretty much can't be killed."

"How is that possible, though?" I eye over the black ink tattooing his skin, the Mark of Immortality. "I mean, I know you are because you're a Vampire, but what does that make Stephan?"

Laylen scratches at the Greek-like marks on his arm. "He could be a lot of things. There are a lot of different breeds that get the mark . . . Alex says he doesn't know why his father has it, though. Only that Stephan told him once that he couldn't be killed by anything." Laylen rolls his eyes as I cringe. "Alex didn't even question him, and I'm not surprised. He always did what his father said . . . until in the cabin . . . supposedly." He pauses. "But still, wouldn't it seem normal to be suspicious? Especially when he told Alex that he can't even be killed with the Sword of Immortality, which is supposed to be able to kill *all* Immortals."

"I'm not sure if Alex fully understands the word suspicious," I point out. "He doesn't even understand why I'm suspicious over everything he does . . . but how can I not be after everything that's happened?" I pause, taking an unsteady breath. "I'm not sure who I can trust."

Laylen offers me a sympathetic look and then places a hand on my leg. His touch causes a very mystifying feeling inside me that coils all the way up to my thighs. "You can trust me."

"I know that." I actually mean it, too. Something about Laylen makes him seem like a very trustworthy person, which is what I need at the moment. "What else did Alex tell you?"

Amusement develops on his face. "He told me that you guys took a little trip to the City of Crystal where you discovered that you're a Foreseer."

I rub my hand tensely on the mark on the back of my neck—the inky black circle wrapping the 'S'—the one that brands me a Foreseer. "Did he tell you about the vision I went into while I was down there?"

"He did," Laylen hesitantly answers. "Do you want to talk about it? I know it has to be hard for you to deal with, seeing that happen to your mother."

Images stab at my mind like shards of glass; Stephan forcing my mom to go into the lake, the entrance to The Underworld where she's been tortured by Faeries. "Do you think there's any way she can still be alive? My mom, I mean . . . while I was blacked out I had a dream or something and I saw her . . . she was begging me to help her."

"Really?" he asks and I nod. He stares at me contemplatively. Part of me grows eager, the stupid side probably, thinking he might say yes, there is a possibility that my mother, who I haven't seen since I was four years-old, and can barely remember—thanks to the detachment of my soul from my emotions and the erasing of my memories—might still be alive.

"I don't know, Gemma," he utters quietly, giving my knee a squeeze. "She's been down there for a really long time. . . . but maybe. I mean, there's been some people that I've heard of who've survived the Water Faerie's torture for a really long time without going too insane . . . God, there's even been a few people who've escaped."

"Are you being serious?" I ask. "Alex made it sound like there wasn't a way to escape."

"Don't get mad at him for that." Laylen slips his arm around my back and draws me closer to him. He puts his lips right beside my ear and whispers in a deep voice, "He doesn't hang out with the same crowd as I do, does he?"

I turn my head to the side and our lips nearly touch.

"And what kind of crowd is that? A Vampire crowd? Witch crowd? Black Angel crowd? There are so many crowds in this crazy ass world I've been thrown into."

He grins mischievously. "The everything kind of crowd."

We're so close that I can't help thinking about how amazing it'd feel if he just took me over, owned my emotions; got my thoughts of dying, the end of the world and, ultimately, Alex out of my head for a while. "Is there any way we can find out if she's still alive and where she is?"

"It depends on how brave you are," he says with a wink.

I force a small smile, but thoughts of my mom drowning in a lake of Fey haunt my mind. If she's alive, I need to save her, like she asked me to in the dream, if that's what it was. "Are you trying to get me all riled up for some reason?"

He shakes his head and a grin slips through. "I'm just trying to tell you the truth, so you know what you're walking into."

"I'm not scared," I assure him, which doesn't seem like a lie. "I want answers—real answers—and I'll do whatever I have to in order to get them."

He mulls over what I said, nibbling on his bottom lip, making sucking noises as he draws the lip ring in between his teeth. "Then I say we do it."

"Do what exactly?" I'm practically bouncing with excitement. "I need to know what I'm getting into."

He inclines back a little and his gaze fleetingly glides to the bed. It scares me for some reason, the idea that he might be thinking something that requires me being on the bed. Again I try to sift through my emotions to figure out how I feel about him, but I can't quite understand it and the prickle seems to be stuck in the REM cycle.

"You remember that club we got the Sword of Immortality from?" he checks.

I nod. "Yeah, and I really remember how the bartender spiked my drink with a rufi."

"Well, where we're going is similar, but worse." Worry laces his tone.

I consider what he said, recollecting the Black Dungeon and how I pretty much attacked Alex after drinking that drink. Alex was there to help me, but he won't be this time. I'm not sure I want him to be, either. "You think it's worth it to go check it out? That there might be answers there?"

He nods with confidence. "I think your mom may know more about what's going on than anyone does. I think that might be why Stephan sent her there. That and to keep her away from you."

"I think so, too," I agree. "In the vision I saw—the one where Stephan forced her into the lake—she said she knew things about Stephan that eventually everyone else would figure out."

Plus, I really just want to see my mom. I miss her, even though I really don't know her, and the idea of seeing her again is enough to make me risk anything. The only family I ever had was Marco and Sophia, my supposed grandparents and two of the most cold-hearted people I know.

"Laylen, what happened to Marco and Sophia?" I ask.

Laylen shrugs. "I'm not sure, but I feel like we need to find out. They were part of removing your soul and they might know something as well . . . but no one can seem to find them at the moment."

"So they just vanished?"

"Pretty much," he says. "At least that's what Alex told me. He tried to get a hold of them when we got here."

I frown. "Why would he do that?"

He shakes his head with disdain. "Despite everything, Alex seems to think that Keepers are still trustworthy and the only kind he can seek help from."

"When are we going to—"

"Gemma." Alex's voice floats through the door. "Are you in there?"

"Uh . . . yeah," I call out, shifting away from Laylen, as though I'm doing something wrong. "I'm in here with—"

Laylen covers my mouth with his hand and puts a finger up to his lips, shushing me. "If he knows I'm in here, then he'll know something's up."

"So what," I whisper back, my voice muffled against his palm. "What's he going to do?"

Laylen aims me a "really" look. "Get pissed off. Not let you go with me. Lock you in a cellar and never let you out just so no one else can touch you." At the end his lips tug upward. "You know how he is with you." He removes his hand from my mouth.

I frown. He's right. If Alex finds out about this, he won't let me go. Besides, I'm not even sure I can trust him. "Yeah, I know."

Alex bangs on the door again. "Gemma, can you open the door?"

I feel the prickle emerge on the back of my neck, begging me to open the door and let him in; allow him to see me with Laylen and think something's going on. I consider doing it, but Laylen abruptly gets up from the bed, drops down to his hands and knees and crawls underneath the bed.

I watch him with wide eyes as I scramble to my feet. "Seriously? You're going to hide under the bed?"

"Just pretend I'm not here," he whispers as the last of his legs vanish.

I stand there, stunned, feeling like I'm a teenager hiding my boyfriend from my parents, only I never really had that experience since I'd never had a boyfriend or parents.

Alex knocks on the door again and a breath eases out of my mouth before I walk over to open it up. The second I see him, my emotions entwine together into a very perplexing knot, even though it's only been like an hour since I last saw him. I don't understand why it happens, why I'm so turned onto him when he infuriates me to no end. I'm seriously starting to wonder if because of all those years trapped in an unemotional state, my body and head are now broken, unable to deal with the newfound emotions recently piled onto me.

He looks very uncomfortable for some reason, however the black mark looks like its fading. "Took you long enough."

"I thought you were leaving," I retaliate, leaning against the open door, aiming for nonchalant, but it comes off a little twitchier than I planned.

His eyes narrow, patronizing me. "Now why would I do that?"

"Because you said you were," I reply simply.

He braces his hands on the doorway, invading my comfort zone and my gaze zeros in on his solid stomach muscles as his shirt rides up. "Well, you're the one who kept insisting I was a liar. I'm just living up to my reputation, something I'm really good at."

I try not to stare at his muscles, but thoughts of how they moved as he thrust inside me haunt my mind. I'm still not sure how I feel about having sex, or if I feel anything other than confusion. I wonder if that's normal.

"Did you need something?" I shake my head at the unevenness of my voice.

He elevates his brows with suspicion. "You've been

up here forever. What have you been doing?"

I gesture at my new outfit. "*Changing.*"

His eyes scan down my body, warming every single inch of my skin. His eyes linger a little too long on my chest area then finally land on my eyes and I can't tell what he's thinking at all.

"You look good," is all he says.

"Um . . . thanks, I guess," I mutter, folding my arms over my chest.

His lips smash together as he deliberates something. Then he steps toward me, taking me by surprise as he lines his body with mine and I have no choice except to back up against the door. Fireworks of heat erupt as he pins my shoulders between his arms, his hands resting beside my head.

"Gemma, I don't want to fight with you," he says gently, changing his attitude in the snap of a finger. I'm beginning to understand that he's good at doing that. "I didn't . . . I didn't work to save you only so we could sit here and argue with each other."

His sincerity is puzzling since he's not much of a sincere type of guy. My eyes drift to his head at the dissolving black spot, the brand of his supposed good deed.

"Did it hurt?" I ask. "When it bounced back on you?"

He rolls his tongue in his mouth, like he's restraining a laugh. "Not too bad, but I'm good at handling pain, much more than other things."

"What about the non-pain part of it?" With each ravening breath I take, my chest brushes against his.

He shakes his head and his forehead brushes against mine. We're almost pressing against each other, but there's still a sliver of space between our bodies, a boundary we need at the moment, until some sort of trust can be established.

"There was no non-pain part of it." His voice is strained as he starts to twist the ribbon on my shirt around his finger. "It didn't do anything other than give me a really, really bad fucking headache."

I hate this drive toward him. The invisible pull that I still don't understand. The overwhelming need to touch him, rip his clothes off, bite his lip, scratch his skin and feel his rock-hard body. I should be angry with him, yet I can't seem to get to that place.

My fingertips dare to go to the place my mind is heading, drifting to the top of his jeans, then skimming underneath the fabric. I feel him tense and I tense, too. I'm about to go there and what really surprises me is how bad I want to do it, want to touch him. I can tell he wants to touch me also, his lips are dipping closer to mine as we breathe frantically. My back arches and my chest presses against his, my body and mind wanting more—needing more. I feel starved from something, but I'm having a hard time placing what.

"Jesus . . . Gemma . . ." He lets out a throaty groan and his eyes start to shut as my hand travels lower. I start rubbing him through his boxers until he becomes hard and tugs on the ribbon of my shirt to unlace the front. The curves of my breasts become more exposed along with my bra. My other hand wanders up the front of him, resting on the top of his heart, crushed between our bodies. I can feel it pounding in his chest, racing almost as fast as mine. Our lips brush, the connection sparking, and he lets out another groan, this time louder. Suddenly, I remember that there's a six-foot four, blue-eyed, blond haired, sexy Vampire hiding under my bed. *Shit.* I lean back, pulling my hands out of the top of his jeans.

"Where's Aislin and Laylen?" I ask, breathless.

He blinks and the emotion drains from his expression.

Holding my gaze, he unwinds the loosened ribbon from his finger and pushes back from the door. "Downstairs I think."

Just like that the tension and desire melt into a puddle below our feet.

"Can I talk to Aislin?" I ask, refastening the ribbon.

He shrugs, pretending to be unbothered, but he seems uneasy. "You can do whatever you want."

"Okay, I'll be down in a second." I step to the side and hold the door wide open so he'll leave, even though I don't want him to at all. I want to put my hands back down the front of his jeans and let him completely untie my shirt.

"Fine." He turns his back on me and walks out. "Goddammit, why do you have to be so frustrating?" he mutters to himself, although it's loud enough that I can hear it.

"I have no idea," I mumble back, then quickly shut the door and whirl around to the bed. "Laylen?"

He army crawls from underneath the bed, his soft laughter making me uneasy. He stands up straight, brushing some dust off his clothes. "Fuck. That was really awkward."

I fidget with the ribbon on my shirt. "Nothing happened."

He laughs, rearranging his hair into place. "If you say so."

"It didn't," I argue, but my cheeks heat. "I swear nothing did."

He presses back a smile and strides for the window. "All I know is that those noises are going to haunt me for life."

"I'm sorry," I apologize. "I don't even know why I did it . . . why I'm like that towards him."

He smiles sadly at me from over his shoulder "Because

you two have history together and a connection nothing can compete with."

I tilt my head to the side. "We do?"

His shoulders rise and fall as he shrugs. "Kind of . . . you'll have to ask him about it, though."

I sift through my memories, knowing I'm probably not going to see anything, but trying anyway. As usual, I see blankness, then a few fading clips, however nothing important appears in my mind's eye.

"So now what." I change the subject.

He hesitates, staring out the window. "Well, here's where things get tricky."

"Get tricky?" I step up beside him and peer down at the three-story drop to a mostly vacant asphalt parking lot. "Things have been tricky for a very, very long time."

"True, but they're about to get trickier." He unlatches the window, pushes it open, and sticks his head out, looking down below. "We're not going to be able to just walk out the front door. Adessa set up some charms so if someone tries to come in or go out, she'll know. It's her version of a security system."

My jaw drops as he ducks back into the window. "Oh my God. You want us to *climb* out the *window*. Are you crazy?"

"It's the only way," he says simply, gripping the windowsill. "All the downstairs windows have charms on them, and although I'm not sure exactly what Adessa's charms do if they get set off, I'd really rather not find out."

I stare at the window with uncertainty. It's getting late, the sky is getting grey as the sun plummets below the tips of the towering buildings. "Can't we just tell Adessa what we're doing?"

"Walking downstairs means facing Alex," he remarks, slanting his head to the side to meet my eyes. "Are you ready to deal with that? Tell him what you want and then fight him until he lets you go?"

"No."

"Well, then . . ."

I sigh, shuffle my way to the window, and sit down on the windowsill. "I really do hate heights."

He playfully pinches my leg. "I won't let anything happen to you. I promise."

"I believe you," I say truthfully. "But how are we even supposed to get down there? Do you have some kind of like climbing-down-the-wall superpower or something?" My voice turns mocking. "Or are we just going to scale it with some sheets we've tied together."

"Sheets would tear." He shakes his head, seeming entertained. "And I'm a Vampire, not Spiderman, so no. I don't have any climbing down superpowers." He pauses, blowing out an uneven breath. "You're going to get on my back, and I'm going to jump out."

I start to laugh, but the sound quickly dissolves. "Tell me you're joking. Please." I stand up from the windowsill, shaking my head as I back away. "No way."

"We won't get hurt." He sits down and swings his long legs out the window. "That far of a fall won't hurt me at all. It's a Vampire thing."

"Yeah, but I'm not a Vampire," I say. "The fall *will* hurt me."

"That's why you'll be on my back, so I can break the fall for you." He winks at me. Even though he's adorably sexy, I'm still not hopping on board his death plan.

"I hate heights."

"And I hate biting people, yet I've still done it a few times."

"Laylen . . ." I'm torn between wanting the truth and dying to get it.

He sighs disappointedly. "Do you want me to go alone? Because I can. I just thought, since you've been in the dark for so long, you'd like to be a part of it, however it's up to you."

He's giving me a choice. No one has ever given me a choice. I could seriously kiss him right now because I want to be part of this and help save my mother. "Alright . . . I'm in."

He gives me a lopsided smile. "Good. Now hop on."

I summon a deep breath and do what he says. I slip a leg on each side of his waist, so I have my legs wrapped around his midsection, my chest pressed up to his back, and my ass against the windowsill.

"You good?" Laylen asks as I move around, trying to get situated.

I tighten my arms and legs around him. "I think so."

"And Gemma?"

"Yeah."

"I promise to try and not drop you," he says.

Before I can respond, he dismounts from the windowsill and, the next thing I know, I'm falling.

CHAPTER
THREE

I T'S OVER BY the time I actually acknowledge we're falling. Laylen lands with the gracefulness of a cat, his feet delicately touching the asphalt, and I barely feel the impact.

For a moment, neither of us moves nor breathes. Even the air seems to pause, as if we fell so fast we're waiting for the rest of the world to catch up.

"You alive back there?" Laylen asks from over his shoulder. His arms are wound around my legs, supporting my weight as I clutch onto his shoulders.

I peek open my eyes, crane my neck, and glance up at the window above us. "Yeah, a little bit more of a warning would have been nice, though."

"Then you would have just anticipated it and psyched yourself out," he says. "Unexpected is always the best when there's fear involved."

I'm not sure if I get his logic, but fear is also very new to my vocabulary. I nod and climb off his back then stretch out my legs and pop my neck, alleviating some of the tension in me.

We walk across the parking lot beneath the shimmering stars dusting the desert sky. The sound of rushing traffic and flashing lights surround us, along with rustic buildings. The entire area is decorated with graffiti, the ground is littered with garbage, and the lack of people around makes the scenario uneasy, yet at the same time calm.

"You said that we are going to a place worse than the Black Dungeon," I remark as we make a right down a narrower, more secluded street. "So does that mean there's going to be a bunch of strange creatures with lizard tongues and weird eyes or whatever?"

He glances at me from the corner of his eye as he stuffs his hands into his pockets. "Actually, no. The only things you're going to find in this place are either human or simply have really sharp, pointy teeth." He traces his tongue along his teeth. "No weird eyes or lizards tongues."

"It's a club for Vampires," I state the obvious. I scoot in closer to him as a sketchy looking man wearing a black hoodie walks by us. "How high are my chances of being bit, then?"

Smiling, he drapes his arm around my shoulders. "I wouldn't let anyone bite you, sweetheart. Seriously."

"But there will be people getting bit?"

He goes rigid. "Yes."

I swallow hard. "Will they . . . will the Vampires be killing them?"

He shakes his head. "This is just a feeding ground, a place to feed on willing humans in a closed space where you don't have to worry about getting caught."

I angle my neck back to look at him. "Willing humans?"

He nods once, his eyes focused on the sidewalk ahead. "Vampire bites are intoxicating in ways I can't even begin to explain. Some humans love it . . . it's like a drug for them and so they come to clubs like these to get their next hit."

I picture teeth sinking into my neck. Pain. Then euphoria? If it's true, it sounds kind of sexy.

I push the thought from my head. "So who is this all-knowing person that we're going to see?"

He inches to the left as a sleek, black car rolls up the road, driving close to the curb. "Draven."

"The guy you were so afraid of back at the Black Dungeon? I thought he was dangerous and the reason why . . . the reason why Aislin got bit."

"Aislin got bit because she was a Keeper and most Vampires loathe Keepers." His jaw goes taut as we round the side of a warehouse. The road reaches a dead-end of dumpsters that line the walls of boarded up, metal buildings. "You're not a Keeper, so you should be fine, but I'm not going to try and convince you that what we're doing isn't dangerous. I think you deserve more than being lied to and walking in blindly."

"And I appreciate that," I say. "I'm just a little nervous."

"That's perfectly understandable," Laylen replies as we halt in front of a door on the side of a large, rusty looking warehouse. "But Draven should be able to help us."

"How though?"

"You know how I can control emotions?"

Goosebumps dot my skin, but more from excitement than the cold. "Yeah."

He glances up at the stars in the sky. "Well, Draven has a different kind of gift—or curse depending on how you want to look at it. He can see what's going on in different realms."

"Realms, like The Underworld." I shiver.

He nods, his attention drifting to the door. "So, if we can get him to agree, he should be able to see if your mom's still there . . . it's going to be hard, though."

"I figured as much," I tell him. "Since nothing is ever easy."

He gives me a partial smile and then removes his arm from my shoulder to rap his hand on the door. The sound echoes from the inside, it is the only noise that can be heard around us. I'm about to ask him why it's so quiet when the door swings open and light floods the night.

On the other side of the door is a tall man wearing a hoodie and his dark eyes resembling coals. His skin is extremely pale like Laylen's, his lips are a deep red, and he has a sequence of tattoos on his neck.

"Well, well, if it isn't the *cruor fastidio*." He leans against the crooked doorframe, assessing Laylen with his dark eyes while I struggle to figure out what a *cruor fastidio* means.

"You know I've drank blood, Kameron" Laylen replies, his blue eyes intense and his voice sinking to a low octave. "I merely choose to do it only when necessary."

Kameron shakes his head as he runs his tongue along his teeth. "Blood is always necessary in life, but you really don't have one, do you?"

Laylen glances at me and then to Kameron, remaining nonchalant. "I need inside. Now."

Kameron's eyes devour me. "And who's this lovely creature right here?"

"No one you need to know," Laylen states, inching in front of me so I'm partially hidden behind him.

Kameron leans to the side to get a better look at me. "She looks like a Black Angel, but the nervousness in her bloodstream suggests otherwise," he says and then waits for something. Perhaps for Laylen to deny that I am a Black Angel or insist that I do have hidden wings on my back, but Laylen never utters a word. "Fine, remain silent then." He steps back, getting ready to close the door.

Laylen slams his hand forcefully against it, shoving the door back open. "I said I need in." His blue eyes blaze and his voice is low, sultry, dangerous.

It's giving me the chills and adrenaline crashes through my body. I'm scared, yet excited for things I'm not sure I should be excited for. I inch back, but only because my mind and body are becoming so perplexed. I wonder if it's because Laylen is getting pissed and his emotion gift—or curse—is no longer under his control.

"You know the rules." Kameron draws the hoodie off his head. His hair is black like the night sky and there's a scar running diagonally on the side of it. "I can't let a Black Angel in here. Only Vampires and humans."

"She is human," Laylen breathes through gritted teeth, slanting in toward Kameron. "Now open the door."

Kameron stands upright, trying to stand taller than Laylen, but he lacks the height. "She looks like one."

Laylen backs up with his arms expanded out to the side of him. "But she's not and, if you'd look harder, you'd realize it."

Humor dances in Kameron's eyes. He's toying with us and completely enjoying it. "Prove it. Make her bleed. Black Angels don't bleed."

I wince at the mention of blood and immediately recoil. "*What?*"

Laylen looks over his shoulder and the fire in his eyes makes me cower back even more. For a second I think he's going to attack me, but then he blinks and the Laylen I know reappears. He turns back to Kameron. "No fucking way," he growls.

"Then you're not getting in," he replies and starts to close the door again, about to slam my opportunity to find out about my mom away.

I peel back the bandage on my wrist and stride

forward showing him my fresh wound. "Look, it's almost still bleeding."

He shakes his head. "I want to see your body dripping out blood."

My expression falls. "That's not fair."

"Life's not fair." Kameron pauses with an impish smile on his lips and I can tell he's just messing with our heads. "I want to see Laylen bite you."

Laylen and mine's jaws drop. "No way," Laylen says, seeming horrified. "I can't."

Kameron opens his mouth, showing me his set of teeth, white, glinting, fangs fully in view. "Vampires *feed* on blood, Laylen. That's what we were made to do."

"No way," Laylen repeats simply. "I won't do it."

"Then I'll do it." Kameron's eyes fix on me. "Trust me, if you let me sink my fangs into," he inhales deeply, his nostrils flaring, "that delicious looking skin of yours, I swear you'll be begging me to never stop."

On the inside I squirm, but on the outside I'm surprisingly composed. "You said that I need to bleed, not let you feed on me, so give me a damn knife and I'll show you I have blood in me, even though I'm pretty sure you already know that."

I expect him to get angry, but instead he cocks his eyebrows. "You know, I really didn't believe you were one, but the cockiness and boldness coming out of you right now is making me second guess my original assumption." Kameron starts to slowly shut the door again. "Now bite or no deal."

I almost hiss at him and snap my teeth. I have no idea where my emotions are coming from at the moment. Whether it's from the disturbing environment, or if Laylen's manipulating my emotions. I turn to Laylen and tip my chin to meet his eyes.

I'm trying not to get angry, but the idea of punching Kameron in the face right now is really appealing. He's the one thing getting in my way of perhaps learning something about my mother's whereabouts.

"Bite me," I tell Laylen and his eyes nearly pop out of his head. Before he can argue, I add, "Just scuff my skin with your teeth. You don't have to drink any of my blood, just spill some out."

"Now that's not fun." Kameron pouts as he crosses his arms and leans against the doorway. "I want to see a show."

I glare at him. *Sick, twisted, pervert.*

"It's not for fun," Laylen says, and my attention returns to him. His eyes locked on me and his brows are furrowed. "It's only so you have to let us in."

Kameron rolls his eyes. "Fine. *Scrape* your teeth against her and prove that she's a mere mortal . . . so fucking boring."

Laylen's lip twitches as he stares down at me. His body spasms as he struggles to keep his expression tranquil and I wonder what I'm getting into; how dangerous will this really be? Will he lose control? Drink my blood? Kill me? Do I care?

I stick my trembling arm toward him and his gaze instantly snaps down to it, zoning in on my wrist. In the moonlight, my skin looks white and the bluish purple vein below it is visible.

Laylen's long, cold fingers curl around my wrist and he wets his lips with his tongue. Then he lowers his mouth to my arm and my heart slams inside my chest as his lips part, his neck muscles tensing as a pair of fangs descend from his gum line. He lets out a growl that makes my heart leap and then a groan that makes my stomach somersault. I try to hold as still as I can, but a flurry of

43

emotions—some dark, some fearful, some needy—whisk through me as I watch his mouth brush my wrist.

He bites on his bottom lip, sucking his lip ring into his teeth, and strands of his blond hair fall into his eyes. Seconds later, I feel a sharp, fiery sting as his fangs delve into my wrist and pierce through my skin.

"Ahh . . ." The pain mingled with bliss in my voice shocks me. My muscles tense as blood seeps out of my wrist, two pools of blood trickling a path down my arm.

He doesn't put the fangs in deep, but he doesn't pull back, either. His eyes shut and he lets out a deep, throaty groan that sends a shiver of pleasure through my body. I bite down on my lip hard to keep myself from begging him to sink his teeth into my pulse. It feels so Goddamn good and the idea of them being in further—him being in further—is driving me crazy. My skin is humming, my pulse throbbing, and my mind as well as my body are spinning out of control. I reach up and clutch onto his shoulder with my free hand.

"I can't . . ." he whispers, his breath hot against my skin. "I need to stop . . ."

"Can't what . . ." I breathe, forgetting where I am, what's happening. Nothing other than his teeth and my blood seem to matter.

He pulls away, looking euphoric, like he's high on my blood; his pupils possessive and out of touch with reality. The look makes my pulse hammer even faster and I can feel an emotion drizzling through my veins; a comforting need to surrender myself to Laylen. The lesions on my wrist continue to trickle out blood, a red trail rolling down my hand and onto the pavement below my feet. I cover them with my hand, trying to limit the amount spilled, but only because of Kameron and the fear that the sight of it might cause him to attack me.

Laylen's fingers are trembling as he opens his eyes and releases my wrist. He holds my gaze for a moment and the atmosphere intensifies between us as a connection forms. Ripping his gaze off me, he turns to Kameron. "Now get the fuck out of the way," he orders in a stern, yet subdued voice.

Kameron's demeanor is casual as he steps back, sucking in a breath and breathing in a mouthful of air. "Are you sure you don't want to share?" he asks. "We could each take a wrist."

Laylen says nothing and shoves his way inside the warehouse, slamming his hand against Kameron's chest hard enough that he crashes into the door. I hurry in, pressing my hand to my wrist.

"Oh, fine. Take the fun out of my job." Kameron shuts the door and walks around us, heading for a spiral stairway in the middle of the empty concrete room. We follow him and, with each step, the air grows colder and the atmosphere darker as the roof shifts from dingy, broken skylights to rusty, metal beams. I can hear music playing from somewhere, smell the potent scent of salt and sweat, and feel the ground pulsating below my boots from the rumble of the bass.

We arrive at the top of the stairway and halt as Kameron begins to unlock the multiple padlocks on a solid steel door. Laylen's head is down, his chin tucked in, and I'm worried he's upset about what he's just done. I hook my finger under his chin to get a better look at his expression.

He's not upset. More like intense. His fangs have retracted, his blue eyes appear shades darker, almost like sapphires, and there's blood on the bottom of his lip, a thin trail just beside his lip ring. My blood, waiting for him to lick it.

"You have blood on your lip," I mutter. I reach forward and slowly swipe my finger along the spot of blood. I smear it a little and go over it again until most of it is off his lip and on my finger. I'm about to pull my hand away, when his mouth unexpectedly moves forward and my finger ends up inside it on top of his tongue. Shutting his eyes, he sucks the blood off, licking my finger while he inhales deeply and then exhales.

He moves his mouth away as my jaw drops. I'm shocked and shamefully turned on in ways I didn't know were possible. I pant heavily, my chest heaving. Laylen opens his eyes and his tongue slips out of his mouth again, licking the remaining blood off. "God . . . you taste so good . . ."

Then Kameron utters something about letting him get a taste and Laylen looks away from me, breaking the tension as he glares at Kameron. Clearing my throat, I quickly wipe the blood on the side of my shorts and put my hand back over my injured wrist.

Kameron gets the door open at the same time that Laylen catches my eye as we step over the threshold and onto the grated flooring. There's something in his expression, shame or desire. Perhaps a mixture of both.

I'm freaking out inside, unsure how he feels at the moment or how I feel—how I should feel. The prickle is getting me nowhere, stabbing at my neck and pumping all kinds of disorder through me.

Yet, as I glance around at the room, any thoughts or feelings of anything else float from my head.

Vampires. Everywhere. And they're feeding.

CHAPTER
FOUR

WATCHING A VAMPIRE feed is a strange sight. However, watching an entire room of Vampires suck blood from willing humans is appalling. Yet, in the twisted side of me, the one I'm barely getting to know, it's strangely stimulating.

"Rascauche" by At The Drive-In flows from the speakers surrounding the room. The lyrics and soft tune encompass the large floor and lights shimmer down onto the Vampires' euphoric faces. A lot of them are dancing, but some are simply standing in the light watching the others, doing one of two things that my mind can barely comprehend; touching each other and feeding off the blood of a human. Some have their fangs plunged deep into the neckline of the victim, while others choose the wrist.

"You're on your own now," Kameron calls out over the music, and then disappears somewhere into the crowd, grabbing the hair of a woman wearing a floor-length satin dress. She looks happy to be with him, content, and I wonder if I look the same way right now.

"Good riddance," Laylen mutters, and then makes his way toward a bar at the back of the room, motioning me to follow him. When he reaches the countertop, he scoops up a shot of a brownish liquid that the bartender magically puts down the moment he arrives. He swigs it down, sucking every last drop out with his head tipped back. He licks the brim of the glass with his tongue before dropping the empty glass back down on the counter.

The bartender, a medium height, curvy brunette smiles at Laylen as she wipes the counters down, her lips parting as if she's about to say something.

"Not now, Taven." Laylen says, then makes a veer to the right toward a corridor with blood-red doors and floors as black as ash.

I rush to keep up and he waits for me in the arched entryway. "Are you okay?" I ask as we enter the corridor. The black marble, domed ceiling is laced with red lines that look like blood and there are lanterns and a few chains as well as cuffs secured to the walls.

He nods only once, though his jaw tightens. "I'm fine."

I stay silent, hyperaware of his distant attitude. It terrifies me not only because he's my friend and I'm afraid I've broken him, but also because of the craving soaring through my body, the strange need for his fangs to return to my skin.

Halfway down the corridor, we pass two large men dressed in black suits stationed in front of a shut door. Neither of them acknowledge us and we continue walking, the music from the bar fading the further down we go.

My wrist has stopped bleeding, but there's a drying trail on my hand. "Are you sure you're okay?"

He nods, and then shakes his head, letting out a sigh that seems to clear the tension between us just a little. "I'll get there . . . I just . . . I just hate drinking blood." He avoids eye contact with me. "Yet I don't, which makes me hate it more. And yours . . ." He squeezes his eyes shut for a moment. "God, it smelled so intoxicating."

My heart aches for him, but at the same time his words put a wave of hunger in me; one that wants to feed, or him to feed on me anyway. We're embarking into dangerous territory and, even though I know it, it still takes me off guard.

"You didn't drink it, though," I remind him. "Only drew it from my body."

"Still, I wanted to drink it." His gaze meets mine as we arrive in front of a door at the end of the hallway. There's a colossal, golden and black vase on each side and a mirror above it that reveals our reflections. We look high and sedated. "I wanted to taste you, so fucking bad."

I'm unsure what to say to him. "Okay."

He seems as perplexed as I do. "Okay?"

I'm not sure what we're agreeing to, but it feels like we're agreeing to something. The atmosphere lightens and Laylen's demeanor changes, his posture unstiffening, his jaw loosening.

He hesitates before knocking on the door. "Stay by me at all times," he whispers.

I quickly nod as several latches click, and then the door cracks open.

"What do you want?" a voice snarls through the crack as smoke rushes out of it.

"I'm here to talk to Draven," Laylen states calmly.

The door opens wider and a shorter man with silky blond hair and wearing a black suit steps forward. "Concerning what?"

Laylen tucks his hands into the pockets of his jeans. "Concerning the *donum of obscurum.*"

"You're very brave to come here and say such a thing," the blond guy states, his gaze sliding to me. "Is this an offering?"

Laylen protectively leans in toward me. "No, she's with me."

The guy rolls his eyes and starts to shut the door. "Come back when you have something to offer. He doesn't just share his gift with anyone."

Laylen flattens his hand on the door and shoves his foot into the crack at the bottom, holding it open. "I'll offer him something else, just not the girl."

The guy considers this for a moment, his eyes wandering to my wrist as he licks his lips. "Just a second." He steps back and Laylen removes his hand and foot from the door so the guy can shut it.

I shoot Laylen a puzzled look and he puts his finger to his lips. A second later the door opens again and potent smoke rushes out so quickly I choke back a cough. I'm not sure what kind of smoke it is and I think I might be better off left in the dark with this one.

The door opens wider and a different man stands on the other side with greasy black hair, pasty skin, and he's wearing a tuxedo while carrying a silver platter.

His fangs point out as he grins, gesturing at the room. "Please, do come in."

Laylen takes my hand as we enter the room. My pulse promptly quickens and he gives it a gentle squeeze, then his fingers move lower so they're covering the wounds on my wrist.

The room is small, though broad, with an extensive table down the center that's surrounded by spindle-back chairs. In every chair, a male Vampire sits holding cards, their fangs fully in view. Poker chips are stacked in front of them and there are ashtrays everywhere, covered with cigar butts. Standing behind each Vampire is a woman. They look human, but from a different era, their flowing corset dresses very out of date.

Laylen confidently approaches the table, dragging a very unconfident me along with him. As we reach it, one of the Vampires sitting at the end extends his arm back toward the woman behind him. He grabs the back of her neck and she voluntarily leans down to him. He sinks his teeth into her neck, gripping her waist as his sucks the blood from her vein. Her eyes roll back into her head as her body lifelessly slumps against his shoulder. She groans and pleads in a muffled voice for him to bite her more.

I tighten my hold on Laylen's hand. Then the Vampire releases her and she staggers back, plummeting to the flood with blood drenching her dress and neck.

The Vampire returns to his cards, wiping the blood from his chin with his hand, grinning as he says, "I think I'm about ready for another round."

The other Vampires mumble in agreement and reach for the women behind them. Shaking with fear, loathing, and curiosity, I let out a quiet gasp. Suddenly everyone is staring at us, and I wish I could shrink myself into a ball.

A man with jet-black hair sitting at the end of the table rises from his chair. He's tall, perhaps even taller than Laylen, with broad shoulders and dark eyes that match his shirt and slacks. He has a golden chain on his arm that stretches to a collar that's attached to a woman wearing a silky blue dress.

"So, Laylen," he says, walking toward us and dragging the woman with him. She seems dazed, her bare feet dragging along the floor as she stumbles after him. "To what do I owe the honor of a visit from the one and only known Keeper turned Vampire?" His eyes flick over to me and he drinks me in as he stops in front of us and the woman kneels behind him. "And with such breathtaking company."

Unsure of what to do, I hold his gaze, remaining impartial as I fight the urge to gape at the woman behind him.

"I need your help," Laylen mutters, his grip constricting on my hand.

The man is fixed on me. "With what?"

An anxious breath eases from Laylen's lips. "With finding out if someone is still in The Underworld or if they've escaped."

"I see." His eyebrows arch as he tears his eyes from me and resides his attention on Laylen. "And what made you bring the human? I rarely see you with them, let alone biting them." He skims my wrist.

"The cost of getting in here." Laylen presses his lips together. "Your guard wouldn't accept anything less."

The man snakes the chain around his wrist, forcing the woman to crawl to his feet. "You should be thanking him, Laylen. I can tell by that euphoric look in your eyes that you must have enjoyed it." He glances at me, his nostrils flaring. "She does smell very divine."

Laylen says nothing, however his fingers compress into my skin.

The man grins at me. "Allow me to introduce myself. I'm Draven." My heart constricts in my chest as he sticks out his hand. Despite my wariness, I take it since he's the man who might be able to help me find my mother. He wraps his cold fingers around my hand, slides them up to my wrist and brings my knuckles up to his lips, placing a delicate kiss onto it. Then he inhales, breathing in my scent before letting my hand go. "Yes, very divine," he mutters, straightening back up. "Now explain to me exactly what it is you need to know from me." He jerks on the chain and the collar on the woman's neck bites at her skin, causing her to whimper. "Who is this person in The Underworld that you so desperately seek?"

"Who said we were desperate?" Laylen crosses his arms and maintains Draven's gaze.

Draven motions around at the room. "Look where you are. You'd have to be desperate to be here."

Laylen glances around at the Vampires circling the table. They're no longer playing poker; their cards have been laid down as they watch. "Would it be okay if we spoke in private?"

Draven considers Laylen's request then calls over his shoulder, "Gentlemen, could you excuse us for a moment? It seems we have to discuss something of a serious nature, privately." There's humor in his voice, which makes it obvious that he's enjoying creating our feelings of uneasiness.

The Vampires get up from their chairs without arguing and file out of the room with the women beside them. After everyone's gone, Draven signals at us to have a seat at the table. We silently obey, either out of fear or the need for answers, and sit down beside each other. Draven sits in a chair across from us and the woman crouches beside him with her head hung low, her veil of auburn hair shielding her face.

Draven rolls up his sleeves, deliberately watching us. I notice that he has the Mark of Immortality on one fore arm and on the other arm there's a bizarre looking set of triangles overlapping each other in black and red. Once he's finished, he relaxes back in the chair and studies us closely. "So who's this person you need to find and what makes her so important to you?"

Laylen peeks at me from the corner of his eye. "Her name is Jocelyn . . . Lucas."

My breath hitches in my throat at the sound of my

mom's name and Laylen snatches hold of my hand from under the table, giving it a comforting squeeze.

"Jocelyn Lucas," Draven ponders. "The Keeper Jocelyn Lucas?"

Laylen warily nods. "Yes, that's the one. Do you know her?"

"Know is a strong word . . . more like I've heard of her." A sinister shadow casts across Draven's face as he yanks on the chain, jerking the woman's head onto his lap.

I swallow hard, wondering just how tricky it's going to be to get him to give us the information we need. Laylen said it was going to be dangerous and I'm starting to understand why. There's something in Draven eyes, a darkness that unsettles every bone in my body.

Laylen shoves aside some poker chips and cards to rest his arms on the table. "So do you know if she's still alive?"

"I do . . . However . . ." Draven trails off, looking right at me as he licks his lips and then his fangs point out from his mouth. "This Jocelyn, I'm guessing she's very important to *you?*"

I nod. "She is."

He loops the chain around his wrist, making a spiral up his forearm and the woman is forced to comply with the movement, her head elevating toward his mouth. "Tell me, what would you be willing to give up to find out if she is alive or not?"

I glance at Laylen for help, but his eyes are fixated on Draven as he slips his fingers around the woman's leather collar and draws her neck toward his chin.

"I don't know . . ." Laylen drifts off, biting at his lip ring, his blue eyes blackening.

Draven grins, aiming his fangs out as he sweeps the

woman's hair to the side. "If you want, Laylen, I'd be more than happy to share." With a final grin, he deliberately dips his fangs into the woman's neck.

She gasps as his fangs enter her skin and then clutches onto Draven's legs. Draven's neck muscles work to devour the blood out and her eyes widen before flicking to me. For a second I see life inside her, but it quickly vanishes the longer Draven continues to feed. Blood drizzles down her neckline and the collar of her dress, staining the silky blue fabric a deep red. She moans in pleasure and then whimpers when it's too much to handle, her eyes dazing off as she arrives at a state of contentment. I wonder what it feels like? What kind of sensations run through the body to make someone look that way?

Laylen licks his lips and I feel his weight shift, like he's about to stand up, his fingers burrowing into my wrist. I wrench my hand away from his hold and slam it down on top of his leg, holding him in place.

He winces and his gaze shoots in my direction. He doesn't even look like Laylen anymore, only a shadow of him that's full of hunger.

"What do you want?" I ask Draven, my voice unsteady as I grasp onto Laylen's leg.

With blood on his lips, he frees the woman from his teeth and shoves her to the floor. She falls on her knees, her head low, blood rivering down her neck and dress as it pools on the floor. Draven wipes his mouth with his fingertips, licking the blood off each one.

He unbuttons the top button of his shirt, tugging it down a little, the fabric stained with blood. Then he reaches for a cigar box in the middle of a table next to a stack of poker chips. He lifts the lid off, takes out a cigar, and lights the end, putting it into his mouth and inhaling deeply.

"I want one very simple thing in exchange for me using my lovely gift to peek in on the Fey of The Underworld." He takes another drag of the cigar and greyish smoke fills up the room.

Laylen tears his gaze from the woman bleeding on the floor and focuses on Draven, gripping onto my hand. "And what is it?" He asks.

Draven puffs on the cigar several times, remaining silent, then finally he balances it on an ashtray, the smoke still rising off the end. He crosses his arms on the table and cocks his head to the side. "I want you to feed on the girl."

Laylen quickly looks at the woman on the floor. "I don't think she can take anymore feeding without me . . . killing her."

He shakes his head. "Not on her." His attention targets on me. "*Her.*"

"What?" I cry at the same time Laylen snaps, "No fucking way."

He laughs and its deafening echo ricochets around the room. The woman beside him quivers and falls flat on her stomach, her head resting near Draven's feet. "Then no deal."

Laylen's livid as he slants forward about to say who knows what, but I interrupt him.

"How can we be sure that you know anything at all?" I ask and feel Laylen go rigid beside me.

His lips part and I half expect him to shout at me to shut the hell up, but surprisingly he stays quiet.

Draven's fingers seek the cigar in the ashtray. "When the Lord of the Afterlife makes a deal, the deal is unbreakable. Those are the rules." He places the butt of the cigar into his mouth and inhales.

Laylen tips his head to the side, encountering my

gaze. There's an exchange between us, an agreement, like we're asking each other what to do.

Laylen leans in toward me, keeping his voice hushed. "It's addicting."

Breathe in. Breathe out. "I know . . . if you don't think you can do it, that's okay . . . I'll understand."

"Not just addicting for me . . . I'll always crave no matter what," he clarifies. "But it's also addicting for you, too."

My forehead creases. "I'll become addicted?"

"You could and then you would most likely end up at a place just like this." He gives a fleeting glance to the woman on the floor. "Doing whatever is wanted just to feel the sensations the bite brings."

Sensations? "But Aislin got bit and she's fine."

"Fine . . . but not great." He contemplates. "Besides, Aislin is a Keeper and a Witch. She's stronger in the sense of control and what she can't do of her own freewill, she casts a spell for."

I swallow hard. "I can be strong." My weak voice contradicts my words, though.

He gives me a heart-wrenching look and then cups my cheek, leveling our gazes. "But your emotions are so new . . . I'm worried it might be even harder for you."

"Is this the best way to find out if my mom's alive?" I ask, refusing to give up so easily.

He strokes my cheek. "It is . . . but we can try to find another way."

I press my lips together, deciding, but ultimately, it's not even a choice. My whole life, I've had no one. It's merely been myself, yet it was only a shell of myself. I want more. I want my mom. I want to know where I came from and feel like someone cares about me. I don't want to walk around this world feeling so unloved. I also want to understand love.

"Do it," I utter. "I want you to bite me." I actually mean what I say, too. Maybe it's because of my mom, out of curiosity, or maybe this is just the kind of person that I am—one who welcomes intoxicating, dangerous things.

Draven claps his hands and Laylen jerks away from me, rotating forward in the chair so he's facing Draven.

"Very well played," he says as he claps his hands again, puffing on the cigar. "Give him the sad eyes and show him your heartache." He pauses, assessing us as a cloud of smoke envelops his face. "Although, I might say that they're extremely lovely eyes so it's not quite fair on Laylen's part. They're so intoxicating . . . Violet is such a unique color. You don't see it that often, except for on Pixies and sometimes Fey." He ashes the cigar, tapping it on the side of the glass ashtray.

"She's neither," Laylen hurries and says. "And will you please just get on with it."

"Easy." Draven puts out the cigar in the ashtray, spilling ashes onto the table. "She's agreed to let you bite her. The time will come."

"I don't want to bite her," Laylen makes it clear through gritted teeth. "What I want is to be normal."

"Normal is overrated," Draven remarks. "Now, please, feed on her. I'm dying to see it."

The full reality of what's about to happen starts to sink in. Laylen's going to bite me and it's going to feel . . . well, as far as I've seen good. Yet too good, almost to the point that I might become addicted to the feel of my blood being drunk.

"Tell us about Jocelyn first," Laylen demands. "Or no deal."

Draven shakes his head with a wicked glint in his eye as he traces the triangular symbol on his arm with his finger. "We're not in Keeper's land anymore my dear Laylen. You are nothing except an ordinary Vampire with a very unfortunate mark on your body that brands you good in the world of the bad."

Laylen's Adam's apple bobs up and down as he swallows hard. "Fine." His eyes reluctantly drift to me and, if it were possible, his skin looks even paler. "Gemma, I'm so sorry."

"You don't have to do it," I whisper at the sight of the discomfort in his eyes. "If you don't want to. We can find another way or . . ."

I trail off as he shifts his body forward in his seat, bending his back and moving closer to me. My chest heaves ravenously as anticipation and fear collide inside me and I turn inward to bring myself closer to him. He maintains my gaze as he cups the bottom of my neck softly, yet at the same time with purpose. I wonder if he can feel my rapid pulse. If he can smell the scent of my blood in my veins. What he's thinking. I wonder a lot of things, until he leans in so close I feel the heat of his breath caressing my skin, and then all thoughts are lost as a silence overtakes my body.

"Just breathe and try to relax," he whispers, the pupils in his eyes expanding and taking over all of the blue in his eyes. His lips part, his breathing sharpens and his pointed fangs descend.

My mind tells me that I should be afraid, but my body won't have any part of it, the prickle on the back of my neck stabs wildly, releasing an abundance of emotions. I lean into his touch, his hand tightens around the bottom of my neck and my knees press into his. I know Draven is watching us, but I block him out and focus on my breathing. *Deep breaths. Deep breaths.*

Laylen's head slants to the side, so he's moving in

toward my neck at an angle. When he's only inches away, his tongue slips out and slides across his lips, moistening them and skimming along the tips of his fangs. I feel a tremor in his fingertips as they delve against my skin and I reach forward to grasp onto his legs. I hold my breath as his lips graze my neckline and then squeeze my eyes shut as his fangs pierce my vein.

It's far more intense than just the scrape. Blindingly intense. A body-altering intensity. I fall so fast into the dark that I can't even remember what the light looks like. I hear myself groan, however it barely sounds like me, and an invisible connection seals the inside of my body to him. It guides me forward, forcing my back to arch and I end up pressing my chest against his.

Laylen's fingers stab into my neck and I feel the skin bruising, but the pain only enhances the experience. He feeds on my blood, sucking it out of me and putting it inside himself. My hands clamp down on his legs as I whimper, my body going limp as all the energy is drained from me.

Laylen pauses, the tug from him sucking momentarily ceasing. He groans and I think he's going to stop, even though my mind is screaming at him to continue. However, then he bites down harder, and suddenly, I'm being laid back toward the table. The edge of it cuts into the center of my back and I cry out as he slides me up and sprawls me down on the table, aligning his body with mine as he sucks on my neck, spilling blood all over my skin and clothes. My hands wind around his back and I stab my nails into his shoulder blades, grasping onto him. I can barely see anything anymore besides the color red. Blood red. I can smell it, taste it. It's driving me crazy. I need more of something. My body is being starved.

"Laylen," I manage to choke out, my head drifting to

the side as my legs fall open. His body responds, curving inward and rubbing up against me. His fangs sink deeper, plunging into the arch of my neck. Then suddenly he's pulling away. I think it's over as he wipes the blood off his face with his hand and licks it off his lips with his tongue. I don't want him to be done. I want more—need it. I'm not sure where the sensation is stemming from, what drives it. Regardless, I fasten my legs around his waist and cross my ankles tightly around him.

He opens his mouth and bends his arms, letting his body softly fall onto me, and his lips crash against my own. I can taste salt and rust along with a thousand different things, most of which I have no idea what they are. I open my mouth, letting his tongue slide into it as I clutch onto him for dear life. His hand glides up my ribcage and resides just below my breast, where he grips forcefully. It feels so right, yet through the fog in my head, a voice whispers at me to stop; that this is wrong and Laylen isn't who I'm supposed to be with. Although, I can't remember the name of the person I belong to.

Laylen moves his mouth away from mine, and starts trailing kisses down my neck, licking off the blood while his teeth graze my skin, barely breaking it as I feel gentle stings.

I let him, too. I'd let him do anything to me at the moment. He owns my body and mind as well as my fractured soul. He sinks his teeth into my neck again and continues to drain my blood from me and I eagerly allow him to, until I can't feel my body anymore and I fall into the dark.

CHAPTER FIVE

I FEEL SO cold, like icicles have bronzed my bones, chilled my heart and frozen the veins running beneath my frosted skin. Unbelievably cold.

Am I dead?

My eyes flutter open. The first thing I notice is that the air smells less smoky. Then I notice the grey sky. I gradually sit up, the skin on my upper arm's blazing like it's on fire. I press my hand to the area as I take in the sight of my surroundings. Miles and miles of muddy land, stretching toward the grey horizon that is buried beneath piles of metal objects. Some are small, some large, some with a basic structure while some are so complex it takes a few blinks of my eyes to get them into focus. Some are embedded with jewels, others dull and faded. It's like a junkyard for the collector of strange objects, but where and what is this place?

I unsteadily get to my feet and immediately reach for my neck, shocked when I find that there's no blood on me, no wounds, as if Laylen hasn't bitten me.

"Hello!" I call out, making my way around a massive steel box with the lid crushed in. "Is anyone here?"

Ravens flock from the heaps of misshapen metal

and flee into the dusky sky, sending black feathers to the ground. I begin to walk, weaving around objects and dirt piles, hoping to find some sort of explanation of how I got here and where here is. The walk seems endless, though, and finally I sit down in the dirt.

As a spot on my skin ignites, I remove my hand from it and peek underneath it. My heart stops at the sight of a triangular symbol on my upper arm, black overlapping red. The same mark I had seen on Draven. *Shit.*

Panic soars inside me and something painfully alters in my heart. I feel different—powerful—like I can do anything. The power is stemming from the symbol on my arm. I slowly rise to my feet, ready to do whatever it takes to get out of here and knowing I mean it, even if I have to take another life.

There are so many terrible things flashing through my head right now that they practically swallow up my identity with a blanket of needles.

"Gemma . . ." Someone whispers behind me.

I turn around, glancing at the land behind me. I search for what seems like forever, feathers raining down on my head. When I give up and turn around something smacks me upside the head.

My ears ring and my skull feels like it cracks as I drift into the ground, into darkness.

WHEN I OPEN my eyes, it takes my brain a second to process where I am. There's too much confusion. One minute I'm being fed on, then I'm in some weird junkyard, and the next thing I know I'm lying on warm asphalt, with a very dim lamppost shining down on me as I gaze up at the stars.

"Are you okay?" Laylen's voice sedates me.

I turn my head to the side and find him kneeling next to me, the top of his shirt covered in blood, his eyes like shadows. I feel strangely calm, all things considering, and I have a suspicion Laylen has put the emotion into me.

"Where am I?" I croak, my fingers drifting to the area on my neck that's coated with a warm, sticky substance. I turn my shoulder inward and glance at the place where the symbol was on my skin, but it's gone.

It was just a dream. A nightmare. Thank God.

"We're just outside of Adessa's, in the parking lot." Concern and guilt mask his face. "You blacked out."

I gradually sit up. "Owe." I wince, clutching onto my tender muscles.

"Easy," Laylen says, his voice soothing as he traces his fingertips up and down my spine. "It's going to hurt for a little bit."

I bring my hand away from my neck and hold it up in front of my face. My fingers are drenched in blood. "What else am I going to feel?" I whisper.

"I'm not sure . . ." He struggles for words as his hand rests on the small of my back. "Gemma, I'm so sorry."

I slope my chin up to meet his eyes, then reach up and brush his hair away from his forehead. I move robotically, as if I'm supposed to be doing what I'm doing, not of my own accord, but because my body needs to touch him. "It's not your fault. I'm the one who said to do it."

"But I didn't have to do it," he says and then shuts his eyes as I place a hand on his cheek and run my thumb along his jawline. "Part of me wanted to do it," he admits, opening his eyes. "Part of me has wanted to . . . to bite you ever since you reentered my life."

I'm uncertain how to take his revelation, whether I

should be frightened or feel flattered. Honestly, I feel neither. I feel drained dry, subdued and emotionally empty. "What happened exactly? I just blacked out?"

He nods, smoothing his hand down my back. "It happens sometimes . . . from the loss of blood and emotional overload."

"Did Draven tell you anything about my mother?" I ask, praying to God that all of this didn't happen without a reason.

"Yeah, he . . . he told me . . . he said that she's still there, in The Underworld, fully alive." He looks like he's unsure whether he should be happy or not

I'm not sure if I should be happy or not, either. Yes, she's alive, but she's also been down there for a very long time. I think of the dream, although now I'm starting to wonder if it was a vision I somehow entered without a crystal ball, something I've been wondering if I can do for a while. "So she's still alive?"

He nods, but then quickly adds, "But Gemma, Draven could see if she was still there, but what he couldn't tell me is what condition she's in."

"Condition?"

"Whether she's continued to be sane or if she's lost her sanity to the torture," he tells me uneasily.

My mouth forms an 'o.' "So she might be crazy?"

"She might," he says. "But she might not."

"I'm not sure what would be worse," I mumble. "Finding out she's dead or knowing she's been down they're all along, yet she's crazy."

He sits back on his heels as he rubs his hand across the top of my head, like I'm his pet or something. Emotions begin to surface inside my body again, the faint stab of the prickle is evident, but it's not completely clear how I actually feel about any of this; if maybe it's simply an illusion built on a massive abundance of stimulation I've been feeling.

"You're going to have to take it easy," he tells me, helping me to my feet. "You've lost a lot of blood."

I slowly nod my head, mesmerized by the sound of his voice. "Okay."

He ducks his head to look me square in the eyes. "Are you sure you're all right?"

"Yeah." I clutch onto his arms when the world suddenly sways. "I'm just a little lightheaded and tired."

"It'll wear off for the most part," he states quietly. "Most of the lightheadedness and exhaustion will anyway, but a few things will stay."

I understand way too well what he means because the other things are lingering inside my body right now, causing me to gravitate toward him. If I weren't so tired, I'd probably be begging him to bite me again. "Now what do we do?"

He slips his hand underneath my arm and supports my weight, leaning me against his chest. "Now we try to figure out how to get into The Underworld to save your mom."

I grasp onto him to keep from crumpling to the ground and we begin to make our way toward Adessa's building. "And how are we supposed to do that? Go visit another Vampire with a unique gift?" I ask.

He seals his lips together as he guides me around a parked car. "I'm not sure exactly how to find that one out, but I think I might know someone who does."

My shoes scuff against the gravel as I fight to keep them moving "Who?"

We stop at the bottom of the building and he glances up at the window we jumped out of earlier. "Alex," he says.

I freeze and glance up at him. "You think Alex knows how? Why? I mean, wouldn't he have said something . . ." I trail off, realizing that what I've just said is probably one of the stupidest things to leave my mouth. "Never mind." I pause. "So what? We just ask him and hope he tells us the truth."

"I think you could probably get him to." Laylen's mouth turns downward. "If you play the situation right."

"What do you mean?"

"I mean, Alex cares for you, and if you ask him in the right way, he might let it slip out if he knows anything."

I let out a sharp laugh and it echoes around the abandoned parking lot. "I think you're a little mistaken about how much Alex really likes me. In fact, sometimes I think he hates me, yet he feels obligated to be around me, to protect me." *Because of the electricity,* but I keep that reason to myself since no one really knows about it.

Laylen looks at me disbelievingly. "Do you really believe what you just said?"

I shrug, resting my head against his shoulder as my eyelids grow heavy. I want him to wrap his arm around me and hug me so I don't feel so distorted inside. "I don't know what to believe when it comes to Alex. He's confused me from day one."

"Maybe that's because you're equally as confusing." As Alex's unemotional voice floats over my shoulder, every ounce of my oxygen dissipates.

I hyperventilate as I glance up at Laylen. He doesn't look worried or upset or afraid. As a matter of fact, his face doesn't register anything and it's an eerie sight to behold.

"You know, I honestly shouldn't be surprised," Alex says, and I hear him walk up behind us. "I saw it in both of your eyes the moment you saw each other; you obviously have some sort of connection." Jealousy drips into his voice.

"You shouldn't," Laylen calls over his shoulder. "You and I both know it's inevitable. I will always screw you over, Alex."

What are you doing? I mouth to Laylen.

Laylen shrugs. "Ask Alex. Ever since the day I turned, I'm nothing except an evil monster." He starts to turn us around with his hand on my back. "Even though I've never actually done anything."

"You're a Vampire." He's right behind us, standing so close that I can feel the heat emitting from his body. That's it, though. Just heat, no sparks or overwhelming electricity magnetizing me toward him. Wait. What happened? Where's the electricity?

I plant my feet firmly to the ground to avoid turning around to face him, however Laylen has all the control at the moment and makes us turn around.

All I can do is tilt my head to the side, cover my neck with my hand, and hope that it's dark enough that Alex can't see the blood.

We face him below the stars and the crescent moon while Laylen has his arm around me. I feel out of touch with reality, unlike myself, as though I'm standing in a delusional world.

Alex's attention immediately darts to my neck. "What's the matter with your neck?"

"I have a kink in it," I say stupidly, but I'm exhausted and can't come up with anything better. "A really bad kink."

From beside me, Laylen shakes his head and Alex's expression hardens. "What the hell happened?" He reaches forward and, before I can react, he pries my fingers away from my neck.

At first he simply stands there, holding onto my hand,

staring blankly at the wounds on my neck, two holes covered with dry blood. Blood is also smeared all over my chest area along with the scratches from where Laylen dragged his teeth. I can feel his pulse hammering through his fingers or maybe it's my own. Usually I can feel us together, always in tune, but I feel detached. Numb. Connected to another and so very damn perplexed.

Alex's eyes lift to Laylen. "What the hell did you do to her?" He steps forward, his grip constricting on my hand and cutting off the circulation.

"What you always thought I was going to do," Laylen says evenly and, if I didn't know any better, I'd guess he was doing it on purpose. "It's what you've been waiting around for." He inches closer to Alex while still holding onto my back and forcing me to move forward with him.

"Damn straight I was," Alex growls and I slouch back. "I always knew what you really were. A killer."

Laylen stiffens and his fingers press into my back, digging into my skin as if he's centering all his anger to that one spot. They stand tall, breathing profusely, glaring at each other. I'm stuck in the middle and I know this is going to end badly if I don't do something to stop it. I decide to take charge, even though I'm not sure who I'm saving.

Slipping out from underneath Laylen's arm, I shuffle forward and position myself between them. I place a hand on each of their chests, the touch not fazing either of them, and then I shove them back. They barely budge, but it's enough to divert their attention to me.

"First of all, I made Laylen bite me," I tell Alex, steadily holding his gaze even though it's terrifying to do so. Not just because of his anger, but because, without the electricity, I feel strangely out of my element, like I'm stuck in a temporary state of vertigo.

"You didn't make me," Laylen intervenes, putting weight on my hand as he leans in.

I shoot a glare at him. "But I told you to."

He rolls his eyes, yet keeps his lips fastened. I return my focus to Alex who looks utterly confused.

"If you'll just go inside with me," I say to him. "We can sit down and I'll explain everything."

I expect him to argue, let his rage rain down over me, however rather than do so, he shakes his head, steps back, and says, "Okay."

Confused, I nod, lowering my hands from their chests. "Okay then." Maybe Laylen was right. Maybe I do have more influence over him than I thought.

We head inside, Laylen on my right side and Alex on my left, with thoughts of both of them floating around in my head and, honestly, at the moment I couldn't say who I have feelings for anymore.

CHAPTER
SIX

I SHOULD NEVER assume things. This is the lesson I learn the moment we step foot into Adessa's living room. It's a beautiful room that has shelves built into the walls with the black and white tile on the floor that goes well with the velvet couches. There are little knickknacks sporadically placed all over the shelves, the apothecary table is decorated with candles, and the chandelier above my head glistens. I'm taking it all in when Alex turns to me and takes me all in; the blood drenching my torn shirt, the open bite marks on my neck, and the scratches on my chest. Jesus. They go all the way from the hollow of my neck to the curves of my breast. It looked less severe in the darkness, however, in the light, I look like a train wreck.

His eyes widen, his chest puffing in and out as he shakes his head. "I don't . . ." A million different emotions flash across his expression, and for a second, I feel the tingle of the sparks reemerge. Yet, as quickly as they appear, they vanish as Alex rushes forward.

I skitter to the side as he dives into Laylen. Laylen stumbles back as Alex slams his head into his chest and both fly across the room and ram into the wall. The sheetrock cracks against the force and splits from the floor to the ceiling.

Laylen quickly regains his footing, standing up straight, and he shoves Alex. Alex recovers swiftly, his boots squeaking against the tile as he stomps toward Laylen, whose appearance I'm sure is making the situation even worse. His hair is damp with sweat and a little bit of blood, his shirt soaked in it. His skin is stunningly more smooth and healthy looking than before, his lips an even deeper red, probably from my blood. His eyes are blue again, but a deeper blue, like the ocean instead of the sky.

"I can't believe you fucking bit her!" Alex shouts as he heads for Laylen who refuses to back away. "Of all people, her."

"I told you that I told him to do it!" I cry, moving forward, but I gasp and step back as Laylen rams his head into Alex's chest, wrapping his arms around him, and making them fly backward onto the apothecary table. It instantly buckles beneath their weight and they roll around on the floor; a violent ball of punches, kicks, curses and bruises as they crash into the shelves and the sofas.

"Stop!" I demand, leaping out of the way as they roll to my feet. "This is ridiculous! You guys are acting like lunatics."

Suddenly, Aislin and Adessa appear in the doorway, looking sleepy-eyed and kind of annoyed. Adessa has on a long, navy blue robe and Aislin is wearing a pink plaid pajama set.

"What in the world is going on?" Aislin cries, her bright green eyes extensive as she takes in the broken furniture, shattered figurines and cracked walls. Then she glances up at me and the color drains from her face. "What on earth?"

"Um . . . I think—"

"*Subsisto,*" Adessa screams with her hands out in front of her. Sparks shower from her fingertips and soar across the room toward Alex and Laylen.

They fly away from each other, Alex landing by Aislin's bare feet and Laylen beside mine. He smacks his head on the floor and I peer down at him as he blinks up at me. There's a moment that passes between us, a need that wants to be fed, but there's still a part of me that rebels against the urge. I won't let it happen right now; not in front of an audience.

"What the hell are you two doing?" Aislin asks as Alex stands up, dusting wood chips and glass out of his hair. He's dressed in the same t-shirt and jeans as when I saw him last, only now the jeans are torn at the knee.

Alex wipes his bleeding lip with his arm and then shakes his head. "He fucking bit her." His voice trembles and he lacks his usual composure, alarmingly so.

Laylen gets up, brushing his hair out of his eyes, and Alex instantly moves toward him like he can't control himself.

Aislin grabs the back of Alex's shirt and holds him back. "Laylen bit Gemma?"

He motions his hand at us. "Obviously. Look at her . . . And him."

"Oh my God. I thought another Vampire did that." However she lacks the confidence to be believable, as if she's in denial.

I could try to lie, but everyone in the room knows what happened. It's written all over the both of us in blood and the euphoric state in our eyes.

"Laylen," Aislin whispers, tucking strands of her golden brown hair behind her ears. "Is it . . . is it true? Did you bite her?"

Laylen looks away to the wall and I become hyper-aware of how much of a mess we're really in. Not only is Alex pissed off because I've been bit, but Aislin looks as if her heart has been crushed.

Aislin releases Alex's shirt and steps back with her chin tipped toward the floor. "Oh."

Laylen drags his fingers through his hair and then, staring down at the floor, hurries out of the room. Aislin chases after Laylen, or maybe just runs off in the same direction, about to burst into tears. Adessa takes one look at Alex and me, then turns around and walks out of the room.

Smart woman. I envy her at the moment.

I'm highly aware that Alex is right behind me, standing only inches away from me. The sparks rise and then diminish as if they're trying to breathe again yet can't quite get enough air. I wonder what caused the sensation to fade; what's the reason they're barely there when they've been so strong before?

Finally, I turn around and face Alex. He's already watching me, his hands in his pockets, and he looks strangely uncomfortable.

"Why?" he finally says, then he waits, for what I'm not sure. An explanation. For me to deny it. For me to say I'm sorry and that I hated it. None of those would fit, though, because all of them would be a lie.

I sink down on the remaining upturned sofa, my legs unable to bear my weight. "I needed to find out if my mother was still alive and if she was in The Underworld."

With a pucker at his brow he sits down on the other end of the sofa as far away from me as he can get. "Where did you go?"

I shake my head and shrug. "Some place where Vampires feed on willing humans."

"So who bit you?" he asks through gritted teeth.

I'm not even sure why he's asking. "I think you know who it is already, since you just tried to kick his ass."

His muscles spasm as he works to stay calm, finally getting up and pacing in front of me. "I know, but I needed to hear you say it."

"Why?"

"Because I do."

"He only did it because I told him to," I say quietly, scraping some of the dried blood off my arm with my fingernails. "It was the only way Draven would tell us about my mother."

"Draven" he says tightly, stopping in front of me. "That's who you went to see?"

I nod once. "I guess he can see stuff in different realms."

"I know that." His voice is clipped as he drops back down onto the sofa, leaning against the armrest. "But what I don't get is why you two would act so stupidly."

"It wasn't stupid," I retort, my head snapping in his direction. "I was just trying to find out about my mom . . . and she may help us, you know. She may know things, since *your father* put her there for a reason."

"So what," he snaps, scooting closer to me. "Find another way, then. Don't go to some sketchy Vampire and Lord of the Afterlife to get your answers. Jesus, do you know how dangerous that is, especially if he figured out who you are."

"So what if he does," I say. "He gave me the answer I wanted. She's alive, Alex. My mom's alive."

"That doesn't matter at the moment," he says and fury storms through my body. "We don't know for sure what the star's power is for, and until we do, we need to be careful. The more people who know about you, the easier it'll be for my father and the Death Walkers to find you. Not to mention people like Draven would love to get ahold of the power you have in you." He reaches to take my hands, but then spots the blood on my fingers and pulls away. "Do you know what people would do to get ahold of that kind of power? What they would do to you?"

I tap my finger against my chin, bitterness seeping into my voice. "Hmm . . . I bet I can guess. How about break my soul, my heart, my memories—my whole freaking life—and also ruin everyone whoever mattered to me."

His lips part in shock. "I don't . . ." he trails off, shaking his head.

I push to my feet. "Besides, that's not even what you're mad about. You're pissed off because Laylen drank my blood and now I'm going to be addicted to getting my blood drunk." I back toward the door, shaking with rage, but I'm not quite sure where it stems from. "Well, you know what. It was worth it because I know my mom's still alive and that's all that matters to me."

He rises from the couch, and I turn to run. I think about running out the front door, running away from this mess—my feelings—because there's too many of them inside me. I feel so much right now, I swear I'm going to explode.

The problem is that my emotions are strongly linked to people in this house and it makes running away impossible, so I do the only thing that I can. I race upstairs, lock myself in my room, and cry as confusion takes over my heart.

CHAPTER SEVEN

A LEX TAKES MY hands in his. "Tell me you want me."

We're standing in front of the lake, the moon reflecting in the dark, still water. The chilled wind smells mossy and the water softly lulls. "Tell me I'm the only one you love."

"I don't even know what love is," I reply, staring out at the water.

He frees one of my hands, fixes a finger under my chin, and angles my face toward him. "Tell me you love me, please," he begs.

I open my mouth to speak, but then someone walks up behind me and I turn around, briefly breaking Alex and mine's connection.

Laylen hikes up the shore toward us, bare foot and shirtless. "Gemma, I need you," he says as he reaches us. "Please, come with me."

He holds out his hand and I want to take it, but I also don't want to let go of Alex's hand. With my free hand I reach for him, but Alex tightens his hold on my other hand and pulls me away

"No, please don't," he pleads. "I need you."

I glance back and forth between them as Laylen slips his fingers through mine. I hold onto both of them, knowing I'm going to have to choose, knowing that I can't have both—that I don't have the right to.

I STAY IN my room for two days. I don't shower. I barely move, only getting out of bed to stare out the window and watch the city move through time. Adessa brings me food, which I barely eat. Other than that, no one else comes to see me, although I sense both Alex and Laylen walk by a few times. The strange connection I have with them thrives the second they get close, but neither ever enters. It's like I'm back to the old Gemma, the lonely, isolated one, and for the moment it's what I need because I don't know how to deal with everything inside me.

I watch the sun rise and set. The more time goes by, the calmer I get and I wonder if I should just stay in bed forever. Eventually, though, I start to stink and the grossness of the dried blood coating my clothes and skin gets to me.

As the sun descends behind the hills, marking the second day to pass since Laylen bit me, I climb out of bed. The lights of Vegas vibrantly sparkle through the window, lighting up the room, but it's still dark enough that it's hard to see so I flip the light on. I take a thin-strapped, black shirt from the dresser along with a cream and black striped skirt, and then I make my way out into the quiet hallway.

I'm not sure which door belongs to the bathroom, but I luck out and it's the first one I open. I peel off my clothes, wincing at my stiff muscles, then turn on the water. As I wait for it to heat up, I look at my reflection.

My violet eyes are bloodshot and, even though the holes in my neck have began to heal, there's dried blood all over it. My shirt is torn, exposing more of my breast than I'm comfortable with and my brown hair is tangled around my face. The only thing that is somewhat comforting is that the scratches on my neck, from where Laylen's fangs scraped me, are almost invisible. Still, I look hideous. It's a simple as that.

I climb into the shower and scrub the blood off my body with a loofa. I scrub so hard my skin hurts. I scrub and scrub, the water beneath my feet tinting red as it whirls down the drain. I want to scrub everything off my body, including how I feel. Because, through my erratic, perplexed, emotions, I feel dirty and wrong and I want to feel right again, or as right as I've ever felt anyway. What I want is to feel the void inside my body shrink. I want someone to comfort me, hold me, and hug me. God, when did I get so needy? I never needed anyone before, although I also never felt so bruised and emotionally torn up, either.

Hot tears spill out of my eyes as I rinse my face off and then sink down into the tub. I hug my legs against my chest, letting the showerhead pour water on me, wishing it had the power to erase my misery—erase me.

I sob into my knees, my body shaking and shivering as I try to sift through the last couple of days. I let Laylen bite me merely so I could get something I wanted. I hurt Laylen and Aislin and pissed off Alex by doing it. Am I that bad of a person? Completely greedy and selfish. Who am I? I don't know.

My head suddenly shoots up when I hear the bathroom door open. I tense as a shadow forms on the other side of the shower curtain.

"Gemma," Alex says.

I try to shut off my tears, but tears never want to seem to turn off when you want them to, so instead I work to maintain a balanced voice. "Yes."

He hesitates and I can see his shadow moving, his hand rising in front of him. "Are you okay?"

My lips quiver. "Yes."

"Are you sure?"

"Yes."

He pauses. "Okay."

I let out an exhale, glad he can't see me, see what I mess I am. I allow the tears to fall freely as his shadow shrinks as he moves away. However, then the entire bathtub suddenly darkens, his shadow expanding over me when he draws back the curtain.

He grips onto the edge of the curtain, staring down at me naked in the tub, hugging my knees. There are droplets of water on my face and tears pooling in my eyes and my hair drips in tangles down my back.

"You don't look okay," he says, keeping his eyes on mine. "You've been in your room for over two days. Aislin said you probably needed space—that it would take a few days for the . . ." He shuts his eyes, gathering himself before opening them. "For the sensations of the bite to wear off. That's how it was for her." His gaze sweeps over my face. "But now I'm wondering if she was wrong."

I don't know how to respond. I did need time; I chose to stay in the room, but while isolation might have been a good thing for Aislin, I don't think it was that great for me. I've had too much of it during my life.

I want to tell him this, but when I open my lips all that comes out is a quiet sob. "I'm sorry." I'm not even sure what I'm sorry for, but it feels like it needs to be said so I go with it.

"Gemma . . ." He reaches for the faucet and shuts the water off. Then he leans back and slips his hands into mine, helping me to my feet. I bite my lip as I stand naked in the bathtub before him, feeling self-conscious. "You don't need to be sorry." He tucks strands of my wet hair behind my ear. "I get why you did it."

I'm a little shocked. "You do?"

He nods, smoothing my hair out of my eyes. "I just wish you would have found a different way—an easier way. Yet, I understand how it feels . . . to want to see your mom again."

The way he says it, makes me wonder. "Do you not know your mom?"

He presses his lips together, releases me, and then takes a step toward the towel rack. "My mom disappeared when I was younger." He grabs a towel off the rack and turns back to me

I can suddenly feel it; the sparks and the elated electricity reuniting wholly with my body. It's wonderful and heartbreaking, welcome and, yet, unwanted. "What happened to her?"

He grips the towel in his hand. "I have no idea." He lets the towel fall open. "How about we talk about what we're going to do about your mom?"

I wrap my arms around my body as the cold air gets to my dewed skin. "Why? Are you going to help me?"

"Lift your arms up," he instructs and I hesitantly obey. "I was thinking about it, but only if we do it smartly." He wraps the towel around my back and then drags it across my sides, wiping away the water.

"Why, though?" I wonder, fighting my eyes to stay open as he moves the towel along my ribs, my hips, my stomach, and back, drying off my body. "Why would you all of a sudden help me? You're acting very strange right now. Too nice."

"I've always been helping you, Gemma. It just might not always seem like it, especially when your emotions get in the way." He pulls on the towel, moving to the front of me, and begins to wipe off my neck. "And I'm trying to be nice because you deserve nice."

I swallow hard as his hand holding the towel wanders toward my breast. "Your emotions get in the way sometimes, too. You can be so hot and cold."

He stares at my chest as he begins to dry it off. My nipples harden and a gasp escapes my lips, even though I fight it. "I can't help it," he says softly, moving his gaze and hands away from my chest. He wraps the towel around my body and secures it in a knot at the top. Then he moves back and holds his hand out. "It's how I've been taught to be . . . detached." He stops as I set my hand in his then he helps me out of the tub. "I can't help it and I don't want to help it. Besides, I'm beginning to believe that everything I was taught is bullshit."

He's being so cooperative and the surprising thing is that he seems genuinely nice at the moment. "I want to believe you," I say. "But it's hard to after everything that's happened."

"I know," he says simply and then he winks at me even though he looks sad. "Give me time, though, and I'll change your mind."

"We're always arguing, though," I point out.

He winks again and this time a smile shows through. "Don't pretend like you don't like it—that it doesn't get you all turned on."

I don't say anything because he's partially right. We stare at each other for a moment and I can hear us both breathing erratically. Taking a step forward, he carefully backs me into the sink and sweeps a lock of my hair away from my face. When his gaze meets mine, my body nearly melts as electricity spirals through it. I decide that, despite whatever I said, I did miss it. A lot.

He leans in toward me, tracing my jawline with his fingers. "You bring it out of me, you know. Before you, I could completely control everything I feel, but you . . . you drive me crazy."

"You drive me crazy, too," I agree, my voice a lot less steady than his. "You make me so frustrated . . . and I don't know if I should, or if I even can, trust you."

I wait for him to get angry, but he seems to be very distracted by my neck, his gaze is glued to it as he sketches his finger back and forth across the healing teeth marks.

"Did it hurt?" he asks, pressing down on the marks.

I wince, but only because the contact of his skin makes my body flame hot. "Not really."

His eyes glide up to mine. "Did it feel . . . good?"

"Honestly?" I ask and he nods. My breath falters. "It felt good, bad, and . . . confusing."

His hands glide up the front of my neck, his skin agonizingly hot as it stops at the top. "Did you do anything else?"

"I don't know."

"Yes, you do."

"I know, but I don't want to tell you."

He pauses and I feel his hand tremor. "I *need* to know. It'll drive me crazy if I don't."

I swallow hard. "We kissed."

His grip tightens on my neck, not enough to choke me, but enough that it's intense. "Just kiss?" he asks and I nod.

He loosens his grip slightly, pressing his thumb against my pulse. "Does this feel good?" he asks in a husky voice. "When I touch you?"

I shake my head as hot tingles coil up my legs. "I don't know."

His other hand touches my knee and then slips up the front of my towel, his fingers delving into my upper thigh. "How about this?"

Unbearable heat spreads up my leg and causes me to tremble irrepressibly. "Maybe . . ." I fight to tell him the truth; that he gets to me in ways I can barely grasp. That no matter what happens, if he wants me, then he'll eventually get me because battling my emotions and the sparks will break me down in the long run.

I unintentionally gasp as his breath catches, and then his hand inches higher. I lean back against the mirror. "Alex . . . what are you. . . ."

I drift off as his fingers touch between my legs without slipping into me, merely resting just outside. I bite down on my lip as every single one of my nerve endings blaze with fiery heat and every thought inside my head dissipates

"I can't take this anymore," he says in a breathy whisper as he leans in closer, his eyes glossed over. "I want to be angry with you, but I can't stop thinking about how I need to make you mine again and how I really don't deserve you because of everything I've done to you—all the lies I've told." His lips hover above my mouth as his chest lines up with mine, burning me with ecstasy and driving me crazy. I grip onto the countertops, struggling to cling onto reality.

"How do you think I feel?" *I groan. Hold on, Gemma. Don't let go. You need a clear head . . . clear . . ."*I never know what you're thinking . . . what you want . . . what's the truth . . . what's right and what's . . ." I drift off as his fingers slip inside me. My body bows into him and the towel slips loose before falling to my waist, my bare chest pressing against him.

His fingers start to gently move inside me. "Just trust me okay?"

I shake my head because I don't entirely trust him or myself and what I'm feeling, but I don't argue because I can't. I want him to keep doing what he's doing, feeling me, touching me, diminishing the void inside me. Giving me the human connection that I crave.

His fingers keep working as I struggle to breathe. I clutch so tightly onto the counter that the edge stabs into my palms. Finally I let go and grab onto his shoulders at the same time his hands slide around my back. He pushes on it, forcing me to move closer to him.

My body arches into him so he can touch me even more, even though he's already touching me all over. It feels like there's something missing in the midst of it all. Another connection I'm being deprived of. Then his lips come down on mine and I understand. I needed him to kiss me in order to breathe, function, and be whole again. The entire time the electricity was gone I felt so out of whack, so incomplete, and incredibly wrong. I need Alex, however the question is, do I need him because I want him or is it because of the electricity and whatever's causing it?

I shove the thought out of my head as his fingers push me into blissfulness. As I scream out, he trails kisses down my jawline, my neck, and my breast; sucking hard on my nipple before returning his mouth to mine. He kisses me fiercely. Forcefully. Until my lips are going to bruise. My body and mind unwind and for a moment everything seems perfect. Complete. Whole.

Then I start to regain my composure, however, I don't want to just yet. I want to lose control, drift away, feel every emotion amplify and leave.

I reach for the bottom of Alex's shirt as I pull back my lips.

"What are you doing?" he asks blinking, his lips swollen as he slips his fingers out of me.

I don't say a word as I start to tug his shirt over his head.

He opens his mouth to argue, but then clamps his jaw shut, deciding against it before he then rips his shirt over his head. My hands glide up the front of his lean muscles, trace the lines of the golden flames trimming a ring, the Mark of the Keepers branding the side of his ribcage. He crashes his lips into mine and steals the breath out of me. I writhe my body against him as I slide my hand to the top of his pounding heart. The feeling of it hitting my palm fuels me with desire and I reach for the button off his jeans. He jerks his lips away and the lack of control in his eyes is undeniable. Like the first time we had sex when he lost control of what he was doing. I'm losing control, too, and I don't give a shit. I want, no, *need* him to be inside me now, and I don't even completely understand why. It's like I'm drowning in emptiness and being with him is the only way to save me.

I undo his button and slowly unzip his jeans. He moans, a deep, husky utterance of desire. There's a pause where our eyes collide and we pant, deciding what we should do next. So much has gone on and in the end I know I'll end up as confused as when this all began. Somehow, I can't seem to care.

I want this.

Him.

He must think the same thing because suddenly he's kicking off his jeans along with his boxers. He rips the towel from my body and his hands slide up my legs, spreading me open. I bite down on my lip, waiting in anticipation for him to thrust inside me. Instead of sliding into me, though, he dips his face down toward my open legs. I gasp as his tongue slides inside me, my body curving upward of it's own accord.

"Alex . . ." I grasp handfuls of his hair, unsure what to do or where I should channel this vulnerable, helpless energy to as his tongue slips inside me, filling me like his fingers did earlier. It's almost too much, my emotions are out of my power. I writhe against his tongue, fighting to breathe and function as I'm pushed over the edge. I scream so loud I'm sure the whole house can hear it.

As I catch my breath, his tongue leaves me and seconds later his lips crash against mine. I barely have time to regain my breathing as our tongues twine together, our bodies welding and becoming almost one as he thrusts deep inside me. It doesn't hurt as bad as the first time, but I'm still tender. I jab my nails into his back as I hold onto him, splitting the skin open on his back, clawing into reality. Our bodies dampen with sweat as they move rhythmically together and our breaths grow ragged.

I don't have any control over what I'm doing or feeling. All I can do is hold onto him and, even though I'm not sure I want to, trust him not to break me.

His lips leave mine as he licks and bites a path down my neck, to my collarbone as his hand grips my breast. He grazes his finger over my nipple and so much heat coils through my body that I can't even think straight.

With one final thrust, my body and mind spiral out-of-control and I grab onto him as euphoria takes me over. I let my head fall back and it slams against the mirror. I think I hear the glass shatter, though I'm too far gone to care.

Moments later, Alex buries his face into the crook of my neck, his body tensing. Once he relaxes, he places kiss after kiss onto my skin, sucking on it, making a path to my mouth.

With one last kiss, he slips out of me. His hands grip my waist as he guides me off the countertop, then he stares over my shoulder. I follow his gaze, turning my head, only to find that I did shatter the mirror. Glass is everywhere, behind me, in the sink, on the counter.

I turn my head back to look at him, opening my mouth to say something, but I can't find anything to say.

He combs his fingers through my hair, tugging my head back a little, and forcing me to look at him. "I didn't mean for that to happen," he says. "I just . . ." he trails off. "I don't know how to deal with how I feel around you. You simultaneously piss me off, turn me on and frustrate me. No one's every done that to me before."

"Me, neither," I admit. "But then again, I've only been able to feel those things for a few months so . . ." I frown, unsure how I feel anymore, whether I want to be driven by a grudge or let it go.

His green eyes fill with something I can't quite place while his fingers linger in my hair. "I don't want you running off to Laylen for help," he says. "I want you to come to me."

I look down at my legs wrapped around his waist, so close to him physically, yet mentally we're still incredibly far away. "I honestly still don't know if I can trust you." I look up at him. "I mean, sometimes I ask you questions and you give the vaguest answers. Also, when we first met . . . the stuff you did and said . . . it's hard to forget."

"I'm sorry," he utters quietly and it's a weird moment because Alex isn't the type of guy that says sorry a lot. "I'm sorry all of this happened. That you had to go through everything and that I'm a total douche who you have to feel this crazy electricity feeling with."

I swallow the lump lodged in my throat put there by the intensity in his voice. "It went away for a moment, you know. When Laylen . . . when he bit me."

"How did that . . . how did that feel?" He seems torn with wanting to hear the answer or even asking the question.

"Weird. Crazy. Unnatural." I shrug. "Honestly, it kind of made me feel empty." Some of the tension leaves his face, like he's relieved by my answer. "But I still don't know exactly how I feel about you or what's driving what I do feel."

He eyes me over, seeming undecided, as if he's having an internal battle with himself. Then he grips my waist and lifts me off the counter.

He reaches for his jeans on the floor. "Get dressed," he says as he slips them on.

I reach for my clean shirt folded up on the counter beside the sink. "Okay." My voice is tight, figuring we're heading back to where we started. He's being distant and I'm sure he's going to start shutting down. Goddammit. Why do I do this to myself?

He slips his shirt on over his head and then heads for the door, and feelings of shame, guilt and irritation flood me.

"Where are you going?" I tug the shirt over my head. "Are you leaving?"

He pauses, glancing over his shoulder as he grasps the doorknob. "I'm going to go find the one person that I know of who can get us into The Underworld."

I start to smile, a full, real smile. "To find my mom?"

He nods. "But don't get so happy yet. First we have to deal with the person who's going to help us." He jerks the door open as I slip the skirt on. "And it's going to be a pain in the ass.

91

"Why?" I tie the top of the skirt.

He looks unhappy as he steps into the hall. "The only Foreseer I know who's not afraid of breaking the rules."

I point my finger at myself. "Me?"

"No someone who is experienced and knows the history." He steps out into the hall and I follow. "We're going to find Nicholas."

CHAPTER EIGHT

"YOU WANT TO bring Nicholas here?" I frown as I trot down the stairs behind him, gathering my damp hair into a side braid "Like the pervert Faerie/Foreseer/likes-to-invade-my-personal-space, Nicholas? The one who became a mirage and made me believe he was you more than a few times?"

He glances over his shoulder, nodding. "That would be the one."

I shake my head as we enter the living room. It's miraculously been put back into place, the walls mended, the chairs fixed, and the apothecary table looks like it's never been touched. "Do we really need him, though?" I ask. "Isn't there anyone else who can help us?"

"My connections in the Foreseer world are very limited." He flops down on the couch, shaking his head. "Trust me, Gemma. He's the last person I ever want to go to for help, well besides someone like Draven." He glances up at my neck and I have the urge to cover my neck and hide the two small, healing bite marks on it. "Foreseer's can travel anywhere at any moment, which is why Nicholas was able to randomly show up back in Colorado. You remember the crystal ball he used to get us into the City of

Crystal, right?"

I sit down on the couch beside him. "How could I forget? I nearly broke my damn arm."

He presses his lips together, draping his arm on the back of the sofa. "Well, that crystal ball allows them to travel *everywhere*."

I perk up a little. "Everywhere as in places like The Underworld?"

His fingers brush the back of my neck and begin tracing soft, circular patterns. "That's what I'm not one-hundred percent sure of. I'd guess yes, but I never like to guess about things. The only way to really find out is to talk to a Foreseer who knows the history."

"And you think he's going to willingly help us?" I frown doubtfully. "I've only met him once, but I'm guessing he's not the kind of person to just hand over information."

"I know."

"So . . . what do we have to do then? How do we get him to cooperate?"

His fingers trail around to the front of my neck, up to my cheek where he finds a loose strand of my hair and coils it around his finger. "We have to bring him here."

"And then what?" I wonder. "We just go down there and get my mom? I'm guessing it's not going to be that easy."

He offers me a sad smile. "It's not . . . that place is dangerous. More dangerous than anywhere you've ever been."

"Then who's going to go to this place?" I ask. "Me?"

He shakes his head. "But I can't go, either. It's going to have to be someone we can trust to keep an eye on Nicholas since he'll have to take them there. Someone like Aislin . . . and Laylen, I guess."

I elevate my eyebrows at him and he releases my

hair before shifting uneasily back in the chair. "*You* trust Laylen?"

His shoulders lift and fall as he shrugs. "If he's with Aislin, then I'm sure he'll be okay."

"You sound like you don't believe it yourself," I remark, studying him over. "What are you up to?"

He narrows his eyes. "I'm just trying to help you. That's all. Jesus, can't you simply trust me?"

"Trust is something earned," I say.

He glares at me, his green eyes smoldering. "Like when I sacrificed myself against a *memoria extracto* so you'd be okay?"

I evade the question because he's right, yet distrust stabs at the back of my neck. I can't seem to shake the feeling for some reason, even when he proves otherwise. "Why won't you go?"

"Because I'll be going somewhere else." He stands to his feet and extends his hand out to me. "Now come with me. Let's go get Nicholas and get this whole thing over with."

WE GO INTO the back room where Adessa stores her supplies on rows and rows of metal shelves that are stacked with boxes, elaborate objects, and glass jars filled with disturbing looking things.

Aislin joins us, seeming cheerful as ever, yet I can feel the awkward energy between us. "Hey, Gemma," she says.

I smile, but it feels forced. "Hey."

She glances at my clothes. "You look good in what I picked out. Very Black Angel like."

I look down at my boots, skirt, and tank top. "That's

why you picked me out such a Gothic wardrobe? So I'd look like a Black Angel?"

She nods, picking up a box embedded with miniscule, silvery diamonds. "I thought it would help you blend in."

I want to tell her I'm sorry, yet now doesn't seem like the time. Maybe when Alex isn't around perhaps.

She lifts open the lid and sniffs the inside of the box. "So what are we doing exactly? Trying to figure out what my . . . what Stephan is doing?"

Alex quickly fills her in, letting her know his plan. Something about her reaction unsettles me to no end, especially when Alex says that I'm going to use a Foreseer's crystal ball to summon Nicholas here.

"Are you insane?" I gape at Alex. "There's no way I'm doing that."

Alex rolls his eyes, like I'm being absurd, but I'm not. "You want to get your mom back, right?"

"Of course," I reply, propping my elbow onto a shelf. "But not by using a crystal. Every time I've used one I've seen stuff I'd rather not and, besides . . . didn't you make some promise to Dyvinius that I wouldn't use my power until I was trained."

Aislin's examining a jar that looks like it has a chicken leg or something in it. When I say this, she nearly drops it on the concrete floor. "You did what? She rebalances the jar in her hand. "Alex, why the heck did you do that?"

I stand up straight and step toward Aislin. "Wait. What happens if he breaks it?"

Aislin sets the jar back down on the shelf and fidgets with the straps on her floral, pink dress. "He'll end up having to go to the City of Crystal to do—"

"Aislin," Alex warns, spinning a steel ball balanced on a podium. "Don't."

I scowl at him. "Are you seriously trying to keep things

from me?"

He stands up straight and steps in front of me. His nearness forces me to crane my neck back to look at him as he backs me against the shelf. "This is for your own good."

"Why?" I ask as the edges of the shelf press against me.

"Because you won't do it if I tell you." He puts a hand on each side of me, pinning me between his arms.

"How do you know that?" I cross my arms. "Maybe I won't mind whatever's going to happen to you."

He rolls his eyes again. "Yes, you will because, whether you'll admit it or not, you care about me."

I open my mouth to protest, but I can't get any words to come out. A faint stab reveals at the back of my neck and unexpectedly I realize that I do care about Alex, despite the bad that's happened between us.

"Please just tell me," I practically beg, gripping onto the bottom of his shirt. My knuckles brush against his muscles and the contact singes my skin. "I want to know what we're getting into."

The side of his mouth crooks up into a lopsided smile. "All you need to do is use your power to get Nicholas here, then you can leave the rest to everyone else."

"I could go to The Underworld, you know," I tell him firmly. "I'm not completely incompetent. Besides, it is *my* mom we're going after. It should be me who goes and gets her."

He sighs and places his hand on my cheek, his thumb grazing a line across my cheekbone. "Regardless of everything you've done over the last few days . . . walking into a Vampire Lair . . . you still have the star's energy inside you, and until we know for sure what the hell it's being used for. . . . Why my. . . ." He swallows hard. "Why my father wants it, then we need to keep you safe. Furthermore, the last thing we need is for the Queen of The Underworld to get her hands on you. She's almost as bad as Demetrius and his Death Walkers."

"Are you sure there's not another way to bring him here?" I ask. "I mean, don't you guys use phones or something?"

The corners of his lips quirk. "I'm pretty sure there's no service in the City of Crystal."

I want to roll my eyes at him, but I don't. What I want to do is hug him because I have this feeling something really bad is about to happen. "Just promise me you're not going to die," I whisper.

He seems pleased by what I say. "Never."

"What about the Kingdom of Fey," Laylen suggests, abruptly appearing in the doorway. He leans against the door frame and his arms flex as he crosses them. "You could always just go there and get him."

The second my eyes land on him, I know that the sensations of the bite has changed me somehow. He's wearing all black again, his standard uniform, and his lips look a little swollen as if he's been kissing someone or feeding. The thought makes me insanely jealous and, for a brief moment, I feel compelled to run to him, beg him to fold his arms around me, and sink his teeth into my veins. It actually physically hurts not to do it, yet I manage to keep my feet firmly planted to the ground.

I clear my throat, attempting to also wipe the tension building within me. "Kingdom of Fey?" I ask.

"It's where the Fey live," Aislin explains, staring at the spot of concrete on the floor as she shuffles her sandals against it. "Since Nicholas is part Fey, he goes there sometimes, but I don't think he's very fond of it because . . . well, because the Fey can be . . ."

"Everything's a joke to them," Alex interrupts, his fingers possessively touching my hip as he moves around behind me. "There's a lot of running around in circles." He gently guides me closer to him, his eyes fixed on Laylen as he situates my back against his chest. "Besides, you know they aren't very welcoming to anyone who isn't full Fey. They even give Nicholas shit, which means he doesn't usually hang out there."

"So you what?" Laylen crooks his brow and steps inside the storage room. "Just summon him here, using *her*." He nods his head at me. "Then you go pay your debt for breaking the promise and Aislin and I go with the crazy Faerie into The Underworld."

Alex's chest presses against my back and his other hand touches my waist. "Unless you have a better plan."

He shrugs, stopping just in front of us, and I ball my hands into fists to keep from touching him. "I just want to make sure you're good with it because you're the one who's going to have to pay the debt. Everything else is easy compared to that."

"I wouldn't go so far as easy," he says. "But I get what you're saying and I can handle it. Besides, it's the quickest way and we need quick."

"Alex," Aislin starts, but then stops when Alex shoots her a glare. "Fine, you know what? Do whatever you want. You always do anyway." Her voice is full of venom as she backs up to the shelf behind her with her hands up.

"I really wish someone would let me in on what the hell's about to happen," I say and Alex's fingers leave my waist.

I shift uncomfortably as I turn around, very aware that Laylen is just behind me. "Ummm . . . What if Nicholas doesn't show up as Nicholas . . . what if he mind fucks with my head again?"

Alex's expression plummets. "Shit, the damn mirage thing." He contemplates the dilemma and then his gaze diverts to Aislin. "Any ideas."

Aislin sighs and then turns toward the shelf. "Always turning to the Witch." She rummages through the unique collection of stuff stacked on the shelves and finally selects a small, bronzed box about the size of her palm. "What would you guys do without me?" she asks, turning around with the box balanced in her hand.

"Probably be confused all the time," Laylen says, winking at her.

She smiles, but it's tight. Then she walks forward, her eyes glued to the box. "Now I'm not one-hundred percent sure if it'll work, but it's supposed to give you clear, undiluted sight, so we'll see."

"You know, I love you to death," Alex says. "But every time you say you're not one-hundred percent sure, it makes me worry I'm going to grow a third arm or something."

"Hey, that only happened once," Aislin protests, removing the lid from the box.

"Or temporarily change into a frog," Laylen says with a small smile.

"I was only trying to turn you into prince charming," she says, her green eyes lighting up as she smiles up at them. "It's not my fault I didn't read the fine print."

Laylen causally leans against the shelf. "You know, I still crave the taste of flies sometimes."

"I bet you do," Aislin's mouth threatens to turn upward as she reaches into the box.

The whole conversation reminds me again how much I've missed out on and how I'll never get it back. I won't share moments with them of misplaced spells and games or whatever else children do. I only have now and I'm not really sure what to do with it since it pretty much owns me at the moment.

Alex temporarily removes my necklace so Aislin can splash some silvery dust in my eyes and chant her magic words. He puts it back on me and Aislin splashes some in Laylen and Alex's eyes as well as hers. Then Alex moves over to a shelf and searches the bottom row. Bending down, he scoops up a crystal ball and then walks back over to me, balancing the illuminating crystal structure in his palm.

I wipe my eyes with the heels of my hands and blink against my blurry vision. "Are you sure you want to do this?"

He nods. "Now shut your eyes and place you're hand on it . . . the sooner we get this over with, the sooner we can have answers."

I swallow hard, torn. Is this what I really should be doing? Should I really risk it? Risk whatever waits for us in the future?

"Think of somewhere safe to go," Alex instructs with his fingers wrapped around the glass. "A safe place."

I'm seriously considering stepping back and really thinking about what I'm about to do because I do care for Alex. I really do. The feeling I'm experiencing—the desire to protect him—makes me hesitate.

"Maybe I should—"

Before I can react, he grabs my hand and places my palm onto the glass. I feel a hot energy swoop up my body before it slams against my head and my heart. It feels like my limbs are being detached from my body as my pulse accelerates. Seconds later, I'm engulfed by a bright, warm light and being swept away into the unknown.

CHAPTER NINE

I'M NOT SURE what went wrong, but something is definitely wrong. All I can see is light. Everywhere. I'm not falling or floating. I'm not even moving, I'm simply sustained somewhere within it.

"Where am I?" I whisper, moving my arms and legs, desperately trying to get my bearings.

"You're in your future," someone says from behind me.

My feet suddenly plant against the ground and I spin around to squint through the light. The smell of lilacs, rain, and forest smother my nostrils and I know, even though I can't see him, that there's an extremely annoying half-Faerie standing behind me.

"Nicholas," I call out, wrapping my arms around myself. "I know it's you."

He doesn't answer, but I can feel him next to me, the heat of his body radiating all over me.

"What is this place?" I rotate in circles, searching the light for him, but I'm blind everywhere I look.

"I already told you, it's your future," his voice purrs in my ear and I flinch, swinging my arm around.

I only hit air and curse under my breath. "How do you

know it's my future?"

His voice touches my ear again. "Because I do."

I glance around at the pale light. I can't even see my own body, can barely feel it. "How can this be my future? There's nothing here."

"Is that what you see?" Nicholas's breath encircles my face. "Nothing?"

My instincts warn me to be cautious as I remember how far he pushed me the last time we were in a vision together; how he tried to touch me and take advantage of me.

I open my mouth to tell him I don't know, but as if my voice no longer belongs to me I say, "I see light . . . It's everywhere." Shit. Where the hell did that come from?

"Are you sure that's all you see?"

No. "Yes."

There is a pause. "Then I guess that means your future's dead."

Dead. "What!" I exclaim. "How do you reach that assumption?"

"Let's go back," he says, evading my question. "I have some business to take care of with Alex."

Before I can respond, I feel his fingers slide through mine and he pries my arms away from me. Then I'm jerked back and he slams me against him, his arms enfolding around me.

"Let me go!" I wiggle my shoulders and arms, but he tightens his hold, trapping me against him.

He kisses the top of my head and I hear him breathe in the scent of my hair. "God, the things I could do to you right now." His voice is deep and full of desire; it makes me want to gag.

I lift my leg, bend my knee, and swing my foot forward hoping to kick him, however all I touch is air.

"Nicholas, I swear to God—"

His lips come down over mine and I feel vile and gross inside. I try to lean back, but he only moves with me, keeping us pinned together, as he attempts to snake his tongue into my mouth. I open my lips and bite down hard, feeling his tongue rupture open and bleed.

He only laughs. "You're seriously going to pay for that."

His hand starts to trail down my back, groping me, and forcing me against him. The prickle stabs at the back of my neck and everything feels wrong. I'm terrified. Disgusted. With him and myself.

"Please don't," I beg, writhing my body as tears threaten to spill out. "Please just let me go."

"Don't worry," he whispers in my ear. "I'll be gentle."

As his hand reaches my ass, a sharp, deafening noise echoes in my head. I hear Nicholas curse and then the lightness intensifies as I'm jolted back.

WHEN I OPEN my eyes again the light is gone. I'm lying in the velvet sofa with my head in Alex's lap and he's staring down at me with a concerned look in his expression.

"Are you okay?" he asks, tracing his finger down my temple.

Panic flares through my body as I glance around the room. "How did I get here? I thought I was in the storage room?"

"Yeah, but you fainted," he says, brushing my hair out of my eyes. I wince at the aching pain in my skull. I feel nauseous and sick as I try to decipher what happened. "And you hit your head on the corner of the shelf before I could catch you." He checks my eyes, leaning closely. "I'm worried you might have a concussion."

I shake my head while I gradually sit up and he leans back to give me room. My eyes immediately drift to the sofa across from me where Nicholas sits.

He's wearing a navy blue T-shirt and a pair of tan cargo pants. His sandy blonde hair sweeps over his forehead, his golden eyes twinkling and his smile is devious.

I narrow my eyes at him, but he only shakes his head and smiles. *Watch it,* he mouths. *Or I won't help.*

Alex follows my line of gaze and then he stiffens. "When did you get here?"

"He showed up in the vision," I explain through gritted teeth. I want to wring his neck, but I also need his help. It's wrong to let him have so much power over me, although there's nothing I can do about it other than succumb to him. "In grand, creepy Nicholas style."

Nicholas's grin broadens and his dark gaze skims over my body. "You know it."

"But that's not allowed," Alex interrupts, putting his hand on my knee while his fierce gaze remains on Nicholas. "Foreseers are not allowed to go into another Foreseer's vision without permission. Even I know that."

"Maybe I did have permission," Nicholas says with a sly grin. "How do you know for sure that I didn't? Maybe Gemma begged me to show up there?"

Alex arches a brow at me, wondering what's going on. I want to tell him, so I can watch him punch Nicholas in the face because I know he will, yet then Nicholas probably won't help me, either.

I shake my head and lean into Alex, wanting to shut my eyes and let the electricity lull me to sleep. "It's nothing. He's just being a creeper."

"Don't pretend you don't like it." Nicholas winks,

relaxing back in the chair with his arms spread out on the back. His attention focuses on Alex who protectively inches closer to me. "So is there a reason you let her use the crystal ball again? Or did she just decide to do it on her own and let you suffer the consequences for it? Personally, I'd love to think it was the latter."

Alex and I exchange a look that seems to tell me he's preparing himself for something terrible. His expression flashes with worry, and Alex rarely looks worried. "It wasn't the latter." He forces his gaze away from me and his fingers on my knee tense, his nails jabbing into my skin as his other hand clenches into a tight fist. "We need your help." It sounds like it's killing him to say it.

"Help with what?" Amusement dances in Nicholas's eyes.

"With getting into The Underworld," Alex says through gritted teeth.

A smirk forms on Nicholas's face as he absentmindedly traces the Foreseer mark on his wrist, moving around the circle and ultimately the 'S' in the middle of it. "And who says I know how to do that?"

Alex shrugs. "I know your kind have a way of getting everywhere, including to different realms."

"True," Nicholas says. "But even if I could get you there, who says I want to help you?"

Alex slides his hand up the front of my leg, finds my hand in my lap, and laces our fingers together. I catch Nicholas watching the movement and for a moment jealousy burns in his eyes. "I'm sure there's some sort of bargain we can work out."

Nicholas's attention transfers to me. "I'm sure I could figure out something that you have that I want."

Alex angles himself in front of me, obscuring me from Nicholas's view. *"Not her."*

"And what if I said that was the only thing I'd take."

"Then I'd kill you."

My head whips in Alex's direction, but his eyes stay on Nicholas. Nicholas holds the gaze steadily, though the longer it goes on, the more uncertain Nicholas gets, and finally, he slumps back looking really fidgety.

"There is one thing I'd love to have," he says. "And if you can get it for me, then I'll be your golden ticket into the land where torture is welcomed with opened arms along with insanity." He pauses, bringing his foot up onto his knee. "But I have to ask, why The Underworld?"

"That's not important." Alex squeezes my hand, sending sparks up my arm. "Just tell me what you want."

He dithers, thrumming his finger against his lip. "I'd like some *fraxinus invisibili.*"

"What the hell's that?" Alex asks.

"Ask your Witch," Nicholas replies. "She'll know what it is."

Alex glances at the doorway. "Aislin, can you come in here?"

A minute later Aislin enters the room with Laylen trailing at her heels. I discount the pull toward him the best that I can, especially since Aislin looks like she's been crying, her eyes red and her cheeks swollen.

"What's up," she says, sounding hoarse as she reaches the middle of the room, keeping her distance from Nicholas.

"Do you know what *fraxinus invisibili* is?" he asks her.

Her expression plummets as she sits down on the edge of the apothecary table and Laylen sinks down on the armrest of the sofa right beside Nicholas. "Yeah, its invisibility ash."

Alex looks confused. "Why the hell do you want that?"

he asks Nicholas.

Nicholas shrugs, jiggling his foot that's on his knee. "Who knows when it'll come in handy?"

Alex and Aislin trade a look. "It's what he wants in exchange for his help," he explains to her.

"But what if he can't help us?" Aislin turns to the side so she's facing Alex. "What if I give it to him and then he runs?"

Alex glances at Nicholas and then demands, "Tell us how to get into The Underworld and then we'll talk deals."

Nicholas lowers his feet to the floor. "I don't really think you're in a place to give orders since I'm going to be taking you away soon, but if you must know, getting into The Underworld requires a lot of Foreseer power and an *Ira*."

"What the fuck's an Ira?" Alex asks.

Nicholas shrugs, nonchalantly kicking his feet up onto the apothecary table. "A very powerful crystal ball. One that can take you to and from forbidden places, like The Underworld, and in present time, too, without any of the laws being broken."

"And it'll work?" Alex pulls me even closer to him, as if he can't get enough of touching me, as if he's about to go soon.

I bite my nails, nervous at what lies ahead for us. What'll happen to him? To me? To us?

"I didn't say that," Nicholas corrects him. "But it's your best bet."

Alex exchanges another look with Aislin. "How much damage can he do with something like *fraxinus invisibili*?" he asks her.

"Well, if he can get a Witch to help him use it," she replies. "Then probably a lot. He'll be able to go invisible whenever he wants which means he'll be harder to find, yet it'll be easier for him to find us."

Alex's forehead creases as he frowns at Nicholas. "She's not helping you use it."

Nicolas raises his hands in front of him. "I never asked her to. All I said is that I need it."

Alex scoots forward in the chair, still holding onto me so I have to move forward with him. "You know I could just beat you up and force you to help us."

Nicholas's eyes darken with a challenge as his fingers curl around the armrest. "You'd be surprised how much pain I can endure. Besides, you don't have that long before you're officially considered to be going back on your promise." He releases the armrest and taps a watch on his wrist. "Time is ticking."

Alex puffs out a frustrated breath and glances at an antique clock on the wall across from us. "Fine. Aislin will give you the ash after you take me to the City of Crystal. That way you have to come back."

Even though I knew it was coming, I panic, grabbing onto his arm. "You can't go to that God awful place."

"I have to go . . . its part of the promise I made with Dyvinius . . . you already knew this," he says simply.

"I know, but . . ." I trail off as he leans in and rests his forehead against mine.

"Whatever you do, don't trust him," he whispers. "He'll stab you in the back as soon as he gets a chance."

"You're coming back, right?" I whisper. "You're not leaving me forever."

"I would never leave you forever." He lets out a faltering breath. "Eventually I'll be back, however I have to stay there for a while."

Panic owns me at the moment and I can't seem to control it. Everything else that happened between us, the good and the bad, doesn't matter. Only this everlasting second does and the fact that I can't let him go. "Alex, please don't go."

"I have no choice . . . the consequences if I stay . . . well, lets say they're way worse than going to the City of Crystal." He puts a hand on the hollow of my neck right above my locket. "And never take this off. Promise me you won't."

My skin swelters and I'm unable to help myself when I graze my lips across his. "I won't," I whisper against his mouth. I'm about to pull away when he cups the back of my head, tugging gently on my hair, and kisses me hard with every ounce of passion he possesses. Again I wonder just how much control we have over our emotions and how much control the electricity has. I kiss him back with an everlasting hunger. I'm breathless by the time I pull away and I've completely forgotten we're in a room full of people.

Aislin covers her mouth as Laylen clears his throat, staring at the doorway. Alex's lips are swollen as he turns to Nicholas.

"Alright," Nicholas says and slips a ruby-filled crystal ball from the pocket of his pants. He rises to his feet with it palmed in his hand. "Let's go." He winds around the apothecary table and holds it out in front of him.

Alex gives me one last kiss on the cheek and then releases my hand, getting to his feet. I want to grab onto him, pull him back to me, and hold him against me. I fight the urge to do so, trying to decide what's right and what is wrong while fearing what's going to happen to him when he goes. Is this what caring for someone feels like? All this worry and fear floating around inside me, only it's not for me.

"And one last thing," Alex says to Nicholas as he reaches for the crystal.

Nicholas sighs begrudgingly. "What now."

"If you try anything, and I mean anything with Gemma while I'm gone." He jabs a finger against Nicholas's chest. "You'll have to deal with two very powerful Witches and a Vampire who will do anything to protect her."

"Whatever." Nicholas rolls his eyes, though he looks a little worried.

Alex doesn't say anything else as he places his hand on the glowing crystal ball. There's a loud swoosh, then a blink of light and they're gone, along with the electricity.

I miss him the second he disappears.

I miss him so much it hurts.

I've never missed anyone before and I'm not fully sure that I like it.

CHAPTER
TEN

I ASK WHERE Adessa is and Aislin tells me she's tending to her store. Aislin quickly leaves the room to go find some *fraxinus invisibili* from Adessa's storage room.

Once she's gone, Laylen and I sit on the sofa and wait for Nicholas to return. There's an awkward silence between us as the memories of bites and blood linger in our heads.

"So," Laylen finally starts, bringing his knee up onto the spot of sofa to fill up the space between us. "How have you been feeling?" He rakes his fingers through his hair and doesn't bother to fix it, leaving it sticking up all over the place. "God, that was a stupid question. It sounded so much better in my head."

"I'm fine." I pluck at a loose thread on the sofa, forcing myself to focus on the conversation and not memories of him sinking his teeth into me and blood or anything else that's bringing me down. "And it wasn't a stupid question. It was a much needed question . . . things have been really weird between us."

"They have," he agrees and then scoots forward on the sofa until our knees touch, invading the safe zone. I need space, otherwise I'm going to do or say something stupid; like *please, pretty please bite me again.* "And I don't want them to be."

"Neither do I," I agree, blowing out a stressed breath. "You're the only person I've ever felt normal around."

His eyebrows lift in doubt. "Really?"

"Yes, really," I say. "Minus what happened back with Draven, you've always made me feel like a person instead of a star."

He puts a hand on my knee. "Can we forget about what happened and go back to being friends?"

I nod, relieved even though I can still feel a faint pull toward him and his fangs. "I'd like that."

He smiles, but there's reluctance behind it and he lacks the confidence that his words portray. "Then it's settled. No more kissing or biting," he jokes, but his voice is sad and full of guilt. I have a feeling that despite how nonchalant we're both being about it, down the road sometime, it's going to end up being a huge problem.

"I'll never ask you to do that again," I say and then unable to take it anymore, I lean in and give him a hug. "I'll never make you do anything that will hurt you ever again." God, he smells so good, I need to lean back. I give myself a few more seconds and then I pull away. I shake off the sensation to lean against him and tilt my neck to the side. It makes me feel so guilty because of Alex.

Alex. I should be thinking of Alex, shouldn't I? I have no idea anymore. Alex or Laylen? How about both? What the hell is wrong with me?

As I sift through my thoughts of what's right and what's wrong, images begin to flicker through my mind as the prickle lightly begins to poke at the back of my neck At first it's stuff I can already remember, but then suddenly they start to reveal lost thoughts from a place and time I once was forced to forget.

Alex and me picking lilacs in a field; watching other Keepers practice sword fighting in the castle; playing, having fun, smiling.

"Gemma, what's wrong?" Laylen's voice is far away as I begin to feel disembodied.

"I think I can remember some stuff . . . about my childhood . . . about Alex and I being friends."

"You remember?" he asks. "Like actually remember?"

I nod as my vision goes in and out of focus. "They're real memories . . . And I can feel how I felt when I was there . . . God, this is so strange. . . ."

The emotions I experienced during each memory link to my heart, mind, body, and conclusively my soul, the most important part. In the end, it's just Alex and me. Together. Like we were never supposed to be apart and all I can do is drift into the memory, letting it take me over.

WHEN MY SIGHT returns to me, I'm no longer at Adessa's. I panic as I look around at the trees of a forest even though this has happened before. I've gone into a vision without a crystal. But how? How is this even possible?

Thick trees enclose me from every side and a grey stone castle peeks through the top while, far in the distance, the sun shines behind it. It has to be the forest near the lake—the entrance to The Underworld. I can feel it in the air, in my mind, in my body.

The sky is a clear blue and the air smells like earth and musk. Not knowing what else to do, I head for the castle, wondering why I'm here. What am I supposed to see exactly?

I'm about halfway there when a cool breeze sweeps through my hair and kisses at my cheeks. The impulse to go to the castle floats away. Suddenly, I'm turning around, heading in the opposite direction, and going deeper into the forest, my feet moving as if they have their own mind.

I hike for what seems like forever, stumbling over fallen tree trunks and fighting against the unruly, blooming branches. Finally, I come to a stop in front of a steep hill. I need to go up it, yet I don't understand why. Obeying, I move to the side and start searching for something I know is hidden on the hill. After a while, I get frustrated because I have no clue what I'm looking for or how long I'm going to have to keep looking, but then I spot something that makes me pause. A bush budding with violet flowers, growing out of the middle of the hill. I hike up to it, my boots battling the loose, rocky dirt, and then I pick one of the violet flowers. The smell is intoxicating and causes more images of my past to spin in my head. I've been to this place before and picked these flowers . . . I remember the flower in Alex's car and how he told me I used to pick them for him when we were younger.

I squat down and start digging through the damp soil as I inch around to the back of the bush. Behind it is a small hole in the ground. I hoist myself up to it and peer down. There's a ladder that leads to a bottom where a light filters from somewhere.

I take a deep breath and lower my feet to the top step of the ladder. Then I start to climb down, my hands sweating against the cool metal until my feet reach the floor. I immediately spin around, fearing what I'm going to see. Visions have never been kind to me and I half expect Stephan to come charging out to stab me.

I'm standing in a hollowed out room, made of dirt as well as the roots of a tree. There's a rustic wooden table against the back wall where a candle is burning. Next to the table is a metal trunk, and in front of the trunk is a young girl with long, brown hair, violet eyes, and wearing a purple dress. It's me, the younger version anyway. I'm probably around four years old, which means there's a good chance that my soul and memories are still intact.

Sitting across from me is a little boy with his legs crisscrossed and a pocketknife in his hand. He has dark brown hair and bright green eyes that shine like emeralds. It's Alex when he was younger. Alex and me. Together.

"So, what do you think's going to happen?" the younger version of me asks as she plays with a large sapphire, rolling it in the dirt. "After they take me away?"

Alex shakes his head and gently takes the sapphire from her, tossing it across the room into the trunk in the corner. It lands inside, making a soft thud as it hits the bottom. "I don't know, Gemma. I really don't."

"Do you think we'll ever see each other again?" she asks, tracing circles in the dirt with her fingers.

He nods, scraping the blade of the pocketknife into the dirt. "I promise we will, no matter what anyone says."

Tears bubble in the corner of her eyes, and I can actually feel her fear, worry, and sadness stirring with in me as I remember this exact moment. "Do you think Marco and Sophia will be nice to me?" she asks.

"How could they not be nice to you?" Alex says. "No one could ever be mean to you, Gemma."

My mouth turns downward at his words. It's such a nice, free moment between us and I'm a little shocked. This is what we were like together? So comfortable. I almost feel sorry for us, we were too naïve to see what was going to happen to us.

"I have an idea," Alex says, holding the pocketknife up in front of him. "How about you and I become blood brothers?"

She scowls at him and folds her arms. "I'm not a boy."

Alex laughs and I do, too. "Okay, how about blood friends?"

Tears escape her eyes and roll down her cheeks. "What do I have to do to become one?"

"I'll make a little cut on my hand and on yours, then we press them together and make a promise, okay?"

She looks wary. "Will it hurt?"

"Only for a minute," he promises.

She wipes the tears away from her cheeks with her hands. "Okay, let's do it."

She stretches her hand to Alex and he carefully makes a small incision in her palm with the tip of the knife. She winces and I glance down at the small scar on my palm. I never knew where it came from and I once made a joke to Alex about it, saying a guy cut me there. He's known all along what it was from and never said anything.

Alex makes a tiny cut in his palm, then drops the knife to the ground and raises his hand out in front of him. "Okay, put yours up to mine."

She presses her palms to his with a beaming grin on her lips.

"*Forem*," Alex utters. "Now you say it."

She takes a deep breath. "*Forem*."

Alex smiles as he drops his hand to his lap. "There, that's all it takes."

"But what does *forem* mean?" she asks, wiping the blood form her hand with her finger.

"It means—"

"Alex!" Someone yells from above the ground.

The children's eyes become round and Alex jumps to his feet. "We have to go." He holds out his hand and helps her to her feet.

"Do you think your dad will be mad at us," she asks, panicking as they head past me toward the ladder. "For disappearing?"

"I don't know," Alex says. "Let's just hurry up, okay?"

She glances around at the little hideout with a sad look on her face, like she'll never see the place again, and then she nods. "Okay."

They climb up the ladder and I follow them. As I step out from the behind the violet bush, I see Stephan waving his finger as he scolds them. I don't want to see what happens next because I have a feeling I already know. The friendship will get crushed, a soul will be broken, and I'll forget that it ever happened. I know because I can pretty much feel it coming. It's heartbreaking to think about and know that this is what will be destroyed. For a second I find myself wishing I could forget it again and go back to unknowing.

I shut my eyes and sink down into the ground, waiting to be yanked away, thinking I'm going back, but suddenly I'm drowning in darkness.

Evil darkness.

CHAPTER ELEVEN

MY SKIN IS on fire, raging like a desert storm. The heat claws at my skin, bites at it, gnawing it's way into my soul as I fly helplessly through the seemingly endless darkness.

The further I go, the hotter I get until I can't take it anymore. I stretch out my arms, glancing at them, however the darkness is too thick and weighted to see them at all. I open my mouth to shout for help, but my voice is lost in my own head.

I get dragged further into the desolate place and start to give up hope of ever seeing the light of day again. Yet then a light forms around me, lighting up my ghostly pale skin and orbing through the darkness, allowing me to see where I am.

I'm nowhere. Lost in nothingness. Destined to be no one.

As a triangular shape forms on my skin, swirling upward before dipping down in a ray of light, I realize that I could become someone. A strong someone. A powerful someone.

I could become the darkness.

My eyes shoot open and I gasp for air, my skin is

covered with sweat. Laylen's face appears in my line of vision, kneeling to the side of the sofa where I lie flat on my back. He looks horrified, his skin a sickly green.

"What the hell just happened?" he asks, his blue eyes wide beneath his blond hair.

I start to sit up, scratching my arm, even though there's no triangular shape on it. "I have no idea."

He puts his hand on my shoulder and pins me down to the sofa. "Don't sit up until we figure out why you passed out."

"I didn't pass out," I tell him. "I went into a vision . . . I think, anyway" At least with the first thing I saw. The second one I'm not sure of, but the idea that it could be a vision scares the living daylights out of me.

He leans away, taken aback. "But you weren't touching a crystal."

"I know," I say. "But I think I might be able to go in them without a crystal."

He gapes at me unfathomably. "Seriously?"

I shrug. "I'm not sure . . . All I know is that I enter things sometimes, just like I enter a vision, only I don't have a crystal."

"Does anyone else know about this?"

"I don't think so."

Laylen shakes his head incredulously. "Jesus, one minute you were sitting here and the next thing you fell over." His lips quirk upward. "Do you know how much of a pain in the ass it was to catch your dead weight?"

"I'm sorry. I didn't mean to fall over." I swing my legs to the floor, preparing to sit up. "For a second I thought I was just remembering stuff about my childhood, but then, the next thing I knew, I'd entered a vision about my past." I let out a breath, preparing to tell him what else I saw and to ask him about the triangular symbol. I want to know what it represents and if it's a Mark.

"So you went into a vision?" Nicholas asks and Laylen and I jump, startled by his sudden appearance on the sofa across from us. *Damn it.* "Without a crystal?"

This is bad, very, very bad. Nicholas should not have this kind of information on me and I have a feeling he's going to use it against me.

I lift Laylen's hand off my shoulder, sit up, and get a head rush. I blink a few times while I wait for the room to stop spinning in blurs and streaks of color. "Did I hit my head?" I ask Laylen. "When I blacked out?"

"No, I caught you before you did." He helps me sit up and then examines my eyes. "But didn't Alex say you hit your head when you went to get *him*." He nods his head in Nicholas's direction.

I press my fingertips to my head and wince at the tender spot on the temple. "I have a really bad headache."

"So," Nicholas interrupts, marveling at me as though I am the most fascinating thing he has ever laid eyes on. He inclines forward in the sofa and overlaps his hands on his knee "You can go into a vision without the help of a crystal . . . how fascinating."

"I guess that's what I did," I mutter, racking my brain for a way out of this, but my mind's foggy with pain from the earlier fall as well as from the memory I've just witnessed.

"How long have you known you could do it?" Nicholas asks with way too much interest.

I shrug as I scratch my head. "Not too long I don't think."

"Do you know how rare that is?" Nicholas asks. "Jesus, I've never even met a Foreseer who could do it."

"Well, I'm not one-hundred percent sure that's what I can do." I shrug, unsure what to say that would make the situation better. "I'm just guessing."

"No, you can . . . I can sense it all over you now that I know what to look for." Nicholas's eyes devour me, drifting over my entire body, and I wrap my arms around myself as I squirm from his unrelenting gaze. "I've only heard of one other Foreseer who could do it and that's Dyvinius's younger brother," he says. "Who's been a Foreseer for a really long time, and comes from a line of many, many powerful Foreseers. He isn't some girl who just got her Foreseer's mark only a couple of days ago. Do you know how unlikely it is for anyone to be able to do that? You would have to be . . ." He trails off, mulling over something, his forehead furrowing.

"Have to be what?" I wonder, glancing at Laylen. We exchange a curious glance and then Laylen chimes in.

"Nicholas, just finish the damn sentence," he says in a low, commanding tone.

"Very powerful," Nicholas finishes, glaring at him. "You better watch it, Vampire boy. I might be here to help, but I can very easily leave."

Laylen's expression darkens and I note that his lip twitches. For a second, I swear his fangs descend, though then I blink and he looks normal.

"So about the Ira?" I ask, changing the subject, knowing the clock is ticking. The longer I sit and argue, the more time my mom spends down in The Underworld. "Where is it?"

Nicholas smirks as he pats the pocket of his pants. "Safe and sound."

I stick out my hand. "Can I see it?"

He shakes his head. "Not until I get my *fraxinus invisibili.*" His eyes wander to the doorway and I'm surprised to find Aislin's there with a small, velvet bag in her hand. "Do you have it?" he asks her.

She doesn't respond right away, and then, reluctantly, she stomps across the room and drops the bag into Nicholas's lap. He grins and she turns away, looking at Laylen.

"I'll be in the store if you need anything." He eyes glide over me as she turns to leave the room. There's something about her; sadness and pain along with longing in her eyes. It hurts my heart and I turn to Laylen the moment she walks out.

"Go check on her," I tell him. "Something's wrong."

He glances at Nicholas. "What about him?"

"He's fine," I say, waving him off. "Now go."

He dithers momentarily then gets up and hurries out of the room.

"Trouble in paradise?" Nicholas wonders, getting comfy on the sofa. "Let me guess, your beautiful eyes have gotten in the way of their love."

I scowl at him, placing my hands on my hips. "That's none of your business."

His expression lights up with enthusiasm. "So it's true."

"No, it's not true you asshole," I say. "Now show me the Ira."

He picks up the bag on his lap, unlaces the golden ribbon on it, and glances inside, looking pleased before he ties it back up and sets it aside on the apothecary table.

"Show me the Ira," I repeat firmly.

He rolls his eyes yet tolerates me, slipping a shimmering teal crystal ball out of the pocket of his pants. He gives me a quick glimpse of the Ira and by simply looking at it I can feel the power humming off of it, my fingers are itching to touch it to see what I can do with it. "There, satisfied?" he asks, stuffing it back into his pocket.

I nod. "I guess."

His brow curves upward. "Could you feel the power?"

"Maybe," I say coolly, even though my body is still humming from its energy even more powerfully than from the electricity.

"You know it's not as easy as seeing," he says. "I'm going to have to use your Foreseer energy to even get it to work."

"Why can't you use yours?"

"I'm going to have to use that, too . . . it's going to take a lot of power—power that you don't even know how to use yet."

My lips bow downward into a disappointed frown. "If I don't know how to use it yet, then how the hell are you going to get into The Underworld?"

"First off, *we're* going to go there. It's going to take both of us," he explains. "And second, I'm going to train you."

I pull a disgusted face. "Are you being serious?"

He places his hand to his heart." My dear Gemma, I'm always serious."

"No, you're a pervert who pretty much raped me back in the vision," I ball my hands into my fist as shame and disgust nauseously resurface in my body, remembering how he put his hands and mouth on me without my permission. "And the only reason you're still sitting here is because I need you to help me get into The Underworld, otherwise I would have told Alex to kick your ass."

He laughs and rolls his golden eyes. "Like he could."

I straighten back in the seat. "I think you know he could. That's why you won't try it again."

He doesn't argue, but he doesn't appear happy about it, either. "You know, I doubt you'd be so confident if you knew where he really was right now." He shakes his head and I detect a slight flash of light under his skin as his body vibrates. I think he's trying to change into the mirage, but luckily it's not working. "Would it help if I looked like him? You could kiss me and pretend I was him."

I roll my eyes and slump back in the sofa. "If you're trying to do the tricky mirage thing it's not working."

He glances down at his arms, rotating his hands over. "What did you do," he growls.

I smirk at him, but deep down my heart and mind are entering a painful state, as if they miss the electricity—miss Alex. "Wouldn't you like to know?"

We exchange defiant grins as we stare each other down and he drops his hands to his lap.

"You know that confidence is going to come in real handy when I train you. It'll channel your inner energy," he says.

If only he knew just how much energy was inside me. It's a good thing he doesn't, though, because I have the feeling he's the kind of person that would do anything to get his hands on it.

I'M QUICKLY LEARNING that Nicholas has the attention span of a child. After our little argument, we sit down on the living room floor amongst the table and the sofa, as if we're doing a séance. Our legs are crisscrossed as we face each other with an ordinary violet ribbon crystal ball between us. It's the teaching ball, he told me. He said that once I'd been trained properly he'd bring out the Ira, that it was too powerful to train on

He also told me that it would only be him and I going into The Underworld and that it wasn't possible to bring anyone with us besides Foreseers because they'd need their own Seer energy. I asked if I could go alone and he said no. I honestly have no idea whether the words that come out of his mouth are true, but there's no real way to find out.

"Why do you need to go to The Underworld?" he asks as he rotates the crystal ball in his hand.

I hesitate, not sure what to say. Lie. Probably not since he is going to end up finding out when he goes down to The Underworld with me. "To get my mom."

He glances up at me with inquisitiveness. "I met her once. She disappeared quite a few years ago, didn't she?"

"Fourteen years ago," I say, my voice uneven.

"And that's where she ended up?" Nicholas sets the ball down on the tile floor and it wobbles a little, rolling back and forth.

I nod and wait for him to ask how she got there, but he never does and I wonder if he already knows, if maybe he saw it through a vision.

He spins the crystal ball on the floor. "So who's your father?"

Good question. "I'm not sure exactly."

He quizzically raises his eyebrows as he slams his palm down on the crystal ball, stilling it. "You're not sure? How's that possible?"

"When your mother refuses to tell anyone before she gets trapped in The Underworld," I reply dryly.

"So, for all you know, your father could have been some almighty and great Foreseer." He pauses and a mocking grin plays at his lips. "Your father could be Dyvinius."

I roll my eyes. "That's disturbing. He's like sixty."

Nicholas shrugs. "You never know. Some girls have a thing for older guys. Like you and Alex."

"He's only a few years older than me." I move my feet

out of the way as the crystal rolls toward them. "And how can you touch that thing without being sucked into it."

He presses two fingers to his temple, his lips curving upward. "Mental talent."

I let out a slow breath, tired of playing games. "Can we just get on with this? The longer I'm up here, the longer my mother's stuck down there."

He stares at me blankly, cupping the crystal in his hand. "I want you to ask nicely first."

I bite down on my tongue. "Pretty please."

He drops the crystal onto the floor so hard I'm surprised it doesn't break. "So, until we can get you going into and out of visions that you're intentionally trying to go into," he starts in a bored tone as if he's done this many times. "There's really no point in us trying to travel into The Underworld . . . One false move and we could end up in the bottom of the lake, where we'd either drown or get taken to The Underworld by the Water Faeries which means we'd be prisoners there—we have to go in a specific way or we're in trouble. Got it?"

I nod. "So how does it work, exactly? We enter The Underworld through that ball. Then what?" I lean back on my hands. "How do we get the Queen to let my mom go? And how do we get her to let us go? Wouldn't we just end up prisoners anyways?"

He shakes his head. "The Queen can't keep us there—it's the law that comes with using the Ira."

"It sounds kind of difficult."

"It will be," he says matter-of-factly. "It'll take a lot of power and control to pull it off, and I have no idea how you're going to get the Queen to let your mother go."

"Neither do I," I mumble. "But I'll find a way."

He stretches his legs out in front of him. "Sure you will."

"I will." I stare down at the crystal ball only inches away from my feet. "So what do I do first?"

"The first thing that's going to happen is I'm going to go into a vision with you," Nicholas explains, sitting up straight. He holds out his hand toward me as he carries the crystal ball in the other. "Give me your hand so we can go into one together," he says. With reluctance, I take his hand, his skin clammy and cold against mine. "Good, now we need a simple vision to go into. I think it would probably be best if you just thought of a memory. Maybe something from your childhood."

That's not simple at all. "Does it have to be from my childhood?"

"As long as it's simple, it doesn't really matter," he says.

"Okay. . . ." I search for something simple to picture, but all I can see are broken images and darkness.

"Gemma, place your hand on the crystal ball," he instructs, growing impatient. "And channel your energy."

A brief glimpse of my mother and me in a field flashes through my head and I reach out to touch the crystal ball in Nicholas's hand, but I pause. "Wait, how do I channel my energy?"

"The best way is to use your emotions, despite what Dyvinius says," he tells me. "It's quicker and easier, so whatever you're feeling right now, channel it."

I'm a little surprised at his answer, and suddenly, I begin to wonder if the appearance of my Foreseer ability came from the fact that I'd started to experience so much emotion.

I do what he says and channel what I'm feeling, which is a combination of irritation, fear, and longing. As soon as my skin brushes the glass, I'm yanked forward into a tunnel of light. Nicholas clutches my hand and we sink and spin while it feels like I'm being ripped apart. Finally, we reach the bottom and I immediately let go of Nicholas's hand.

I sigh in relief until I take in my surroundings. I'm not in my past, but I think in the future, standing on the main street of Vegas beside a massive pirate ship. The busy city is no longer busy, instead it's dead quiet. A layer of glistening ice covers everything as if a million Death Walkers have marched through and breathed their Chill of Death on everything.

Just like they would if the portal opened up.

CHAPTER
TWELVE

I STAND IN the empty streets as shock seeps into my bones. This can't be right. It can't be. Because, if it's true, then the portal opens up. We don't save the world or the star and everything ends.

"Gemma." Nicholas's voice carries caution as if he can sense something's up.

I tear my eyes off the frozen streets and look over at him. "What?"

"Are you okay?" he asks, stuffing his hands into his pockets, examining me intently. "You've been standing there staring at whatever it is you're seeing for over five minutes."

I swallow hard. "I . . . um . . ." I don't know what to say to him.

"What is it?" Nicholas glances around, even though he can't see anything. It's a rule of seeing visions: only the seer can see what's actually taking place.

To Nicholas everything looks blank and I envy him in a way. I want to erase the image from my mind so I can have my hope back; hope that the world can be saved.

The sky is gray and a frost-bitten wind gusts across streets, blowing snow all over the ground. The buildings still stand tall, though they're glazed with ice and some structures are cracking from the pressure.

"Gemma?" Nicholas says, waving his hand in front of my face. "What's going on?"

I shake my head and blink. "It's nothing."

He raises his eyebrows at me. "If it's nothing, then why do you look like you just saw someone die?"

I'm about to answer when a loud shriek cuts the air. The sound echoes, vibrating the ice, and my body goes rigid as the fog creeps out from the buildings.

"I think we should go," I say, slipping backwards as I move away from the fog. "I think something really bad is about to happen."

Seconds later, a herd of Death Walkers emerge from behind and inside the buildings. Their black cloaks are pulled over their heads, their skin rotting and mapped with bits of muscle as well as veins. Their eyes are like fireflies and their breaths are made of death as they march toward me.

Stay calm. Stay calm. "Can we just go back to the house? *Please.*"

Nicholas watches me as I walk backwards, trembling, remembering what the monsters can do. "You know whatever's out there can't harm you, right?" he reminds me.

I blink my eyes a few times, trying to takes us away, but it doesn't work. "Nicholas, quit being an ass and just take us back. I know they can't hurt me, but I don't want to see them,"

Nicholas taps his finger on his lip, glancing in the direction of the Death Walkers, his shoes scuffing against the icy road as he takes a step forward and the fog winds around his feet. "I don't think so. Whatever's scaring you, I think you should face it. It'll be good practice for when we go to The Underworld."

I glare at him, my heart thumping in my chest as the Death Walkers march closer. Fog twists around us, spinning in circles, clouding the buildings surround us. I hold my breath, backing away, but they move faster and end up hurrying by me, one by one. My breath fogs out in front of me as I stay as still as a statue with my arms tucked inward. Deep down, I know they can't touch or see me, however there's too much fear inside my body to risk otherwise.

They all manage to walk by me without so much as glancing in my direction and I'm about to let out my breath when two tall men wearing black cloaks step out into the streets. The taller one with darker hair and eyes has a scar in his cheek and I immediately recognize him as Stephan. The shorter one with longer hair and a slouchier posture, though, I'm not sure of.

Their cloaks swish behind them as they stride toward me. Stephan carries something in his hand; something razor sharp and made of shimmering metal . . . The Sword of Immortality.

"Shit . . ." I breathe. Nicholas starts yammering about something, but I zone out, watching the vision play out before me.

"I wish you wouldn't carry that around," the man says to Stephan as they walk down the middle of the road lined with frozen cars. "It makes me nervous."

"It makes me nervous when I'm not carrying it around," Stephan replies, rotating the sword in front of him. "It's the one thing that could end all of this." He gestures around at the frozen, desolate street. "And this is what you wanted, isn't it Demetrius. To end the world and rule it."

Demetrius. Oh my God. Demetrius and Stephan together. I think deep down I knew this is how things would end up, but the question is why? Why did Stephan end up siding with him? Why did he start seeking the star for bad instead of protecting it? And how can I stop him from making all this happen?

"Yes, but who is left to get ahold of it?" Demetrius laughs as he swishes his cloak behind him. "The ice killed everyone off who was still left around."

"There are a few Keepers around who might try." Stephan says. "Do you remember when Octavian made this after the vision was first seen?"

Demetrius laughs again, throwing back his head. "He was so convinced that if he created it, I'd never be able to pull off what he'd seen. Too bad for him, he didn't see you coming. Jesus, Foreseers think they can see everything and make some sort of difference."

"Well, that was the doing of my parents." Stephan touches the scar on his left cheek as they stop just short of where Nicholas and I stand. "They though if they cut off the mark, it would change things—change who I was—but they couldn't change the blood that runs through my veins, could they? Although, it did help keep my hidden from Octavian. Once the mark was gone, my part in it couldn't be seen."

The scar on his cheek is a mark that was cut off by his parents? I cringe at the idea, and then cringe again at the idea of what kind of mark would make a parent cut their child's face just to get rid of it.

"That mark is a gift," Demetrius tells Stephan as he turns to face him and reaches out to touch the blade of the sword in Stephan's hand. He pricks his finger on the end of the blade and smiles as he spills his blood on the snow below his feet. "My parents seemed to understand this—understand who I am and what I was meant to do."

"Yes, but your parents weren't Keepers," Stephan

replies venomously as he wrenches the sword away from Demetrius's reach. "Mine were. In their eyes, to have a child who bears the mark was a disgrace, which is why they so stupidly tried to cut it off." His jaw sets tight as he stabs the sword into the ground and the ice cracks below the blade.

They continue to walk again, heading past us, and I turn to follow them with my eyes.

"It's a gift," Demetrius says. "We've been chosen since birth by the mark—since before birth—to free him and everyone else who was bound by his sentencing." He raises his hand in the air and his expression glazes over as he shuts his eyes.

"And now we have," Stephan says thoughtfully as he lightly traces his finger down his scar.

"Yes, and now we have," Demetrius agrees, opening his eyes and lowering his hand to his side.

"Gemma," Nicholas says and I gasp, almost forgetting he is there.

I fling my hand over my mouth and hold my breath. Suddenly, Stephan stops, his head tilting to the side and he glances over his shoulder.

He holds up his hand, signaling for Demetrius to stop. "Just a second."

Demetrius pauses, his gaze sweeping the buildings. "What's wrong?"

"Please, get us out of here," I hiss at Nicholas as Stephan starts walking back toward us.

Nicholas wavers. "I don't know . . . I kind of like being alone with you."

"Nicholas," I hiss again, grabbing onto his arm. "Get us out of here. *Now.*"

Stephan's getting closer and I don't understand what's going on. He's not supposed to be able to see or hear me, but I swear he can sense that I'm here."

"What are you doing?" Demetrius calls out, but Stephan doesn't reply as he continues moving toward us, grasping the sword as his eyes scan from side to side as if he's searching for something—for us.

I dig my fingers into Nicholas's arm and jerk him closer to me. "There's someone in this vision that I'm pretty sure can either see or sense that we're here and, if he can, then it's very, very bad."

His eyes widen as he takes my hand, abruptly looking anxious. "Okay, let's go."

I cast one last glance at Stephan as he picks up his pace, charging at us and I know something's very wrong. It doesn't look like he can see us because he's looking in the wrong direction, but he can obviously sense us.

"Nicholas . . ." I say, tripping backwards as Stephan reaches out for me. I open my mouth to scream, but then Stephan abruptly stops.

He's only inches away from me and his eyes fasten right on mine as a slow smile curls up his lips. He touches the scar on his cheek with the tip of the knife, cutting a thin layer of skin off, and drawing blood. "You have it, too," he whispers, then his eyes divert to my upper arm.

My skin ignites as I'm hauled backward, fading from the vision, but it's enough time to see it. The red and black triangular mark on my arm.

CHAPTER
THIRTEEN

I TRIP OVER my feet, but quickly regain my balance as I land back in Adessa's living room. The fear of what just happened still lingers in my body and has me gasping for air.

"Who was it?" Nicholas asks with very little patience as he gets into my face. "Who was in the vision?" He still has ahold of my hand and I try to wrench it out of his, but he refuses to let me go. "Gemma, talk to me." He puts a hand on each of my shoulders and looks me directly in the eyes. "Tell me who it was that could sense us . . . It's important."

My chest heaves as I work to compose my breathing. "Why would anyone be able to sense us like that?"

"Because . . ." He pauses, eyeing me over. "Because it means the vision has already been seen or told to the person who was in the vision."

I'm not surprised. I know Stephan has been told visions of the future and how the world will end, which is why he was supposedly protecting the star. Now, though, it's beginning to make more sense. He wasn't protecting the star, he was holding onto it for himself.

"Tell me what you saw," Nicholas commands,

roughly squeezing my shoulders. "And tell me how you saw it. Normal Foreseers aren't able to just walk into other Foreseers' visions."

"I've got to go ask Laylen something." I duck out from his hands and head for the doorway.

He catches me by the arm and his fingernails pierce into my skin. "Who was in the vision, Gemma? You need to tell me."

"No I don't," I say. "What I saw . . . it doesn't concern you."

I tug my arm away from him and scurry out of the room. Nicholas doesn't follow me, surprisingly, but I'm glad. I need to talk to Laylen alone. I find him in one of the rooms upstairs on a bed, reading a book. He's on his side, propped up on his elbow, his boots kicked up on the footboard. His legs are too long for the twin bed and he's nearly falling out of it.

"Hey," I say, shutting the door, checking my skin in the light to make certain there's no symbol on my skin. Thankfully it's bare, the only thing there is a cluster of freckles. "I need to talk to you."

He peers up from his book. "Hey, what's . . ." He quickly sits up, shutting the book as he lowers his feet to the floor. "What happened? You look upset."

"Something bad happened when we went into a vision." I drop down on the bed beside him. "And Nicholas is getting suspicious that there might be something wrong with me."

Laylen sets his book down on the nightstand. "You think he knows about the star's power?"

I shake my head. "I don't think he knows what exactly it is, only that there's something different about me and my Foreseer power."

"Well as long as he doesn't know exactly what it is,

then I think we're okay." Laylen pauses, sucking his lip ring into his teeth. "Although, I'm not really sure it's so great that he knows so much about you."

I nod in agreement, but then remember I have bigger problems to discuss than Nicholas. "There's something else I need to talk to you about . . . something I just saw in the vision." I shiver as I remember what I just left. "Laylen, I think I just saw the end of the world."

It gets so quiet; I can hear the sound of our breaths and our hearts.

"The end of the world," Laylen whispers, rubbing a hand tensely down his face. "Seriously?"

I nod. "Covered in ice."

"Then the portal opens up."

"At least from what I saw it does," I say. "But then again, Alex already told me another Foreseer told the same vision, which is the same thing Nicholas said."

"But I always thought maybe he was lying," he mutters, staring the floor. "But I guess not . . . the portal opens and the world ends."

"Unless we change it . . . somehow." I recollect the vision and Demetrius's conversation with Stephan. "Why would someone try to cut a mark off their child?

Laylen's head snaps up. "Why would you ask that?"

"In the vision," I say. "Demetrius and Stephan were talking and they—"

"Wait a minute," Laylen cuts me off, lifting his hand in front of us. "Hold on. They were there—Demetrius and Stephan were there together?"

"Yeah." I give him a quick recap of what I've just seen.

Laylen looks utterly shocked when I finish. "So what you're saying is that the scar on Stephan's face used to be a mark? One that he was born with?"

"Yeah, but what's the mark for?" I ask. "And why

would his parents cut it off?"

Laylen swallows hard, his throat muscles bobbing up and down. "Maybe it was his Immortal mark . . . but I'm not sure. From what I know, you have to have some sort of supernatural blood in you to bear the mark; such as Vampire." He glances down at the Mark of Immortality on his arm.

"Maybe he is something," I tell him. "And he's hiding it . . . maybe that's what the mark is." I pause, summoning the courage to ask. "What exactly does a red and black triangle represent."

His face twists with puzzlement. "I have no idea. I've never heard of such a thing . . . why do you ask?"

"Well, I first saw it on Draven and then, when I blacked out, I saw it on me," I tell him, my voice shaking with my nerves. "And then, just barely, when I was going out of the vision, Stephan stopped in front of me, touched the scar on his cheek, and told me I had one on me, too." My hands tremble as I fear what this all might mean. "And when I looked down on my arm, it was there."

"I'm not sure . . ." Laylen rubs his hand across his jawline, deliberating my words with worry lacing his demeanor. "Gemma, honestly I don't remember seeing it on Draven, either.'

I touch my forearm. "He had it right there."

"Maybe I missed it." He sounds unconvinced, though, and it makes me uneasy, like he either thinks I'm crazy or is worried that there might be something wrong with me.

"It couldn't be a symbol of Immortality, could it? Maybe it's the one that makes him Immortal amongst the Immortals."

"Maybe."

I sit in silence, trying to figure out what it all means, not just with the symbol in question, but also with the future. The fact that Stephan wants to end the world, using me, and the fact that he can't be killed . . . what other option does this leave me with except that I'll end up being the person solely responsible for ending the world? And then what? I'll either die in the frozen streets or be killed with the use of the star's energy.

"Are you okay?" Laylen asks.

"Yeah, I'm fine." I sound hollow and I'm not sure why. Yes, I just saw the end of the world, but Alex has told me about it before this. Still, he made it seem possible that we could stop it and now it doesn't seem realistic. I'm going to be the thing that makes it happen.

"Gemma, we'll figure something out," he assures me, brushing his finger across my jawline. "We'll get to your mom and maybe she'll know something . . . how to stop Stephan. I mean, he put her in the lake for a reason. I can have Aislin look around to see if we can figure out what kind of marks there are that would be bad enough that someone's parents might cut it off."

"I think I better get back to Nicholas and my training." I stand up from the bed and trudge for the door.

"Gemma." Laylen gets to his feet and trails behind me. "Are you sure you're okay? You've been through a lot within the last few weeks. I'm worried you're going to break apart."

I force a tight smile, letting the hollowness seep into my body. "I'm fine," I repeat and walk out. However, what I really want to say is that I think I'm already broken.

CHAPTER FOURTEEN

I'VE STARTED HAVING this reoccurring nightmare, but it doesn't just happen at night. It goes on during the day as well. In it, my mom is begging me to help her, save her from the treacherous place she's been imprisoned in. Each time I can see The Underworld and what it looks like, a secret cave buried beneath the lake; a place sculpted out of rocks, mud, vines, and a home for water Fey that thrive on torturing. Every time I manage to make it there, to my mother, who's trapped in chains and secured to a wall. Yet, as soon as I come close to reaching her, the triangular mark appears on my arm and, instead of saving her, I suddenly want to kill her.

When I wake up, I sometimes continue to feel the dark filling me.

This isn't my only problem. I also have to deal with Nicholas who is a pain in the ass. It's been two days of excruciating training, falling into and out of visions. I need a break from seeing things I don't want to see and I need a break from perverted Faeries. What I really want is for this to all be over and I'm doing everything I can to make that happen, even if it means taking a risk or two.

Aislin and Laylen have been spending a lot of time

together, looking through books and asking around about marks and the strange triangular symbol that no one seems to know about. Laylen even asked some of the Vampires if they knew if Draven had one and either they don't know or are denying it.

The biggest void is inside me, though, created from the absence of Alex and the electricity. Two days without it and I swear I'm feeling more sluggish, less enthusiastic, and emotionally drained.

Nicholas and I are sitting on the black and white tile floor of Adessa's living room with a simple crystal ball between us. He's wearing stonewashed jeans, a green shirt that makes his golden eyes look brown, and his sandy hair is fluffed up at the top because he keeps messing with it. I have my hair down today because I couldn't find anything to put it up with and no makeup on as usual. My black shorts are too short while the purple and black striped tank top is a little too tight; both selected from the Black Angel themed wardrobe Aislin picked out for me.

"Try again," Nicolas demandingly commands, motioning at the crystal ball. He's growing impatient and I'm growing flustered, a bad combination.

"Okay." I take a deep breath and extend my hand out to Nicholas, my other hand hovering over the crystal ball. "Stop being so bossy."

"Don't pretend you don't like it." Nicholas takes hold of my hand and unnecessarily intertwines our fingers, making my blood boil. "Do you have an idea where you're going to take us?"

"Yeah, I have an idea." I shut my eyes and brush my fingers across the cold glass of the crystal ball, knowing that what I'm about to do is wrong. I need to know, though; I need to see her.

I pictured what I've been seeing in my nightmares

over and over again because I need to see if my mom is still my mom or if her sanity is too far-gone.

I need to know how it all ends.

"SO WHERE'D YOU take us?" Nicholas rubs his hands together, appearing intrigued as he glances around. "Somewhere good I hope."

"Um . . ." I'm at-a-loss for words.

We're standing in a tunnel, the muddy walls dripping with musty water and moss. Vines hang from the ceiling and water flows below our feet. It looks much different from in my dreams, strangely more unrealistic than anything as if it was created from a haunting fairytale

"I think I . . . I think we might be in The Underworld."

His face reddens with anger as he shuffles toward me. "You what?"

I open my mouth to tell him that I'm sorry, even though I'm really not, when a shriek reverberates through the tunnel and my head snaps in the direction it came from.

"What's wrong?" Nicholas follows my line of gaze, even though he can't see anything. "Is it a Water Faerie?"

I squint through the darkness at something white. "I'm not sure . . ." I move forward, straining my vision. "It's something white and wavy and . . . or more like Ghostly and boney . . ." My face falls as I step back. "Shit, I think it is."

Nicholas tugs on the back of my shirt and pulls me to the side of the tunnel. He presses his back against the wall and then shoves me back by flattening an arm over my chest.

"What's wrong with you?" I hiss. "We're in a vision, so they can't see us."

He quickly shakes his head, his wide eyes searching around us in terror. "It'll be able to sense I'm here."

"*How?*"

"Water Faeries are Fey, so it'll be able to sense I'm here because I'm part Fey." He presses himself against the dirt wall as far as he can go with his hands flat out to his sides. "And if it does. . . ." He shudders.

"And if it does then what?" I press, eyeing the Fey heading toward us. Its face is a skull, its fingers bone, and its feet are hidden by wispy pieces of fabric that brush against the dirt as it floats.

His chest descends as he releases a breath. "Look, there are certain reasons—rules—that don't allow me down here. And I can't take us out of here, because I can't—my Foreseer power is no use down here."

I glare at him, stepping away from the wall and moving in front of him. "Then how did you ever plan on helping me save my mom?" His silence says everything and I shake my head, putting my hands on my hips. "You weren't ever planning on it, were you?"

More silence and I want to smack him.

"I can't believe this," I say, pacing the area in front of him "You know what, actually I can. Still, though." I huff in frustration, the prickle stabbing violently at the back of my neck while I feel like wrapping my fingers around his neck. "You are seriously the cruelest person I've ever met . . . playing me like that . . . over my mother."

He shrugs. "You should have known better than to believe someone like me." He glances down the tunnel as if he senses something. "Faeries are a tricky breed."

I look over at the water Faerie nearing us, and then return my attention to Nicholas with a dark look in my eyes. "You know what, I think I'm just going to sit here and let it find you. You deserve it, you know, for messing with my head."

He scowls at me, but there's fear in his eyes. "Look at you . . . you're starting to sound as cruel as me."

I shrug. "But only with you."

"Yeah, but you're new at this and you're going to lose," he says.

"You think so?" I question, pointing over my shoulder. "Because the water Faerie's right behind us."

His eyes snap wide and he takes off down the tunnel. Shaking my head, I run after him, leaving the water Faerie in the distance. He continues to run with me chasing at his heels until we reach a dead-end, the tunnel opening up onto a wide room carved out of rock. In the middle of the hollowed out space is a throne made of stone that has a back spiraling up to the ceiling like a slide.

Nicholas keeps running until he trips over his feet and I slow to a stop, I laugh at him.

"Well, that was smooth," I say, staring down at him with my hands on my hips.

He glares at me, opening his mouth as he gets to his feet, but I hold my finger up as someone walks into the cave.

Her head is hung low, her brown hair tied in a bun on the top of her head, and she's wearing ratty pants with a t-shirt. She walks up to the throne and starts dusting it off with a white cloth. As she glances up, I catch the sight of her bright blue eyes. It's my mother.

I gasp. "Oh my God."

Nicholas brushes the dirt form his jeans as he steps up beside me. "What is it?"

"My mom," I whisper, inching forward.

Moments later another woman enters the cave. She's

wearing a long, elegant, white dress and her eyes are two sunken holes. Her frosty hair veils down her back and she holds her head high as she crosses the cave floor

My mom bows as she walks by her, and then backs away as the woman sinks into her throne. She has to be the Queen of The Underworld.

"Where are they?" The Queen's voice echoes out.

"I think Sarabella is bringing them in," my mom answers quietly with her head still bowed as she stands in front of the throne.

The Queen stares at the arched entryway of the cave. "Does anyone know why they're here?"

My mother shakes her head. "They haven't said anything yet."

Nicholas taps me on the shoulder, and demands for me to take us away, but I disregard him, my eyes are glued to the vision unfolding in front of me. When does this vision take place?

Another scream rings out and then a tall, thin-framed woman with the same frosted hair and pale skin as the Queen, strides into the cave accompanied by a tall, lean guy with messy brown hair and green eyes. On the other side of her is a brown haired, violet eyed me.

"Alex and me . . ." I gape. "What the hell?"

Alex remains close to me as we follow the woman across the cave and to the throne.

"Thank you, Sarabella," the Queen says.

Sarabella smiles, her mouth a toothless hole. "You're welcome my Queen," she breathes, and then sweeps the tail of her white dress across the floor before she turns around, exiting the cave.

The Queen taps her fingers together, her eyes secured on Alex and me, her mouth set firmly in a line. "So, you two are the humans who dared to enter my world without my permission." Alex starts to speak, but the Queen holds up her hand. "Silence. I do not want to hear your excuses. All that's important is that there are going to be consequences for what you've done." She glances us over. "You look familiar," the Queen remarks to Alex. "Have you been here before?"

Alex shakes his head and intertwines his fingers through mine. "I haven't."

"Are you sure?" The Queen's empty gaze bores into Alex. "There's something about you that's so . . . familiar."

Alex shakes his head again. "I swear, I've never been here before."

"Tell me then, why you've entered my world?" she asks.

My mother steps out from behind the throne and the vision version of me smiles, my violet eyes lighting up with excitement.

"For her," Alex tells the Queen, giving a nod at my mother.

My mother stares robotically at us. "I have no idea who they are, my Queen."

"She doesn't know who you are," the Queen says with a grin.

"That doesn't matter." Alex steps forward, pulling me with him. "We need to take her."

"That's impossible," the Queen roars, hammering her fist on the armrest of the throne. The ceiling shakes from the bellowing sound and pieces of loose rock fall to the ground. "No one ever leaves The Underworld. Ever! Something you probably should have considered before you entered here."

"We entered here in a way that you have no control over whether we get to leave or not," Alex says with an arrogant grin.

"You better watch your tone, boy," the Queen warns, leaning forward in the throne. "I've cut off the tongues of those who dared show such disrespect to me." But then her grin fades. "Which one of you is the Foreseer?"

"What do you mean?" Alex asks, discretely inching himself in front of me to block me out of the Queens restless gaze.

"Don't play stupid with me, boy. The only way you could enter my world and still get out is by entering with the Ira, something that can only be used by a Foreseer. So, is it you? Or is it her?" The Queen's gaze lands on the vision version of me. "Tell me, girl, what is your name?"

"Gemma," I tell her in a surprisingly confident tone as I step forward.

"Gemma, would you please explain to me what your interest in this woman is?" She gestures her hand at my mother who's knelt down on the ground.

"She's . . ." she trails off. "We just know her,"

She glances at my mother. "Why would I let you take my best slave? Are you really that stupid? Did you really think you could simply walk in here and persuade me to hand over someone because you know her?"

Alex reaches in the pocket of his jeans and retrieves a sparkly blue object. I shuffle forward into the cave, squinting to see what it is. I need to find out so that Alex and I can come do this exact same thing and free my mother, which is hopefully the end to this vision.

It's sparkling blue and I've seen it before . . . somewhere. Oh my God. I saw it in the mysterious hideout. I was holding a large, sapphire gem and Alex took it from me and tossed in into a trunk. Is that what I need? When I come here to save her?

I'm waiting to find out when Nicholas lurches up behind me and shoves me against the wall, his fingers wrapping around my throat. I'd almost forgotten he was there and he takes me completely off guard.

"Take me back," he demands, leaning into my face as his nails cut through my neck. "Or I'll kill you where you stand."

"Let me go," I choke as I shove my hands against Nicholas's chest, but it barely fazes him. I try to glance into the cave, but he tightens his grip and my air supply is nearly cut off.

"Take. Us. Back." He demands. "I swear to God, Gemma, if you don't, I'll kill you."

Determined to win, I hold on for as long as I can, trying to watch what's going on in the cave, knowing that I'm missing something important. As my vision starts to spot and I can feel myself verging to the point of blacking out and probably dying, I give up and blink us away, knowing there's a good chance I'll never find out how it ends until I have to go through it in reality.

Whether we're able to free my mother or not will have to remain a mystery till then.

CHAPTER
FIFTEEN

A S SOON AS we land in Adessa's living room, I take off in a mad sprint toward the doorway, but Nicholas grabs onto the back of my shirt and jerks me back. The force gives me whiplash and I trip backwards, landing on the floor hard.

"Don't even think about it," Nicholas breathes hotly as he lowers himself down on top of me, trapping me on the floor beneath his body. "You aren't going anywhere until we get something straight."

I open my mouth to scream as I buck my body beneath his weight, but he slaps his hand down on my mouth and places his arm over my neck so my airflow is limited. I raise my arm up and elbow him in the ribs, yet he only laughs.

"Nice try," he says, bending down to bring his face closer to mine "But it's going to take a lot more effort than that."

"I hate you! You're a liar and the cruelest person I know!" I attempt to scream against his hand as I lift my leg managing to kick him pretty hard in the shin.

"I'll take that as a compliment." He releases his arm from my neck, infuriated, and slaps a hand across my cheek. My skin stings and my ears ring while he grins wickedly. "I don't know about you, but I could do this all day," he says. "In fact, I think I might take you back home with me and tie you to the bed for a while." He presses his nose to my cheek and smiles at me. "God, the things I could do to you."

Panicking, I bite down on his hand, sinking my teeth into his clammy skin. He lets out a high-pitched shriek and his grip loosens enough to allow me to get my leg up a little and I quickly knee him between the legs as hard as I can. He cries out in pain, his face reddening as he falls to the side, grabbing his manly parts.

I slip out from under him and run for the doorway. "Laylen!" I shout.

Nicholas staggers to his feet and chases after me. I feel his fingers graze my back right as I step up the stairs and then suddenly he's wrenching me back toward him again by the back of my shirt. I fall on my knees on the first stair and slam my head against the wooden step.

"Help!" I scream, clawing away from him as my head throbs. "Goddammit let me go!"

Laylen appears at the bottom step as if out of thin air. He takes one quick look at Nicholas lying on top of me as I try to crawl my way up the stairs and grabs Nicholas by the back of the neck, prying him off me. I skitter to the side of the banister as Laylen shoves Nicholas down to the floor on his back.

"If you ever touch her again," Laylen stands over him, "I'll fucking break your legs off."

I could hug Laylen right now and maybe in a few minutes I will. I work to catch my breath as I cup the bottom of my neck that I'm sure is going to have fingertip sized bruises on it when morning rolls around.

"Are you okay?" Laylen glances over my body, shaking

his head at the wounds on my neck.

I nod, rubbing my cheek that Nicolas slapped. "Yeah, I think so."

"I'm going to fucking kill him," Laylen says when he sees my swollen cheek, and then he turns back to Nicholas.

As Laylen reaches for Nicholas he rolls to the side and hops to his feet before running into the living room. He stands in the corner, putting the crystal ball into his pocket.

"Don't you even think about it!" Laylen runs for him, knocking over the sofa as he leaps over it.

Laylen lands only feet away from him, Nicholas winks at me, and then evaporates from the living room, taking the Ira and my ticket to The Underworld—and my mother—with him.

CHAPTER SIXTEEN

AFTER NICHOLAS LEAVES with the Ira, Laylen makes us some coffee and we sit down in the kitchen while I explain to him in detail what happened, not just with the vision, but how Nicholas isn't even supposed to be in The Underworld and he was pretty much playing us all along for God knows what reason.

"I still can't believe it," Laylen mumbles, shaking his head. "Why would he go through all that trouble to hang around here if he was never planning on taking you there? It's such a waste of time."

"Well, he did get that invisibility powder stuff out of it, but still . . . he got that in the beginning so why stick around?" I shake my head, feeling so Goddamn frustrated and powerless. My head and cheek are swollen, and I'm so damn jittery it's ridiculous. "And I never got the Ira . . . yet I know we get to there somehow. . . . I saw Alex and myself in The Underworld trying to save my mom, so there's got to be a way to do it."

Laylen contemplates while fiddling with his lip ring, twisting it back and forth. "Alex was there . . ." He takes a sip of his coffee, dazing off into space. "Maybe that's where we need to start, then."

"With Alex?" I give him a quizzical look as I take a gulp of coffee from my mug and the warm liquid spills down my throat, soothing my insides. "But he's in the City of Crystal and I'm not sure how to get him out of there since I have no idea what he's doing down there."

He tenses. "Well, with what you saw, he kind of has to be here to make it happen. He also has to have that gem you saw."

"Which, from what my memories are telling me, Alex and I had once in a hideout hidden in the forest, but I don't know exactly where it is because my memories haven't connected that part yet."

"Alex should know, though," Laylen points out. "Let's just hope the gem's still there."

I frown as I set my mug on the table. "The frustrating thing is that Alex is in the City of Crystal for pretty much no reason."

Laylen shakes his head. "That's not completely true. Because of Nicholas's involvement, you now know that you need to have the Ira to get into The Underworld. It just sucks that *he* has it."

"I know." I mutter and sip on my coffee.

Laylen adds a spoonful of sugar to his coffee and stirs it. "I say we start with Alex and get him back here. Then we'll make a plan to get the Ira and the gem. We just need to find a way to get into the City of Crystal."

The idea of going there again doesn't make me happy, but saving Alex does. So does the idea that he and I will be going into The Underworld to save my mother, even if she did look completely hollow, I still have hope that somehow, through all this, she'll come back to me and be able to help figure out what Stephan's up to. Or maybe, if I'm lucky, get the star's energy out of me.

I set the cup down and take a deep breath. "I can

probably get us into the City of Crystal, but I'll need one of those ruby-filled crystal balls Nicholas is always using."

Laylen cocks his head to the side. "You think you've learned enough about your power to be able to do that?"

I shrug, pretending to be casual, although on the inside I'm terrified that I won't be able to do it or I'll mess something up. If I can't get it right, then what? My mom and Alex stay trapped wherever they are. "There's only one way to find out."

Laylen gets up from the chair, deeply thinking as he takes our empty mugs over to the sink. He rinses them off and turns around, leaning against the counter. "I know someone who probably has a lot of them."

I get up from the chair. "Who?"

He gives me a small smile. "The person who owns the house we're staying in. I think she's got a whole room full of crystal balls."

LAYLEN WAS RIGHT. Adessa does have a whole room full of crystal balls and she more than willingly lets us into it. I have the suspicion, though, that Laylen might be messing around with her emotions since at first Adessa seems reluctant, then suddenly she's all too happy about the idea of taking us into the room concealed behind the shelves lining the walls of her store.

Once we're in it she begins searching the seemingly endless amount of shelves that line the walls from front to back. Every time she dips down to look at the bottom row on the shelf her braided hair that runs halfway down her back brushes against the concrete floor. She's also wearing a patterned dress with heels that make clicking sounds as she walks around and the noise reverberates around the room deafeningly.

"Why do you need this?" she asks, sliding a few jars and unique figurines out of the way.

I open my mouth to explain our dilemma to her, but Laylen shakes his head, exchanging a secretive glance with me as I pick up a strange looking clay eye. "Gemma just needs to look at one, for her training."

My eyebrows dip down as I set the clay eye back on the shelf. I don't get why he's being so secretive with her when it's obvious that she's helping us.

Laylen crosses the narrow room and stops beside me. "We need to be careful who we tell," he says. "Adessa doesn't know about you, Stephan, or the star."

I glance at Adessa as she wanders to the back section of the room and then I lean into Laylen. "Why does she think we're staying with her?"

He shrugs, collecting up a two-headed horse statue from the shelf, and peeks under the bottom like he's checking for a price sticker. "I just told her we needed help."

"You don't trust her?"

"No, I do, but it's always better to be careful."

I nod as he sets the statue down. "You know what, you're right. I need to start working on doing the same . . . I let Nicholas know too much."

"That's because he has the power to fuck with your head," Laylen tells me. "He's always running around in circles and talking in vague sentences. It confuses people and makes it easy to slip up."

"Well, I need to work on it," I insist. "Regardless of how tricky he is."

"I think I found it," Adessa declares and we look in her direction as she walks toward us, carrying a miniature crystal ball with rubies floating in it. Red rays of light shimmer around the tiny storage area as the ceiling lights reflect against the glass.

Adessa offers me a small smile as she gives the crystal ball to me and I try not to grin as I take it from her because, for the first time, things actually seem like they're going to be easy.

I SPOKE TOO soon. Way too soon. Yes, we got the crystal ball, but using it is turning out to be a pain in the ass. After Adessa gives us the crystal ball, Laylen and I return to the living room. We ask Aislin to join us, figuring we all should go to The Underworld together because there's power in numbers.

"I don't get it." I shake the crystal ball like a magic eight ball and on the inside the rubies swirl in a funnel. "I've gone into a crystal ball completely by accident, but this feels impossible."

Aislin flips the page of the book she has opened up on her lap and tucks a strand of her golden brown hair behind her ear. "You know, there's a lot more marks that I'm sure a lot of people would want to remove. However, there's nothing on this mysterious triangular symbol."

"I know," Laylen agrees. "I can't even think of one off the top of my head. Usually they appear later in life or something happens and they . . ." He drifts off, stretching his arm out on his lap and staring down at the Mark of Immortality.

Aislin glances up from the book and gives a fleeting glance at the mark. Then, looking guilty, she quickly sets the book down on the table between the three of us. "I'm going to go up to the library and get another book." She stands to her feet. "This one's getting me nowhere."

"Adessa has a library?" I ask after Aislin leaves.

Laylen bends his arm back and wraps it around his stomach so his mark is hidden. "Yeah, it's up in the attic. Nothing too fancy, but there's a lot of books. The problem is that most of them stick strictly to the Wiccan history and there's not much about other marks in there."

"What kind of book do you think you'd need for something like that?"

"Honestly, I'd go with a Keeper's book, since Stephan's a Keeper and a lot of the Keepers' history is mixed with other marks. In fact, there was once a mark of evil. It had a different name, but that's pretty much what it stood for. It was directly related to the Keepers' blood. I think the man who had it, though, died or something and it killed all the bloodlines linked to it."

"So you think it's extinct?" I ask.

He nods. "Yeah, from what I've been taught it is."

I set the crystal ball down on the apothecary table and give it a good spin, causing the rubies to clink against the glass. "I can't even feel any energy from it."

Laylen reaches for the crystal ball. "Did Nicholas say anything while he was training you?" He scoops it up and turns it in his hand. "Like maybe there's some magic words," he teases, but he looks sullen, which is exactly how I feel. The more time we're up here messing around with this thing, the more time everyone stays trapped. It's also more time that the star remains inside me, which means the more time the Death Walkers and Stephan remain at our heels.

"When he was training me with the regular Foreseer crystal ball, he said something about channeling emotions," I say. "That it would help."

Laylen encounters my gaze and we exchange a penetrating look before our concentration focuses on the crystal in his hand.

"It doesn't hurt to try, right?" he asks, peering up at me.

I waver because it might not hurt to try, but it could hurt for me to channel up certain emotions around him. Sure, things have been okay lately, but I'm still concerned that the tie I felt with him will surface.

He pats the sofa. "Come sit down by me. Let's see if we can try something."

I'm nervous, but I still get up and meander around the table to the couch, dropping down beside him. "What emotion should we aim for?"

I tuck my hands underneath my legs and shrug, anxious over how many ideas pop into my mind, ranging from an orgasmic feeling to an idyllic state of rapture. "You pick one."

He dithers, his eyes all over me, then ultimately he sweeps my hair off my shoulder. "We could go for calm because I really do think you need it, but I don't think that's going to channel up much energy."

I tense as he inclines inward toward me until his chin lightly grazes my shoulder. "I agree . . ." I lose my voice as his lips gently caress my skin.

"I really tried," he whispers hoarsely. "I know I should stay away . . . and there's Aislin . . . and so many other reasons, but God you smell so good . . . I haven't been able to stop thinking about your scent since I tasted your blood." He breathes a path up my shoulder, heading toward my neck.

My head falls to the side. All this time I've been so curious to know what it feels like to be bit and now, well, I sort of regret it. Yet I can't go back from what's already happened.

I slip my hands out from under my legs and grip onto his legs as his lips move across my skin, hardly touching yet it's enough to send flutters throughout my body. It feels so wonderful, to the point that it steals my breath away, and I end up gasping for air.

He groans and then drops the crystal ball onto my lap so his fingers can find my waist. "We should stop . . ." he trails off as he presses his nose into the arch of my neck.

My eyes slip shut and I start to helplessly fall into his arms. "We should. . . ." I agree, telling my body to move away, but I feel the prickle poke at the back and I know I need to let whatever's emerging make an appearance.

I hold my breath and wait as Laylen's fingers reach my rib cage.

I wait as his mouth heads for my lips.

I wait until a vile sensation builds inside my stomach.

I wait until I can feel it, the heavy weight crashing upon my chest, pressing me down—the weight of my guilt.

I gasp, realizing just how wrong this is and that I shouldn't be doing this, not when I have feelings for Alex and Aislin has feelings for Laylen.

"This is wrong," I say and start to lean away when I feel the hot energy surging through my bloodstream like liquid fire "I think I . . . I . . ." My body goes limp as something deep within me roars. There's a rough tug and I hold onto Laylen's hand as he moves his mouth away from me. I hear him say something, but then we're sucked away into the crystal ball, falling down, down, down into the unknown.

CHAPTER
SEVENTEEN

I MANAGE TO land somewhat gracefully, catching myself with a very minor stumble and Laylen lands effortlessly beside me, gripping onto my hand. We're standing in a cave with charcoal ceilings and a translucent crystal floor. A midnight river with bits and pieces of gold in it flows beneath the floor. Maroon crystals hang from the ceiling and rubies wave across the snow-white walls.

"Is this the City of Crystal?" Laylen asks in awe as he glances around.

I shake my head in disbelief as I put the crystal ball into my pocket. "I really didn't expect to actually get us here . . . but this has to be it. I mean, I haven't been in this area before." I slip my fingers from Laylen's and stroll up to the wall, feeling the smoothness of the porcelain. "But where else could we be?"

Laylen strides up to the side of me and picks at a chipped section in the wall. "I think you're right."

I step back, looking from left to right. Each side is the same, paved with broken multicolored pieces of glass, but the one to my right heads toward a bridge. Beside the path is an edge that leads to a very short drop off.

"The question is, which way?" I say. "And what are we

even looking for exactly?"

He studies both directions, his head turning from left to right. "I just want to say first, that it's not going to be pretty."

"What's not pretty?"

He locks eyes with me. "Where Alex is."

I swallow the lump forming in my throat. "Why? Where is he?"

He circles around me and then drapes an arm around my shoulder. Guilt immediately soars through me from his touch because I want him to touch me more intimately. "There's this crystal ball in the center of the city that channels the energy to all the other crystals. That's where he is."

"In the crystal ball?"

"No, outside it."

I pull a perplexed face. "So what's the point of him being down here, then?"

He tugs on my shoulder and guides me closer to him and I have the strangest compulsion to ask him to let me go, yet conflicted by my desire, I keep my lips sealed. "The crystal ball uses human energy to fuel it," he explains.

I crane my neck, tipping my chin up, and meet his blue eyes. "*What?* And no one bothered to mention this to me?"

He offers me an apologetic look. "Alex had his reasons for doing it, I'm sure. He wanted to help you."

"But not like this," I say, shaking my head. "Not by fueling a crystal ball. It's absurd." My heart aches inside my chest, not just at the multiple ideas of what exactly is required to fuel a crystal ball, but also because the electricity has been missing for days now and I desperately miss it for reasons I both do and don't understand.

Laylen searches my eyes with a creased forehead and

then he removes his arm from around me. "We should get looking for him." He veers toward the left, away from the bridge. "It's a big city and I'm sure it's going to take a lot of time."

We walk in silence for a while, following the glass path. He looks like something's really troubling him and, despite the fact that I don't want to admit it, I think I might know what it is.

I'm just about to open my mouth and tell him that we should probably talk about what we're feeling because it's getting really complicated—at least for me—when I detect the sound of approaching footsteps.

Laylen and I freeze simultaneously then we whirl around, looking behind us to where the noise is coming from.

"Is someone coming?" I whisper.

"I think so." Motioning his hand at me, he scoots us over to the side of the path, where we step off the ledge and down onto a frosty blue, smooth surface that's as slippery as ice. He takes my hand, and we hurry over to one of the short pillars rising out of the ground that is pointed up at the top. We cower down behind it and hold our breaths as we wait.

The longer we wait, though, the quieter it gets. Finally, Laylen ducks his head low and, placing his fingers on the ground he peeks around the side of the pillar.

"No one's there," he hisses.

"They must have gone somewhere else," I whisper, hovering over him to look for myself.

"I knew you'd show up here," Nicholas breathes in my ear.

Every single one of my nerve endings tingle and my back stiffens as I jolt away from his nearness. I end up landing on Laylen's back. Luckily, he's strong and he flips us around, grabbing my hand, and pulling us to our feet.

I start to spin around toward the Faerie, when he grabs me by the waist and an overwhelming floral sent stenches up the air.

"Try anything funny," Nicholas hauls me against him, "And I'll have you out of here before you can even take your next blink."

"Fuck you," I say and bend my arms up so my fingers reach his hands, then I aim them downward and dig hard.

He doesn't so much as budge. "Feisty, I like it."

"Nicholas," Laylen says calmly as he stations himself in front of us with his arms slightly out to the side. "Let her go now before you end up getting hurt"

He spurts a laugh. "Hurt me how? I can have us out of here before you even take your next step." Keeping one arm secured around my waist, he holds up a crystal ball filled with rubies.

Laylen steps forward, but then halts, debating what to do.

"Wise choice," Nicholas says, putting the crystal ball into his pocket and then wrapping both his arms around me. Our bodies are aligned completely and I can feel things that I really don't want to feel . . . bulging in certain places. It's disgusting and vomit burns at the back of my throat.

"What do you want?" Laylen asks his hands are just to the side of him. He appears composed, but I can see that he's flexing his fingers, as though he's considering taking a hit at Nicolas. He could probably reach him in a few more steps, the pillar being the only thing between us. However it's still enough time for Nicholas to take us out of here and the last thing I want to do is end up alone somewhere with him.

Sliding his hand up my ribs and then my neck, he

sketches a finger across my cheek. "I have what I want right here." He dips his mouth next my ear. "Are the nightmares getting worse?" he breathes, stroking my upper arm. "Can you see the symbol clearly?"

I go rigid. "W-What?"

He laughs against my ear.

"You're going to pay for this," Laylen says in a low tone that conveys so much warning it actually sends a chill down my spine.

Nicholas strengthens his hold on me, his chest rising and falling as it repeatedly crashes against my back. "I'd like to see you try, you pathetic excuse for a Vampire. You can't even bring yourself to drink blood."

Laylen's lips expand to a slow grin. "Want to bet?"

Nicholas laughs. "You're so enter—"

Laylen launches forward so fast he's nothing except a blur and, seconds later, Nicholas is jerked from my grasp. Laylen doesn't bite him, but he does bring his fist up against the side of his head and knock him out cold. Nicholas's body slumps to the ground and Laylen steps back, wiping the sweat off his forehead.

His fangs descend and then retract as if he's deciding whether he wants to bite him. Then choosing not to, he slumps over, grabs onto Nicholas's arms, and drags him behind the pillar.

"The last thing I ever want to do is taste his foul blood," He says, standing upright.

"I don't blame you." I pause, watching Nicholas's chest rise and fall as he sleeps off Laylen's punch. I can't help thinking about what he whispered moments before Laylen leapt on him, though. How did he know? Not just about the nightmares, but about the symbol? "We should probably hurry before he wakes up."

Laylen nods and then takes my hand as we head back

to the path. We walk for what seems like an eternity and the more time that passes, the more worried I get that someone's going to discover us. I'm starting to get discouraged, which is a horrible feeling, when I feel it. A spark. It's soft at first, like a delicate kiss, but it increases in intensity the further we continue to go down the path until finally my body is drowning in heat.

"Alex is close," I whisper, glancing around at the walls and floor. "I can feel it."

"What?" Laylen asks, studying me with a mystified expression.

I'm completely engulfed in feeling it again, so welcoming and familiar. I've never had familiar before and it makes me feel content. "I can feel him through the electricity."

"The electricity?"

"It's a story for another time." I tug on his hand as I start to speed up down the path. "Now come on. We have to hurry."

We run, following the invisible current of electricity, going further into the cave. With each step, the current grows and becomes more charged and at the same time I become more eager and excited. God, I've missed this. I've never really missed something before and knowing I'm going to have it back soon pumps adrenaline through my body at a toxic dose.

By the time we reach a door, the current is flowing so powerfully that I know Alex has to be behind it. I'm actually shaking from the energy coursing through me, it owns me, consumes me, possesses me to the point that nothing else matters.

I need to feel more of it.

I need to see Alex.

What I need is to feel like I'm breathing again.

I let go of Laylen's hand, turn the door handle, and push the door open, starting to smile. However, what's on the other side makes my mouth turn back down and my stomach churn. All the excitement evaporates and my eagerness alters to paralyzing fear.

There's a massive crystal ball about the size of a football stadium flaring brightly within the enormous space of the cave. Attached to the crystal, solely by chains, are people. Alex is front and center, chains wrapped around him from head to toe, binding him to the crystal ball.

And he looks dead.

All of them do.

CHAPTER
EIGHTEEN

T HEY'RE ALL DEAD. Alex is dead. I can't breathe.
I can't live.

"Calm down, Gemma." Laylen's voice is sooth-
ing, yet distant. I feel my legs turning into rubber and the
room begins to sway. "They're not dead."

I straighten my legs back up. "Are you sure?" I choke
out while I stare at Alex's slackened body; his shirt's off
and his jeans hang loosely at his hips. His head is tipped
down so all I can see is his hair. *Is he awake? Dead? Alive?*
"They look . . . he looks dead."

"Yeah, I'm sure. The crystal's collecting energy from
them," he explains, his hand brushing my back. "If they
were dead, they wouldn't be useful."

I nod and then I'm running to Alex at a pace I didn't
even know I was capable of. When I get closer, I realize
that not only are chains securing him to the crystal ball,
but so are tubes. They're embedded all over his body,
sucking his life and blood.

I immediately start pulling the tubes out of his skin.
"Laylen, can you break through these chains?" I ask as
he moves up beside me. With each tube I remove, a hole
and blood trail is left on Alex's skin. They're not too deep,

though with so many, they have to be painful.

"I think so," Laylen says, gripping onto the chains.

Alex's eyelids suddenly shoot open and my breath catches. His normally bright green eyes are dull and he looks incredibly weak. I've never seen Alex look so weak. It is strange and heartbreaking as well as completely disconcerting. It makes me realize how much I like the confidence he portrays most of the time and how safe it makes me feel. I realize a lot of things at that moment; about me, about him, about us. I can feel something shifting inside me; chains breaking, my body drifting closer to him and farther from another.

"Are you okay?" I ask, cupping his cheek.

He opens his mouth to speak, but no sound comes out and his head bobbles around, like his neck is too weak to support it.

Laylen bends the metal links and snaps the chains like twigs. I reach up to help Alex and he falls onto me like a hundred and eighty pound bag of bricks. I almost buckle to the floor, but Laylen catches him and supports the majority of his weight.

"Excellent catching skills," Laylen jokes, flopping Alex's arm over his shoulder.

"Hey, I never claimed to have them," I protest, grunting as I attempt to carry some of Alex's weight. "Besides, I'm not a half-Vampire, half-Keeper who is freakishly strong."

"Would you two stop joking around," Alex says with a smidgeon of humor in his voice as he leans against me and I slip his free arm around my waist. "Can you get us out of here before we get caught?"

I start to retrieve the crystal ball from my pocket, but Alex shakes his head and then nods at the massive crystal ball exploding with energy, a enormous glowing orb radiating around the pallid, seemingly lifeless people. "Don't use your power too close to this . . . it could kill you."

I nod and we head for the door, Alex dragging his feet as we walk. Laylen holds up most of Alex's weight and we move quickly, distancing ourselves from the gigantic crystal ball. Once we're a safe distance away, I retrieve the crystal ball from my pocket while Alex works to hold himself up and gather his own balance. Laylen grabs onto my arm and I touch Alex, making sure they both go with me.

I'm getting ready to shut my eyes when the glass of the crystal ball frosts over with flakes of crisp ice. I hear a crackle moments later and I glance up just in time to see a stampede of black-cloaked Death Walkers storming our way, glazing the land with a sheet of ice and rapidly dropping the temperature to well below freezing.

I start to shake and chatter, the electricity simmering to a murmur as they ascend toward us, their yellow eyes glowing fiercely.

"Shit," Laylen says when he turns and notices them. "Gemma, get us out of here."

"I-I'm t-trying," I chatter as I fight to hold my hand steady, noting the tint of blue my skin is taking on. The Chill of Death. I've experienced it once and I don't want to ever experience it again.

As I attempt to find my energy and some sort of emotion to feed off of, I spot a blond haired, golden-eyed half-Faerie in the midst of the Death Walkers. Traitor! Not only does he play us, but now he's also siding with evil.

I grasp tighter to Alex as his skin starts turning and alarming shade of purple. He's too fragile, even with his Keeper blood, to withstand the cold and I need to get us out of here. I shut my eyes and picture Adessa's living room, the purple velvet couches, the strange figurines everywhere, and the black and white checkerboard floor. Then I let my mind and body sync with the faint spark still thriving between Alex and me. It's so weak, yet the emotions it brings out of me are more potent than any other emotion I've ever felt.

I want to hold him. Make him feel better. Kiss him. Touch him. Breathe in his scent. Feel him rocking inside me, being part of me, being connected with me in every way possible.

"Gemma . . ." Laylen's voice is full of fear and panic. "Jesus, please . . ."

I hear a sharp noise like a thousand glass cups shattering against concrete and I open my eyes. Fragments of porcelain crack apart from the ground and fly through the air, unable to withstand the pressure of the ice.

My eyes open wider as the porcelain rushes towards us in a wave of sharp glass, the ground breaking apart. I hear Alex and Laylen shout out my name as the pillars snap in half and topple over, slamming against the ground and bursting across the ground.

We're running out of time and soon we're going to be sucked into the floor or taken out by the Death Walkers who are managing to avoid the opening with little effort, their feet hovering over the floor. Nicholas has disappeared and I wonder if he has gotten sucked down into the hole that's forming.

Alex suddenly slides his arm off Laylen. Laylen continues to watch the wave of glass roaring closer to us with wide eyes as Alex limps toward me. My heart rate starts to still, my breath suffocating as my blood pressure drops with the temperature.

My breath puffs out in a cloud and envelops my face as Alex places a hand on each of my cheeks.

"Pretend they're not there," he says. "Pretend it's just you and me and no one else."

The look in his eyes and the delicacy in his words send a torrent of calmness through my body along with the desire to be near him. I can feel us being magnetized together as my body and mind connecting with the energy of the crystal.

I reach out and find Laylen's arm as Alex continues to hold onto my face. I think I've done it, but a set of bony, stone cold fingers seize hold of my arm and the energy is blown out by a vapor of cold.

I scream as the Death Walker wrenches on to me and my Foreseer power counters, strengthening. I feel like I'm going to rip apart and I'm not even sure if I'm still holding onto Laylen and Alex. My body becomes numb, brittle, tired, and worn.

I let out another scream as images pound through my head. Mountains . . . Adessa's . . . desert . . . snow . . . lake.

They move so fast I lose complete control and disappear into the midst of them.

CHAPTER NINETEEN

W HEN I OPEN my eyes again, I'm lying face first in a field of grass. I push up, brush the dirt off my legs and arms, and then glance around at the lake, the cloudy sky, and the shallow hill as well as the stony castle near the horizon.

I start to walk forward, wondering where everyone else is when Laylen rises from the grass. His blond hair shimmers in the sunlight snaking through the cracks in the clouds.

"Jesus, how the hell did we get here," he says then makes a repulsed face when he spots the grey stone castle towering in the distance. "And why here?"

"I'm not sure," I say, stepping in front of him, the grass circling around us. "I lost control or something . . . the Death Walkers' ice was making my power shaky." I shield my eyes with my hand and glance around at the field and then the trees. "Where's Alex?"

"Right here." Alex coughs. He stands up in the grass just a little ways away from us and then hobbles toward us. There are dark circles under his eyes and he, of course, still doesn't have a shirt on. The holes in his skin are more defined and his Keeper's Mark is bright against his somewhat pale skin. His brown hair is damp with sweat and he looks like he's about to hurl.

He spits in the grass and then hunches over, bracing his hands on his knees when he reaches us. "What the hell happened back there? And why was Nicholas with the damn Death Walkers in the City of Crystal?"

I can tell he's in a lot of pain. I've never really understood compassion or giving comfort. I went years and years without being touched, feeling nothing, and then when I finally did, I was too old and all of my emotions left me confused. However I step forward and start rubbing Alex's back, tracing my fingers up and down his spine. Laylen tries to ignore the fact as much as possible, but I catch him noting it. Alex tenses momentarily, but then his muscles unravel as he embraces and melts into my affection.

"It might have something do to with the fact that Nicholas was playing us." I sketch a line up and down his spine. "He never even intended to help me get to The Underworld—he's not even supposed to be there, which means he's pretty much been lying and will probably continue to lie about everything. He could have been working with the Death Walkers this entire time."

Alex elevates his head. "What?"

I sigh and the three of us sit in the grass as I begin explaining what has been going on for the last week while he was trapped in the City of Crystal. I tell him about the visions, how I saw us freeing my mom. I tell him about my nightmares and the triangular symbol. He doesn't know what it is, either, but he doesn't seem too surprised by the fact that his father's scar is actually from a mark that's been cut off. He says he didn't know, but that he's sort of glad, at least that way he has something to justify what his father's doing—going to do. There are a few times where

I swear he looks like he's tearing up, but he shuts it off quickly, a true pro at hiding his emotions. As I watch him battle them, I start to notice just how similar we are. We both fight our emotions and act as if we don't understand them. While I understand my reason, I can't help thinking about what could have caused him to want to turn his own emotions off.

AS SOON AS I get done telling him about what happened in The Underworld, Alex takes us straight to the hideout. It's like he can remember it as if we've been playing in it only yesterday. When we climb up to the flourishing violet bush on the hill, we climb down the ladder and step into the dark. Memories instantly flood me and I realize that we spent a lot of time down here together.

Alex disappears into the darkness and seconds later I hear a match strike. He blows the dust off a candle and lights the wick. The glow orbs around the room and he places the candle down on top of a table, and then heads over to the trunk in the corner.

"It's still in the same spot?" I ask, peering over his shoulder.

He lifts the lid up and begins rummaging through it. "That was the last time I ever came down here. You went to live with Marco and Sophia and I just didn't see the point anymore." He avoids eye contact with me as he searches for the gem.

There are a lot of silly objects inside it; a rock, a leather bracelet, and what looks like a bouquet of pressed flowers. At one time all of this stuff meant something to us, tied us together along with our friendship.

I lean back and trace my finger down the palm of my hand. "Alex, what does *forem* mean?"

The muscles in Alex's back wind up as his entire body stiffens. "What?"

"That's what we said to each other when we were in here." I reach around him, take his hand, and then turn it over. I brush my finger along the minor scar in the center of his palm. "You said we were becoming blood brothers and then we said forem."

I hear Laylen clear his throat fairly loudly. I look over at him and he appears uncomfortable, shifting his weight as he stares at the floor. I open my mouth to say . . . well, I'm not really sure what. And I never do get to find out because he abruptly wanders over to the ladder and climbs up.

"What's his problem?" I ask Alex as he turns around, clutching something in his hand.

He shakes his head and lowers himself onto the dirt floor, pulling on my arm and steering me to sit with him. "It's nothing." He takes a deep breath and then opens his hand, showing me a shimmering blue gem.

"Thank God." I skim my fingers on the clean-cut edges. "What is it exactly?"

"It's the *Cruciatus* diamond."

"Does it do anything?"

He encloses his fingers around the gemstone. "The Queen used it to suck the fear out of people before one of the Keepers took it from her."

"But how did they get it from her if it's so hard to get into The Underworld?" I wonder.

"A long time ago things worked differently," Alex sighs tiredly. "The Queen used to be able to come up to the castle to discuss matters of business and to make truces with the Keepers. That's how the Keepers ended up sending people down there as a punishment. This," he pinches the gemstone between his thumb and his finger, "was used during a bargain between the Queen and the leader of the Keepers at the time."

"How did you and I end up with it?"

He rolls his tongue in his mouth as he tries not to smile. "You and I stole it."

"When we were friends?" I question, letting him know that I've been remembering more and more.

"How much do you exactly remember?" he wonders curiously.

"Not that much," I answer. "Just a few images here and there, but there seems to be a lot of us together when we were young."

Alex squeezes his eyes shut and drops the gem onto his lap, exhausted and looking like he's about to tip over.

"Alex," I say softly. "Are you okay?"

He remains silent, leaning his weight on his arm as he props it against the ground.

I place a hand on his shoulder and give him a gentle shake, concerned with how weak he looks. "Alex, can you hear me?" The electricity pulsates through us as I watch his chest lift and then descend with each frail breath he takes.

Then his eyelids lift open and his eyes collide with mine. A rush of relief sweeps through me and I start to pull my hand back, but he slips his hand over mine and positions my palm over his heart.

"What are you doing?" I whisper, loving that he's touching me, but still worried about how exhausted he looks. The holes in his skin aren't healing, either, they're fully open, and some of them are still bleeding while others are mixed with dirt.

"Shhh . . ." He shuts his eyes again and his other

hand finds the back of my neck. He draws me forward and presses our foreheads together. "I just need a minute, okay?"

I nod my head and then shut my eyes, too, the electricity elevating in voltage. My breathing becomes ragged the longer we stay touching and my hands itch to do things to him, inappropriate things.

When I feel him finally shift back, I open my eyes, only to find that he's leaning in again.

"Do you know how hard it was?" he breathes, his palm resting on my neck, his thumb smoothing across the sensitive area.

"I'm sorry you had to do that." I place my finger over a small hole in his chest where one of the tubes was embedded. "I really am, especially since you had to go there pretty much for nothing."

He shakes his head. "Not that . . . I've already told you that pain isn't a big deal." He brushes his lips across mine. "Being away from you . . . it gets harder and harder . . . I swear to God it actually feels like I'm dying."

I don't know what to say at his honestly raw admittance and he doesn't give me time as he crashes his lips against mine. I gasp while I glide my hands up the front of his chest, feeling his soft skin, which gets hotter the longer we kiss. He threads his fingers through my hair, tugging on the roots so he can tip my head back. Deep down I know that now is not the time or place, but then again I've seen the end of the world; I know it's coming and moments like these will come to an end.

I let him lie me back into the dirt and lower his body over mine, pinning an arm on each side of my head as his tongue explores every inch of my mouth. I bite at his lip, but ball my hands into fists, resisting the compulsion to stab my nails into his flesh—he's already got too many wounds at the moment.

The feel of his chest heats something deep within me and, as he positions his hands over my wrist, enfolding his fingers around them and restraining then down beside my head, I about come undone. I writhe my hips against his, lust and desire flooding my body at the intensity that is so overwhelming I can barely think of anything. Nothing other than him and I exist in this moment. Together. Something inside of me whispers that this is how it's supposed to be.

Forever.

He pulls back a little, his lips red and swollen, his hair a mess, but his skin looks healthier. Strangely the holes in his skin have sealed together so there are nothing more than tiny, fingernail sized scratches.

I wiggle one of my arms out of his grasp and run my fingers over his chest. "You're healing."

He kisses me softly. "I know . . ." Another light-as-a-feather kiss and then another and I can barely breathe through the fog in my head and the lack of oxygen in my system. "I can feel the energy healing me . . . Keepers heal quickly anyway, but this . . ." His tongue slips inside mine and I knot my fingers through his hair, pulling him closer. He puts a sliver of space between our lips, yet it's only to utter, "The electricity makes it so much better."

His weight pushes down on me again and I return my arm to the side of my head so he can wrap his fingers around my wrist and pin me down once more. Knowing what I'm doing, he briefly smiles against my lips before he kisses me with so much force it feels like my body blazes as brightly as a shimmering piece of silver in the sunlight.

We kiss until our bodies liquefy from the red-hot heat, until we're verging on the point of ripping each other's clothes off. I'm just about to undo the button of his jeans when a scream rips through the air. I freeze. I know the sounds far too well.

Death Walkers.

Alex is on his feet before I can even register what's happening, then grabbing ahold of my hand, he lifts me to my feet, his strength suddenly back.

"Where's Laylen," I say, glancing around at the dimly lit cave.

"I'm not sure." He looks worried as he stuffs the gem into his pocket and rushes over to the trunk. He selects a small, silver-bladed pocketknife from the bottom, and then dashes over to the ladder, glancing up at the land above.

"Stay behind me at all times," he commands, gripping the knife in one hand and the step of the ladder in the other.

I nod and follow him up the ladder, wishing I had a knife of my own so I could at least try to protect myself. I hate this feeling of being helpless yet I seem to experience it a lot.

I stay behind him as he told me to while he slides down the rocky hill and then winds through the bushes and trees. We can't find Laylen anywhere and the farther we walk, the more worried I get that he might be in some serious trouble.

More clouds have rolled in and the sky is nearly black. I can hear the sound of thunder rumbling and the snap of lightening as it blazes across the sky. As we reach the heart of the trees, rain begins to trickle down from the sky and splatter on the leaves and dirt, making the ground a muddy mess. Shriek after shriek echoes through the forest, growing louder as we hike further.

Finally it becomes so deafening that it's evident we're close to one of them. Stopping behind a large tree, Alex sticks his hand out to hold me back, pressing the knife out in front of him.

"Gemma, if anything happens—"

"I know, I know. Run. Hide. Save myself," I say because he's always telling me this. Usually it's because of the star, but now I wonder if his concern for me might be deeper.

His mouth quirks in amusement. "You and your sarcasm—" A shriek silences him.

Then we hear it. The voice. A very familiar one belonging to a traitorous, tricky, devious half-Faerie, half-Foreseer. Alex puts a finger up to his lips and then pushes me back behind him so I'm pressed up against the rough bark of the tree trunk.

"I can't believe this," Nicholas says. "I can't believe she managed to drag all of us here with her."

There's a pause.

"Well, it would have been a lot better if she hadn't dropped us in the middle of the lake," Nicholas says, fuming.

There's another long pause and then he starts cursing under his breath. Raindrops pour down on top of us, soaking our skin and clothes at the same time that it pitter-patters against the canopy of leaves and branches above our heads. I'm drenched and it's smothering a lot of the noises, but I clearly hear a shriek on the other side of the tree.

With the knife to the side of him, Alex peeks around the corner of the tree trunk then quickly leans back and shakes his head.

Who is it? I mouth.

He shakes his head, and then rubs his hand across his face, attempting to erase the uneasiness in it.

"I know, but where are they?" Nicholas continues on.

Another shriek shakes the trees and ground around us, causing leaves to break from the branches. The temperature rapidly shifts and the raindrops turn to ice droplets that ping against our skin. Alex holds his arm above my head, shielding me from them, but many of them still hit me and welts begin to form all over my skin.

"Would you stop doing that!" Nicholas screams and I'm starting to question if he's having a one-sided conversation.

Either that or he speaks Death Walker.

My eyes widen at the thought. Shit, does he? I aim a pressing look at Alex and mouth, *Death Walkers*.

He looks reluctant as he presses his lips together, refusing to answer me. The strangest fear starts to rouse inside me as I realize that we still haven't found Laylen and that Alex looks like he's going to be sick.

"Would you stop smelling the blood!" Nicholas cries as thunder booms and lightening snaps.

Blood! Oh, no, please, please don't let it be Laylen. I start to run around the tree trunk and dive headfirst into the madness, not caring about anything but making sure that Laylen's okay.

Alex snags me by the arm and drags me back to him. I fight to get away, but he cradles me against his frozen wet chest and I bury my face into it listening to his heart as I feel my own heart pleading to stop beating. Not Laylen. This can't be happening. He means too much to me. So much and I need him.

"He tried to attack me first." Nicholas snaps and it's overlapped by the sound of the crisp raindrops. "It was self-defense. Besides, you would have frozen him to death anyway."

There's a pause and it becomes pretty clear that Nicholas can be verbal with the Death Walkers. The only other person I've seen do this is Stephan and it makes me wonder why? Why can they communicate with them and the rest of us can't?

"So what if Stephan created Laylen?" Nicholas growls venomously. "Creating another Vampire isn't that complicated."

My head snaps up to Alex and he looks down at me. Sympathy and confusion float between us as we try to figure out what to do and what this all could mean.

"I'm not messing around," Nicholas insists. "I know what has to be done. . . . I know, but it might be a little difficult to find her. She's powerful and getting more powerful by the day. She can do things normal Foreseers can't . . . Fine, whatever. Let's go back and I'll see what I can do."

There's a faint swoosh and I swear I can feel energy building and then dissipating before the ice droplets turn back to rain. Minutes later, Alex peers around the corner of the tree trunk as he lets go of me.

Unable to stand it any longer, I shove my way past him and run out into the open.

"Gemma wait!" he calls out, following after me.

I sprint through the rain, splashing puddles and breaking the ice apart on the ground as I run toward a figure lying on the ground. I think I know who it is before I get there, but the irrational side of my mind is telling me I'm wrong

As I approach the lifeless body, Laylen's blond hair comes into view, and I slam to a stop beside him, dropping to my knees in the mud while Alex stops just behind me.

"He's not . . . he's not dead . . ." Tears sting at my eyes as I press a hand to Laylen's heart where a small, wooden stick is lodged. His arms and legs are sprawled out and he looks pallid. Rain soaks his shirt along with blood, and the harder it pours, the further his body sinks into the unstable ground, almost as if it's quicksand. The prickle gnaws at the back of my neck and I start to sink, too. I beg for it to simply take us because feeling this massive hole burrowing into my heart is exceedingly painful, too painful for me to be able to bear life anymore.

Alex crouches down and examines Laylen's body. "He's not dead," Alex says, putting his hands on the stick, and wrapping his fingers around it. "Not yet anyway."

"*Not yet anyway,*" I repeat, horrified, shielding my eyes from the rain as I gape at him. "Does that mean he's going to die?"

"Not if we can get him some . . ." Alex's face contorts as he yanks the stick out of Laylen's chest and tosses it aside into the wet grass

It leaves behind a gaping hole in his chest and I swear to God my own chest—or at least heart—is working to match it. Alex presses his hand over the wound, putting pressure on it as blood gushes out.

"How do we heal him?" I ask, touching Laylen's forehead. His eyes are shut and his skin is icy cold, more than it normally is

"We need blood," Alex states without looking at me.

I glance down at my wrist, rubbing my thumb across my vein. "I can do it," I say softly.

I expect him to argue, but he only nods, pushing to his feet. "Fine." He heads for the trees and I turn my head to look at him.

"Where are you going?" I call out.

He pauses with his back to me, rain showering down his body, droplets beading across his back muscles. "I . . . I can't watch you like that . . . with him . . ." He hikes through the mud and vanishes into the trees.

I turn back to Laylen, feeling the slightest pang of guilt, but then I jump back, startled. Laylen's eyes are open and he doesn't say anything as he reaches for my arm. His body's need to feed and rejuvenate his frail state is overcoming everything else. His fangs immediately slip out from his mouth. He doesn't speak as he lifts his head up, parts his lips, and lets out a weak growl before his fangs plunge into the vein on my wrist. I feel the jolt to my heart instantly and the need to be with him only moments later. I want him to feed off me, need him to do it. His eyes lock on mine as he drinks my blood, savoring the taste of it. His skin looks less and less pale, his blue eyes regaining some of their luster with each swallow and his chest stiches back up. Eventually, I lie down on top of him and let myself head to a place that's only going to bring heartbreak.

A place where I'll eventually have to make a choice about what I want.

Or who.

Once we're finished, we lay side by side in the mud, gathering our strength while we sink further into the forest ground.

"I'm sorry," he says, staring up at the sky, his eyelids blinking against the drizzle of the rain. "I know this has to be hard for you."

I find his hand and place mine over it, watching the lightening in the sky. "It's not your fault."

"But it is," he insists. "I should have been stronger than to let some stupid Faerie stake me . . . the Death Walkers threw me off, though."

"It's not your fault," I press, slanting my head to the side to look at him.

He refuses to look at me, however, fixated on the raindrops falling down to the earth instead. "Where's Alex."

I let out a faltering breath. "He wandered off . . . said he couldn't watch."

He squeezes my hand. "It'll be okay," he says, but I'm not sure who he's trying to convince. Him or me. Regardless, the invisible, magnetic connection that I felt with him the last time he bit me is twice as powerful now and I can only feel it growing with each beat of my heart.

The weight of the rain and my guilt pile on me more and I just keep thinking: *if only I could shut it off.* I try a few times, very pathetically, but give up when the feeling almost builds. Rain crashes down and thunder booms as I keep sinking further and further into the ground.

I'm just about to let it bury me when I realize that it actually is. I'm being buried alive by the mud and rain. Laylen rolls to his side and I hear him say something, but his voice is muddled with the mud oozing into my ears.

"Laylen!" I cry and I feel him grab onto my arm, but the ground only opens up and swallows me whole.

CHAPTER TWENTY

"FEEL IT, GEMMA," someone whispers. "Feel what you really are . . ."

"No, Gemma, don't . . ." a soft voice whispers. I know that voice. It's my mother's.

I open my eyes to the yard covered with metal objects surrounding me. "I don't feel anything."

"That's because you're cold," someone says as I sit up and glance around the junkyard. "And heartless."

"No, she's not," my mother says and she emerges out from behind some metal crates. "She's good and that's why you're so worried."

"Yes, she is," the voice purrs. "She's bad and you'll soon see that I'm right."

"I am not," I argue as ravens flock around my head. "I'm just confused."

"Confused." The voice grows louder and then laughs. "You're messing with everyone's head and playing with their emotions. You're downright evil, which is good . . . it's what I want."

I suddenly recognize the voice. "Stephan."

"Gemma, don't listen to him," my mom begs, not moving toward me, reaching out to me instead. "Please."

"You know you never seem to learn from your mistakes," Stephan talks over my mom as he steps out into the open. "You repeat them . . . which is beneficial for me and what I have planned. It'll make it easier to turn you."

"Turn me," I say. "As in evil? Because that'll never happen."

"You'll see," he states with confidence as my upper arm begins to burn. "I know you have it in you. That's why I chose you."

MY HEAD IS throbbing and I could swear my skull has been cracked open. When I open my eyes, I expect to be buried in the mud, but instead I'm in a small room with sunshine yellow walls, which is decorated with masks, pictures, and a colorful rain stick. The air smells lavishly of rain and forest.

I quickly start to sit up, but I'm jerked back down. I bounce against the mattress, restricted by metal cuffs and chains that are secured to my wrists and legs and tied to the bedposts.

"Shit," I curse. My legs are spread out and my arms are above my head, locked and losing circulation. My clothes are caked in mud and my hair feels crusty.

Where am I? And how the hell did I get here? I don't have an answer for either since the last thing I can remember is sinking into the dirt.

The crystal ball is still in my pocket and I close my eyes to try to Foresee my way out of here, but I can't even so much as feel a charge of energy; despite how much I let my emotions own me. I give up and start jerking on my arms and legs, but the cuffs only bite at my skin. I use every ounce of my energy, trying to get away, until my wrist and ankles rupture open and bleed all over the bed.

"There's no use trying to get away." Nicholas's face appears above me. His arms are crossed, the sleeves of his red shirt shoved up to his elbows, and he has a cut just above his right eyebrow as well as a bruise on his cheek bone.

"What happened to your face?" I ask derisively. "Did one of the Death Walkers beat you up?"

He makes sure to keep his distance from me, leaving just enough room that I can't slam my head against his. "Watch what you say. Remember, I've got all the control here."

I let out an unsteady breath. "Where am I?" I aim for a composed voice, however the fact that he has all the power at the moment makes me extremely nervous. Nicholas is the kind of guy who will do things to me.

"My house," he says simply, motioning at a night-stand beside the bed and an antique oval mirror on the door. There's also a window, but the curtain blocks my view to the outside. I wonder where his home is? In the City of Crystal? The Kingdom of Fey? Somewhere else?

"How did I get here?" I ask. "How did you drag me through the mud like that?"

"I already explained this to you," he says. "It's called mind manipulation, Gemma. You could do it too—make people see things that aren't really there—if you'd just train as a Foreseer."

I swallow hard. I'd almost forgotten how Nicholas could make me see things that weren't real. "But I blocked your mirage power."

"That wasn't my mirage power. God, you know nothing about what you can do." He fakes a pout. "It's quite tragic, really."

"Why did you bring me here?" I make my hand as narrow as possible and attempt to squeeze it out of the cuff, but the metal only bites my skin and I wince. "And what did you do to my power?"

"You can't use your power because of the *praesidium*." He points around at tiny marble sized lavender balls scattered all over the floorboards, the windowsill, and the footboard of the bed. "They trap your Foreseer energy within you," he says, sinking down to the bed.

I arch my back and wiggle my body so forcefully that the bed thumps against the wall. "Let me go!"

He slams his hand down on my stomach, hard enough that it knocks the wind out of me and I cough as I struggle for air.

"I think you know why . . . you understand now, what I am and who I work for." He squats down on the floor so that he's eye level with me and starts playing with my hair hanging over the side of the bed. "I tried to do things the easy way, but you just wouldn't let me."

"Let you what?" I ask, inching my head to the side to get out of his reach. "One minute you're trying to teach me how to be a better Foreseer and the next you're attacking me and chasing me down with a herd of Death Walkers. It doesn't make any sense."

He laughs at my pathetic attempt when I yank so hard on the chains they make a loud snapping noise. I bend my neck up, and aim my forehead for his, but he leaps to his feet and hops back, fury flashing across his face. But then he quickly collects himself and smiles again.

"You're so feisty," he says, his fingers seeking the nightstand.

I glare at him. "Let me go you sick, perverted asshole!"

"Now, why would I do a stupid thing like that?" He opens the top drawer and retrieves a teal crystal ball that shimmers even in the inadequate light.

I freeze. "The Ira." Suddenly there's a spark of light in this very dim, grey situation. I could get it from him. I just need to figure out how to escape with it.

He glances down at it in his hand and then amusement dances in his eyes as he tosses it back and forth between his hands, like he's playing catch. "Oh, I almost completely forgot that you wanted this."

I shake my head. "No, you didn't. You know exactly what you're doing."

He catches the Ira and then taps his finger against his lip. "You know, I could make a bargain with you." He extends his hand toward my face and I twist my neck to the side, cringing as he strokes my temple with his fingers. "You know Stephan wants you really badly." He ravels a strand of my hair around his finger. "And I'm supposed to give him to you . . . but I might break the rules and keep you." He leans down and sticks his nose in my hair, smelling it. "You smell so utterly delicious."

I fling my head in his direction and click my teeth together, trying to bite his finger, but he quickly withdraws his face and hands from my hair. "You know he's going to end the world with me." I know it's a long shot, but perhaps if he understands what's going to happen and the severity of it, then he won't want to help Stephan anymore. "Everyone will die. Even you . . . I've seen it."

"I don't need you to explain what Stephan is planning to do," He snaps, yanking down the sleeves of his shirt. "I understand more than you do."

"And you're simply okay with letting him kill everyone?" I shake my head at him. "Do you even have a heart or are you seriously that cold?"

"I think the real question is just how heartless and cold you are," he sneers.

My jaw nearly drops. His words almost match what Stephan said to me in the dream I had right before I woke up here. Maybe it wasn't a dream, though. Maybe it was a vision.

He leans over me, his eyes nearly glowing like cinders. "Which I think is what this whole thing is about."

My stomach rolls. He knows more than I thought he did. "Why are you doing this? There has to be a reason . . . you can't . . . there's no way you just decided to be evil."

"Maybe I've always been evil. I mean, you barely even know me and, from what you do know, I'm a sick, twisted, perverted asshole." He tucks the Ira under his arm and makes air quotes. "But before you go making assumptions, maybe you should consider how much you know about Stephan. Or about his precious son, Alex. You trust him so much, yet he is the son of the man who ruined your life and so many other peoples that it's absurd. He's supposedly some high and mighty Keeper, yet he has more darkness in him that anyone can comprehend."

"Did Stephan ruin your life?" I ask. "Is that why?"

He shifts his weight, uncomfortable, and I get the impression that I've struck a nerve.

"What did he do to you?" I press.

"I think I'm going to go take a walk." He evades my question and stuffs his hands into the pockets of his pants, rocking back on his heels. "I'd say wait here, but I don't think you'll be going anywhere." He turns his back on me and walks out of the room, taking the Ira with him. He shuts and locks the door behind him as well.

I let out a frustrated scream, tugging on the chains. The praesidium rolls off the footboard and onto the floor, but stays close enough that my energy is uselessly trapped inside me. My battle against the chains goes on for hours until I can barely move my legs or arms and I'm dripping with sweat. Exhaustion takes me over and all I want to do is shut my eyes.

So I do, not knowing where I'll end up, what I'll see, or what I'll feel. However, it doesn't really matter, does it? Because at the moment I don't have control over anything.

CHAPTER
TWENTY-ONE

I 'M BEGINNING TO learn what rage is. I didn't fully understand it like I thought I did because what's stirring within me is definitely rage. It's like a building storm; rolling clouds and thunder, but lightning hasn't arrived yet. It's getting ready to snap its raging energy against the ground, though, and make the world rumble with its bellowing echo.

I'm losing track of time as well as my grip on sanity. Hours stack upon hours, then days upon days. I'm thirsty and hungry while I'm still in my disgustingly muddy clothes, so I smell repulsive.

Nicholas comes in and checks on me occasionally, only unhooking my chains to let me go to the bathroom, which he gives me no privacy for. It makes me feel revolting inside, like something has been taken that I'll never be able to get back. He always makes vulgar comments about me and he feeds me only bread and water. He also likes to keep the Ira on the nightstand, close enough that I can feel the vibrant energy exuding from it, but far enough away that I can't channel it; even though it's useless since the praesidium remains close enough to lock my powers within me.

I try to make several attempts to escape, but always fail and end up paying for it. I quickly learn that Nicholas has a violent streak in him after he hit me a couple of times when I said and did the wrong thing. It doesn't make me back down at all, though. In fact, it makes me more determined to get away and pay him back in full for what he's doing to me.

In the beginning I expected Alex or Laylen to show up and save me. I made a comment about it once and Nicholas informed me that no one could save me. That his house is merely an illusion in the mind and only those he allows to see it can.

There doesn't even seem to be a point in what he's doing. Stephan never shows up to collect me and when I ask him about it, he says he's been detained. Although I think he might be enjoying having me here a little too much.

The strange thing is that he appears to be growing weaker by the day; pallid, his eyes tinting yellow, while his skin looks cracked and dry. It's repulsive to look at and even he seems disgusted by himself. His connection and obsession with me, however, seems to be growing stronger. He's always touching me, trying to kiss me and grope me. I have no idea where his fixation with me is coming from, but I'm starting to think it might be to my benefit if I can find the right moment

Around the six or seventh day, I begin to connive a plan to get away. The one that I create makes me utterly sick, but I don't think I have another choice other than to stay here forever and sink further into my rage.

I mentally prepare myself for what I'm about to do when he walks into the room. He drags a chair from the corner and puts it beside the bed, sitting down.

He slants his head to the side and examines me with curiosity as he props his foot up against the side of the bed. "You know, you're very talented and I have to say I'm quite surprised that you haven't found a way out of this yet.

Oh, I have. I'm just waiting for the perfect moment.

"You can go into and out of visions without a crystal ball," he says enviously. "With a little practice and enough emotion, you could travel anywhere without a crystal ball as well." He pauses, assessing me. "I could teach you . . . we could work together—we'd be amazing together."

I stare blankly at him. "Maybe."

He studies me with a distrusting look on his face. "You don't trust me."

I remain neutral. "You've given me no reason to trust you."

"You've barely gotten to know me," he says. "Maybe I'm different than what you think. Maybe there's a reason for everything bad that I do."

"Prove it," I challenge.

He stares me down defiantly. "How much do you know about the Fey?" he asks.

I bend my fingers downward and itch beneath the cold metal cuff, the skin has been rubbed raw underneath it. "Not much."

"Of course you don't, since you've been spending most of your time with Keepers, Witches, and Vampires." His lips twitch. "And of course there was all that time you spent by yourself unemotionally detached."

I frown. "You know about that?"

He shrugs. "Of course. I'm a Foreseer and can *see* anything I want, something you should learn . . . but that's a story for another time." He drops his foot to the ground and transfers from the chair to the bed, the mattress concaving beneath his weight as he sinks down beside me. "The Fey have been around forever, you know.

Most people think of us as tricksters, which we are, but we can be very serious as well, given the right circumstances, like if our kind are suffering." He brushes his hand over the top of my head. "I'm not sure if you've heard of him or not, but there used to be a man called Malefiscus who was the personification of evil."

I shake my head, letting him pet me because it helps me with my plan. "I'm sorry, but I haven't."

He rolls his golden eyes. "Haven't the Keepers taught you anything?" He withdraws his hand from my hair, but only to tap his fingers on his chapped lips. "Then again, they might not want you to know about it since Malefiscus started out as a Keeper."

"The personification of evil started out as a Keeper?" I ask, remembering what Laylen told me about the Mark of Evil and how it used to exist and was directly related to the Keepers' blood.

"Are you surprised?"

I want to say yes but the more I learn about the Keepers, the more I realize they aren't as good as they portray themselves to be.

He smiles, pleased, and begins petting my head again. "Well, I'll fill you in on the story of Malefiscus so you can get a better understanding of what he was—what a Keeper could become if they ended up switching sides and getting branded by evil." His fingers drift to my cheek and I refuse to look away, knowing I have to do this.

"During Malefiscus's time, there was sheer and utter chaos in the world," Nicholas explains. "He tortured everyone—Vampires, Witches, Faeries. Even humans. He had a whole army of followers and they would go around on killing sprees or trying to persuade people he saw fit to join him."

"There was so much death and blood as well as pain

that the Fey leader of that time decided he'd had enough. There were too many Faeries dying and so he made a bargain with Malefiscus to try to save lives." His fingers roam to my mouth and he strokes his thumb against my lips as he licks his own. "He told Malefiscus that if he would leave the Fey alone, that we would forever be indebted to him—that we would exchange a favor for the Fey's freedom from his chaos."

"Did he agree?" I ask, my lips brushing against the pad of his thumb. He tastes salty while he smells like dirt and murky water.

He nods, sticking his thumb into my mouth, and I just about gag. "Malefiscus agreed to it since the Fey are very powerful and he loved power. So the leader of the Fey and Malefiscus made a Blood Promise." He removes his thumb from my mouth, although he keeps it resting on my bottom lip.

"What's a Blood Promise?"

"Not too long after the promise was made, though," he continues on with his story, discounting my question. "Malefiscus was caught and sentenced to his death. The Keepers made the sentence and supposedly they executed him, but deep down people wondered whether they really did or not. There were a lot of traitors at the time and rumors started flooding that someone had snuck him out the day before he was supposed to be hanged." He pauses and then lies down on the bed beside me, his fingers tracing a path across my stomach, his skin feeling as rough as sandpaper. My gut churns and a slimy chill slithers down my spine, but this is right where I want him; close and distracted.

"Alive or dead, it doesn't really matter because his bloodline didn't die with him," He continues while sketching circles around my belly button as he props up on his elbow and watches my reaction. "It carried through the decades, going completely unnoticed for a while and so no one really knew about it until just recently." He pauses. "It carried on and now resides in a man named Stephan Avery."

He stills and I'm too shocked to breathe. Stephan is the descendant of evil. Alex's *father*. God, what does that make Alex?

"Because his bloodline carried on, so did the Fey's promise to grant him a favor. Only now the favor is owed to Stephan." His fingernails plunge into my stomach and slice my flesh open. Blood oozes out, but I tell myself to shut out the pain. *Shut down.* "I had barely heard of this story and I think a lot of Fey had forgotten as well until surprise, surprise, Stephan came to collect a few days ago," he says venomously. "And he didn't want just any member of the Fey to fulfill the promise. He wanted the Faerie who has the gift of a Foreseer as well."

My eyes enlarge as the severity of the situation that I'm in registers in my head. "He asked you . . . to do what?"

"I think you already know that." He pivots on his hip and aligns himself over me, his fingers stroking the section of my stomach that he had clawed moments ago. I feel my chance arriving and I try to get myself ready for the wretched place I'm about to go. "He wanted me to track down a very beautiful, feisty, and very tortured girl with the most magnificent violet eyes."

"What does he want you to do with me?" *Stay calm. You can do this. You're strong.*

"Bring you to him." He inches closer to me like he's about to kiss me.

I stay as still as I can, despite my initial reaction to squirm and head-butt him. "And why haven't you?"

"Because I can't seem to let you go." He tucks a strand

of hair behind my hair and wets his chaffed lips with his tongue.

"You could just let me go," I dare to suggest. "You could come with me . . . go into hiding with us."

He rolls his eyes. "Alex would never let that happen and you know it."

"I could make him," I say in an even voice. "I have ways."

"You are a devious thing," he remarks and places a sloppy kiss on my cheek. My heart thrashes and my throat burns with the taste of vomit. "But even if you could convince him, I still couldn't . . . I don't have a choice anymore with what I can do to you." He leans back a little and rolls up the sleeve of his shirt all the way to the top of his arm. On the side of his arm, branded in red and black ink is a triangular mark.

"What is that?" I whisper, although I think deep down I already know. I've seen it before in my dream, on Draven, and with all the talk about the Mark of Evil, it's pretty clear what it is; even if I don't want to believe it.

"The Mark of Malefiscus, also known as the Mark of Evil," Nicholas growls, wrenching his sleeve back over it. "I'm branded with the Mark of Evil and I can make you stay all I want, but eventually the power of it's going to take over. It will make me give you to Stephan."

"How did you . . . how did you get it?"

"Stephan."

My body jolts upward as horror slams through me. "What!"

He smiles and it almost looks like a sad smile. For a brief instant, he looks almost human. "Stephan can do a lot more than what people think."

I shake my head and open my mouth to ask more questions, but he places his finger over my lips, shushing me. "No more questions. My time is running out . . ." he looks down at his pale, cracked arm and then his eyes lock back on me. "I have to take you away soon." He leans in to kiss me.

I shove every ounce of revulsion down and lock it in a box inside me. I become a different person, one that doesn't feel, and for a second I feel at home. I kiss him, holding everything in me, and pretending like I'm somewhere else. Somewhere the sun shines and my mood matches it. Maybe on a beach. Even though I've never been to one; the idea of the sand, the ocean, and the heat seem like it would be a wonderful, relaxing experience. I picture myself there, lying in the sand. Someone is with me, but I can't tell who yet. A sturdy male figure with skin as smooth as porcelain. I hold myself there as Nicholas's hands digress all over my body.

He gets more intense the further he goes, but my bound legs and arms are making it hard for me to do anything except lie there.

As he tries to draw our bodies closer, my legs get in the way.

"I'm sorry," I apologize with as much sincerity as I can.

His lips are puffy as he leans back with his eyes unfocused, like he's stoned. It's almost like I have some sort of power over him and I wonder what it is. Regardless, I'm using it to my advantage.

"It's fine," he says and leans back in to kiss me. After a lot of time passes—time where I zone out and my body just moves on its own—Nicholas finally gets frustrated and undoes the cuffs from my ankles and wrists.

"Try anything at all," he threatens, lowering himself down onto me. "And you'll pay severely."

I keep my expression blank as he begins kissing me

again. I allow him to relax as much as possible, and then, when he's about to shove his hands down the front of my jeans, I finally open the box inside me, letting emotions flood out. I lean back and then slam my head forward, ramming our skulls together hard. There's a sickening crack and then Nicholas screams out in pain. I give him no time to recover, kicking him between the legs. His face screws up in pain and he slumps to the side of the bed. I leap to my feet and immediately the blood rushes from my head. The room violently spins in indistinct hues and shapes as I stumble toward the bed and make a run for the door. Halfway there, though, I turn back and stare at the nightstand, at the Ira.

"You know you want it," Nicholas grunts, clutching his goods. "If you leave without it, you'll regret it."

I'm weak and hungry and I feel like shit, but I do want it. Badly. The only thing standing between it and me is Nicholas. I glance around the room for a weapon and spot the rain stick on the wall. I snatch it down and position it in front of me.

Nicholas climbs off the bed, hobbling a little as he winds around to the foot of the bed. He grins at me, raising his eyebrows and spanning his arms out to the side.

"Go ahead," he says with an arrogant grin. "Take your best shot."

Trembling, I shuffle forward and swing the stick at his head. He ducks down and the force of the movement sends me sideways. My feet scuff against the floor, but I ungracefully manage to recompose my balance. I walk a half-circle around him, positioning the stick out in front of me.

He laughs at me as he turns to the side with me, making sure that his eyes stay targeted on mine. "Come on, Gemma. You're a Keeper. You can do better."

I shake my head, redirecting myself to the other side. "No, I'm not . . . I have no mark."

He leans back against the footboard and causally props his elbows against it, unafraid of me to the point that it's almost insulting. "What makes you so sure?"

"No mark."

"Maybe it hasn't appeared yet."

I want to ask him what he knows because it looks like he knows something, but it'll only get me distracted. Taking a step backward, I charge at him. He laughs, skittering to the side like he's dancing, however I twirl around right at the last second and extend the stick out so it comes straight out in front of him. The heavy material slams against his gut and the stuff inside the stick makes it sound like it's raining.

He lets out a sharp cough as he crumples over and I seize the opportunity to bring the stick over my head and ram it down on top of his. The sound is sickening and it makes me feel barbaric, but I've entered survival mode and all that matters is getting the hell out of here alive with the Ira.

I hit him again and again until he's lying on the floor in a pool of his own blood. He's not dead, his chest is still feebly rising and falling, but I've beaten him pretty badly. I drop the rain stick to the floor and back away. I have blood on my hands and even some on my face. I'm a terrible, wretched person. I really am.

I grab the Ira off the nightstand, feeling a thorny vine twist inside my stomach. By the time I step out of the house and away from the *praesidium,* I don't feel like Gemma anymore. I feel dead inside and I let the numbing feeling stay because sometimes, when it all comes down to it, being emotionally detached is better than feeling what really lies inside the darkest spots of our hearts, the one's that we want to deny exist. Yet sometimes they're impossible to ignore.

I walk to the center of the crystal-trimmed yard in front of Nicholas's illusion house. There's a fence carved of rubies and a large tree that grows miniscule pink diamonds. It's beautiful, yet as Nicholas's said, the beauty is just a delusion.

Taking the ruby-filled ball out of my pocket. I hold onto the Ira and shut my eyes. I'm not sure where to go since so much time has gone by, so I do the only thing I can think of.

I shut my eyes and think of the one thing that brings emotion out of me.

I think of Alex.

CHAPTER TWENTY-TWO

W HEN I LAND in the living room of Adessa's, I start to feel alive again, my bones and muscles not hurting so much and my head clears. The air smells intoxicatingly of cinnamon and spices, and the velvet couch looks very welcoming. So does the person on it.

Alex is staring at a book that's open on his lap, but when my feet hit the floor his head whips up. A blistering flame of need combines with desire and I start to run to him, but my knees give out on me and I slow down, bracing onto the armrest of the sofa.

"Where the hell have you been?" He takes in the traumatized state of me as he rises to his feet, dropping the book on the cushion. "And what the hell happened to you?"

I collapse onto the nearest couch and lie down on my side, cuddling the Ira to my chest. "Nicholas."

Alex shakes his head and then storms over to the wall, slamming his fist through the drywall. "I'm going to kill him," he growls with so much fury in him it vibrates across the room and into me, stealing some of my already fading energy.

I struggle to keep my eyes open. "I'm so tired." I raise my arm in the air and hold up the Ira. "I got this from him."

His green eyes widen as he strides across the room and kneels down beside the couch. "You have the Ira?"

I nod, gazing off into empty space as I remember the hell I've been through the last few days. My ankles and wrists are ripped apart from the cuffs while my legs and arms feel stretched. "Yeah, I stole it from him."

"What happened? One minute I left you with Laylen so you could . . . so he could . . . and then Laylen said you just vanished. At first I thought he did something to you, but then I realized that he . . ." he summons a deep breath and shuts his eyes. "That he cares for you. So we searched the forest, however we couldn't find you anywhere, so we came back here." He opens his eyes and sadness abounds within each of them. He hitches his thumb over his shoulder, pointing at the book. "I've been reading and reading on why the hell someone would just disappear, but I was starting to arrive to the conclusion that . . . that you ran away." He pauses, waiting for an answer.

I shake my head. "Nicholas was playing fucking mind games with me." I drape my arm over my head to block out the sting from the bright light. What's been done to me . . . what I did continues to possess my fractured soul. "He took me to his illusion house and tied me to the bed. At first he said it was because of your father, but as the days kept passing and passing, I really started to believe it was for his own benefit."

Alex remains silent for a while, deeply breathing in and out. Finally, the silence becomes maddening and I peer out from under my arm. His gaze penetrates me; my filthy clothes, the warm blood on my hands, along with the purplish blue bruises and deep red scratches covering my body. "Gemma, I'm not sure what you're talking about. I mean I can tell by the way that you look that you obvious went through something really bad, but . . ." He struggles, leaning in over me and sweeping my hair out of my face. "But you've only been gone for a few hours."

I swiftly shake my head. "No . . . no there's no way. I was gone for days. I know it."

His eyebrows furrow as I wince from a sore area on the center of my forehead. "Gemma, I promise you that's not true. I can even get Laylen in here to back me up."

My head pounds as I rack my mind for what the hell could be happening. "But it felt like days. There's no way it could have been only a few hours."

He draws a line back and forth below each of my violet eyes. "Maybe he was messing with you . . . maybe he was making it seem like days had gone by. He could easily do that, Gemma."

I sigh, thinking of how my sanity bolt had unscrewed. "Maybe . . ."I shake my head and sit up as he slants back to give me room. "I hate him. I really do."

Alex slides up on the couch and turns to face me. His fingers find my hips and he carefully lifts me onto his lap so I'm straddling him. "Tell me what he did to you." He scans over my clothes, my wounds, stealing my breath away the longer he stays focused on me. Electricity within me stirs and arouses, along with my emotions that I turned off.

I take a deep breath and tell him what happened, minus the making out details because I'd vomit if I had to say them aloud. There are some things that are better left unsaid and forgotten. The person I became is someone I want to forget.

It takes Alex about a minute before he speaks again. "I'd like to say that I'm surprised," he says, slouching back in the sofa with his hands still on my hips. "But I'm not."

"So you've heard of this Malefiscus?"

He wavers and then hesitantly nods. "When I was little, my father would tell me stories of him."

"So you knew?" Stunned, I slide back to leave his lap, but his fingers press downward, securing me in place.

"Just stories," he insists. "He didn't tell me he was a descendant, only the story of who Malefiscus was and what became of him."

"But you knew about the mark?"

He shakes his head, his pupils like black marbles as he begins to panic. "No, I really didn't. I just knew who he was and what he did . . . my father started telling me stories of him right after my mother left and they kind of became like bedtime stories."

"He told you of evil as a way to get you to go to sleep." I'm stunned. Shocked. And kind of disgusted. All this time I'd felt pity for myself for everything I'd went through when I was younger, but I haven't really thought about what it must have been like to grow up with a murderous traitor. "Alex, that's horrible."

He shrugs it off, staring over my shoulder. "That's minor compared to some of the other shit he's done to me." His eyebrows dip together as he zones out on some distant memory.

I place my hand on his stubbly cheek and he flinches. "What did he do to you?"

His gaze slides to me as his fingers travel up my side, along each bump of my aching ribcage, finally resting on my shoulder. "You don't need to worry about that. It's in the past."

"But I want to know," I say. "I-I want to understand you more."

He smiles sadly. "No, you don't. No normal person

wants to hear about the bad things that were done to someone by their father. They'd rather stay in the dark."

"Well, I'm not normal," I say as his hand covers my hand that's on his cheek. He traces the folds of my fingers and I shiver from his affectionate touch, experiencing a fleeting moment where I feel like myself again, whoever she was. "Tell me," I plead.

"That's another story for another time," he says gloomily. "Right now we need to work on getting you hidden better, especially if my father can brand people. Jesus, there could be a ton of people out there who have the mark. I mean, who knows how many people he branded."

"So you think it's true?" I say, sounding strangled, recollecting all the visions I had about the mark appearing on me. I casually glance over at the spot on my arm where it always appears to make sure I'm still good inside.

"I don't know . . . maybe . . ." He shuts his eyes and his nostrils flare as he inhales sharply. "If it's true, then my childhood would make much more sense."

For a split second, I wonder if Stephan marked Alex, but I've seen him naked and he doesn't have the mark anywhere or a severe scar where one might have been cut off.

"I don't have one if that's what you're thinking," he says, sensing my thoughts. He doesn't sound angry, merely hurt and lost.

"I'm sorry," I mutter, tipping my chin down and staring at my lap while using my hair to veil my face. "I don't know why I thought it."

"Because of everything I've done to you," he says straightforwardly. "You don't trust me or anyone really."

I shake my head and lift my gaze to his eyes. "No, I *didn't* trust anyone, but I'm starting to."

His eyes flare lustrously as he grabs the back of my

neck and pulls me toward him, his tongue slipping out to wet his lips. I think he's going to kiss me, however all he does is shake his head.

"Did he do this to you? Nicholas." His fingers gently outline a pattern down the bruises dotting on my arm and then his fingers circle my torn up wrist.

I nod, the feel of his touch soothing me. "He did."

He clenches his jaw, anger storming through him, and his muscles constrict. "I'm going to kill him for it," he growls.

I nuzzle my cheek against his. "He already paid for it . . . I beat him up really badly."

He pushes me back by the shoulders a little and then lifts my wrist to his lips and kisses my injury. "That's kind of hard to believe," he says between kisses.

"It's true." I shrug, shivering from his kisses. "I beat him with a rain stick."

He seals his lips tightly to refrain from laughing. "I'll take your word for it then, but if I do cross paths with him again, I'll beat him unconscious."

I want to say too late, though all I do is nod because I'm too tired to do or say anything else. Tired of fighting. Of running. Of simply existing. All I want to do at the moment is shut my eyes and go to sleep.

"What are we going to do now?" I ask, my eyelids fluttering shut as I yawn. "I'm guessing we have to leave."

"Now we're going to get you out of here," he replies. "Go somewhere safe—somewhere hidden. Nicholas knows where this is and now that we know he's helping my father, we can't stay here."

I nod and bury my face into his chest while he smoothes his hand up and down my back. "Let me go get Aislin and Laylen to see if we can come up with a plan."

"Okay."

He stands up and secures me to the front of him, carrying me with him as he leaves the room. My energy fizzles with each step he takes as I cling onto him. I keep seeing little images of objects and the color red. I see the mark. I see Death Walkers. I see the end of the world. The images are pulling at me to join them and I keep thinking what if I did? Join them? Join the easy side, the one that chases instead of runs.

"I think something's . . . wrong with me," I tell him drearily.

He says something about everything being okay and that he'll protect me. I keep nodding, but eventually I have to admit to myself the truth.

That in the end this might not work out. That he can try to protect me, but it doesn't mean that things will always end up in my favor. Once I admit that, I sink into a deep state of sleep.

CHAPTER
TWENTY-THREE

T HROUGH ALL OF this, I end up losing myself for a moment. I zone out; not asleep, but not really awake, either. I see a thousand images, dream a thousand horrific daydreams. It feels like I die and come back to life again, over and over. I swear I break and then heal . . . break and then heal.

"Gemma."

The sound of Alex's voice forces me out of my own head and back to reality. I jolt upright as I realize I'm lying in a bathtub, submerged in warm water with my head resting against the porcelain. The faucet is on and a light steam rises around me.

Alex is kneeling down on the tile floor, his arm resting on the side of the bathtub. "Are you feeling better?"

I rub my hand over my face as I sit up and the water beads down my skin. "Where are we?" I have bruises and open scratches on my skin, along with traces of dirt.

"At a friend of Adessa's beach house," he says. "In Maryland."

I hunch over, drawing my knees up to my chest. "Did Aislin transport us here?"

He nods, rubbing his hand down my back. "She

did—you passed out before she even got started." Water drips from his hand onto my skin as he rubs the dirt off me. "Or more like zoned out. Your eyes were open, but you . . . but you were gone." His hand wanders to my arms where he begins washing off the dirt off there, too. "I think you might need to take it easy for a while."

I rest my head on my knees. "I need to save my mom and then maybe I can get this stupid star's energy out of me and be normal for once."

His hand slides over my cheek and I stare at him as he combs my damp locks out of my face. "You need to rest. You're doing too much."

"After I save her."

"Gemma—"

"Alex, please," I beg. "I can't stop thinking about her . . . I dream about her all the time and she needs my help . . . she needs me. She could help us, too. She could know something about the mark and your father—she could know a way to stop the vision I saw from happening."

"But what if she doesn't?" He shuts the faucet off. "It's such a long shot."

I raise my head and turn sideways in the bathtub, grasping onto the sides. "I've dreamt about her and I'm not even sure if it was a dream. It could have been real. She said she could help me—that she knew things. Just like she told your father before he forced her into the lake."

He wipes away some of the water dripping from my eyelashes with his thumb. "But they might just be dreams."

"But they might not," I whisper. "Nicholas said I was powerful and could do amazing things with my power if I was taught right, like travel and see visions without a crystal. What if I can communicate through them to? What if she's communicating with me?"

His finger slides down the brim of my nose and to my bottom lip. "All right, but I'm going with you."

I nod. "I know. Since you were in the vision with me when we were bargaining with the Queen, I'm assuming you need to be there."

He reaches for a washcloth on a small shelf tucked in the corner near the sink. "And I'm making you rest for a day."

"Alex, I don't—"

He places a finger over my lips, the washcloth balled in his hand. "Rest, or no deal."

I narrow my eyes, but on the inside I'm less irritated, understanding that he's worried about me. "Okay, one day," I say against his lips.

He nods and then dips the washcloth into the bathtub of water. "Now, lean back."

I glance at the soaked washcloth in his hand. "Why?"

"Because," he leans in and brushes his lips across mine. "I'm going to wash off all those cuts that damn Faerie put all over you," he says in a low voice.

I do what he says and lean back, resting my head against the back of the tub, the water flowing over my body. I'm completely naked except for my locket and my muscles feel like I've just ran a marathon. Yet, with each touch of his hand, I start to feel better as he moves the washcloth over my body, wiping away the dried blood and mud as he cleans off the cuts. I swear it feels like he's washing away the icky feelings I've been experiencing and the memories of what I did to Nicholas. I feel cleaner, more relaxed, more in tune with him. He's touching me everywhere, even when he's not, the magnetic bond's syncing our bodies together.

I shut my eyes as he works the cloth over my neck, down my chest, over my breasts. I groan, curving upward, but I don't open my eyes, even when his hand moves to the inside of my thighs. Just when I think I can't take it anymore, his hand and the cloth leave my body. Seconds later, he combs his fingers through my hair and begins washing it as he tenderly tugs at the roots.

When he finishes I open my eyes and look up at him.

"Feel better?" he asks, tossing the cloth aside.

I nod, unable to look away from the longing in his eyes. "I do. Thank you."

He stands to his feet and reaches for a towel on the hook near the door, and then he takes my hands to help me to my feet. Like he did back at Adessa's house, he helps me out of the tub and then dries me off. After he secures the towel around me, he carries me to a bed in a room with floral walls and French doors that open out to a deck. The view from the deck is breathtaking; golden sand, amazingly blue ocean and the glistening sunshine. Although I barely get to appreciate it because, as soon as he lays me down on the bed and my head hits the pillow, exhaustion overcomes me and I fall into a deep, dreamless sleep for the first time in a very, very long time.

CHAPTER
TWENTY-FOUR

MARYLAND IS VERY humid. The air is so heavy and dense that it feels like being in a sauna. The little blue house is secluded near a rocky beach where the ocean constantly roars against the shore. It's my first time seeing it and, while I enjoy it, I know that there are many other things to worry about at the moment. Like saving my mom.

Aislin puts up countless charms all over the house, so many that I even set off a few by accident when I simply walked into the wrong areas of the house. One of them turned my skin purple and, when I asked her what the point was, she said it was a distraction. I still didn't get it, though. We also put *praesidium* all over the house and yard and even close areas of the beach; so there won't be any surprise visits from Foreseers.

I've been working my ass off to get the Ira to work, but I can't channel enough energy. It frustrates me to no end and forces me to push past my limits. I've passed out a few times from using too much energy and Alex is getting more and more reluctant to help me.

"You're going to hurt yourself," he said one day after I'd passed out while clutching onto the Ira. "It's not healthy."

"It's not healthy being the star, either," I replied, turning the teal crystal ball in my hand. "I need to be normal."

"I don't think you'll ever be normal," he said begrudgingly. "None of us will."

"Well, then I want to be weird without the star in me," I told him.

That got him to smile, something I've started noticing he doesn't do very often and, whenever I manage to get him to crack one, it seems to lighten his mood.

On top of the Ira problems, Laylen's been getting mood swings a lot, having violent outburst. He even threw a cup across the room because he couldn't find the coffeemaker. It's been happening ever since he almost died and my blood brought him back. I'm beginning to worry that between death and all the blood drinking, his caring, laidback personality has been altered.

I tried to talk to him about it once, when we crossed paths inside the kitchen. He's been avoiding me; he even went so far as to try to turn around when I walked up to him while he was searching for a plate, but I stepped into his path.

"Are you okay?" I asked, reaching for a mug on the counter. I wasn't really thirsty. In fact, I'd kind of planned it out so he'd have to talk to me. "You've seemed a little distant the last few days."

He shrugged, stuffing his hands into the pockets of his black jeans. "As good as I always am."

I rotated the mug in my hand and leaned in. "Laylen, what happened in the forest. That was no one's fault. It had to be done to save you."

He stared at me for a moment and, at first, his expression was unreadable, but then he cut me with a harsh look. "What would have saved me, Gemma, is if you'd have simply let me die," he says. "That's how I want to be saved." He walked around me, bumping his shoulder into mine and leaving me stunned.

I haven't been able to stop thinking about him. It's been over a day and the pain in his eyes when he said those God-awful words remains imprinted into my mind. Not want to be saved? Did he want to die? Does he hate himself that much? The thought hurts at my heart. I can't even imagine what would happen if I told him what I'd overheard Nicholas saying about Stephan creating him. It would break him and luckily Alex seems to agree with me because he's kept his mouth shut. The biggest question I have is why, though? Why would he create a Vampire when there are ton of them wandering around?

It's late, the full moon an orb against the charcoaled sky and the darkened ocean water. I'm sitting out on the deck that extends out from my bedroom, the French doors swinging in the light breeze while Alex sleeps soundly in the bed just inside the room. The stars are glimmering with it and I can't help thinking that this is where it all started. This entire mess. One single star fell from the sky, or a piece of it anyway, and all hell has broken loose. Lives were shattered. Souls detached.

I have a hoodie and boxer shorts on as I sit in one of the chairs, sipping a soda. I'm lost in my thoughts when a tall figure emerges on the beach. It's strange because the beach becomes vacant usually after sunset and I wonder if maybe it's a homeless person looking for a place to stay. Then the light of the moon hits the person's blond hair and highlights his figure even more.

I feel a slight pull toward him and I set my soda down, jumping to my feet. "Laylen!"

He stops, turns to look at me, and then he takes off running down the beach. When he reaches a cluster of cliffy rocks, he makes a sharp veer to the left and heads toward the street that curves beside the ocean and leads to the city limits.

"Shit." I run into my room, slip on my flip-flops, and hurry over to the bed where Alex is fast asleep on top of the comforter.

I give him a soft shake. "Alex, wake up. "

He jolts awake, blinking his eyes. "What's wrong?" He sits up quickly.

"I just saw Laylen leaving," I tell him. "Down the beach. When I called his name, he ran."

Shaking his head, he reaches over to the nightstand and flips on the lamp. "What direction was he heading?" He blinks wearily at me with some serious bedhead going on.

I point over at the north side of the house. "That way . . . he's been acting kind of weird since he . . . since he almost died and then drank my blood."

He swings his bare feet to the floor as he tosses the blanket aside, stretching out his arms. "You've noticed that, too?"

"You've noticed it?" I ask, averting my gaze from his muscles because if I stare at them for too long I'll have no self-control and get completely caught up in him to the point that I'll forget about everything else.

He nods and then stands up from the bed and reaches for his shirt draped over the back of a chair in front of the vanity. He refastens the tie on his drawstring pajama bottoms and then scoops up the keys from the coffee table.

"Let's go look for him," he says and heads for the front door. "I don't know if we really should, because I don't really think he's running away or anything." He opens the door for me.

We step outside and he locks the door up. The chilly

air hits my skin and I pull the hood of my hoodie over my head, jumping to the side when a stream of sparks shoots out of the bushes and threatens to land on my toes.

"Damn it, Aislin," Alex says, pulling me onto the grass out of the way. "I get that we need to be protected, but it doesn't do any good if we get hit by one of her charms."

I don't say anything as we hurry for the driveway. The house is in a fairly secluded neighborhood, where most of the houses on the block have their porch lights on.

"Alex, what if Laylen's . . ." I trail off as Alex opens the car door for me. I climb in and he rounds the front of the SUV that belongs to the person that owns the house. They're letting us borrow it to get around, but most of the time, whenever anyone wants to go anywhere, Aislin just transports them there.

"What if he's looking for blood?" I ask as he hops into the driver's seat and shuts the door. I can't stop thinking about how he said he didn't want to be saved. "What if . . . what if he's suicidal? Or what if he's trying to hurt himself?"

"He might be," he says once the engine is running. "It's in his nature."

"To hurt himself?"

"No, to drink blood."

I reach back and draw the seatbelt over my shoulder, clicking the buckle into place. "Only because of me. If I wouldn't have made him bite me back at Draven's, none of this would be happening."

He backs the car down the driveway, his hands gripping on the wheel as he straightens the car onto the road. "He's drank blood before."

"Only a few times," I point out. "He told me that biting me would be different . . . that I was too innocent and pure; that it would make for a bad addiction."

He swallows hard and drives down the main road, fly-ing well above the speed limit. The houses whiz by and the roar of the tires fills up the quiet cab. I can tell he's up-set and I realize that I should have kept my mouth shut. Too much information is not a good thing when it comes to things like blood, innocence, and me.

I watch out the window as we drive past houses, stores, gas stations, and even sections of the beach. An hour passes and I'm about to give up and tell Alex to go back to the house—that maybe Laylen went back—when Alex makes an abrupt swerve to the right and ramps the SUV over the curb. He skids it across the parking lot, slamming it to a stop in front of the back exit of an older building lit up with neon signs and lights flashing from the grimy windows. I spot Laylen by the back door, tall and lean with his skin gleaming red beneath the glow of the lighting.

"Who's he with?" I ask, clicking my seat belt loose.

"I have no idea." Alex turns off the engine and we hop out of the car, running around to the front of the vehicle.

Alex immediately snatches ahold of my hand when we walk by a group of men loitering next to a rusty truck with the tailgate dropped. The smell of cigarettes pollutes the air and the men make catcalls at me as we pass by them. Alex turns toward them when one of them makes a remark about my ass, but I tug on his arm.

"Come on," I say, dragging him across the parking lot. "Now is not the time."

He shoots a dirty look at me, but continues walking in the direction of Laylen, taking long strides, and I have to jog to keep up. I start to run when we get close. I'm wor-ried who he could be with and what they could be doing hidden in the corner of this rundown place. I think deep down I might really know what's happening, however I won't believe it until I see it for myself.

When I reach him, it feels like all the wind has been knocked out of me. I collapse to my knees, struggling to breathe as I watch him feed off another woman, savoring her blood in pure ecstasy as he drinks it from her veins.

It takes me a few minutes to gather myself enough to stand up and, by the time I rise to my feet again, Alex has already gotten Laylen's attention. He is standing cautiously in front of Laylen with his hands out to the side and Laylen has the woman's neck grasped in his hand, her body slumped back like he's about to dip her. Her black hair is dripping with blood and there are bite marks on her neck and arms.

When Laylen spots me, his eyes bulge wide, his pupils are possessed by darkness as blood drips from his fangs and lips to the front of his shirt. Alex takes a vigilant step toward him, but Laylen puts up a hand and backs up to the side of the building with the woman in tow.

"Stay away from me," he hisses and smears the blood from his lips with the back of his arm.

Alex stops with his hands up in front of him. "I'm just going to check to see if she's okay." He nods his head at the woman and dares another step forward.

Laylen growls at him and snaps his fangs as the woman whimpers, clutching onto his arm for support. "I swear to God, man, if you come any closer, I'll break your fucking neck."

Alex rolls his eyes. "No, you won't," he says, lowering his hands to his sides.

Laylen shakes his head and his lip curls up as he snarls. "Oh, I will. I'd be more than happy to in fact. Maybe it would finally put you in your place."

"And what place would that be?" Alex asks coolly.

"The place where we all live," Laylen spits. "The place

of self-hatred. The place where I live." His dark eyes skim to me. "Where Gemma lives. The place where you feel miserable all the time and utterly hate who you are inside and out. The place where you wish you could get away from, even if it means being dead."

I get what he's saying way too well. There were countless times where I thought about ending it, not seeing a point. Every fucking day was exactly the same, no feeling, no movement inside, no emotion. Then I finally felt it, sadness, for the very first time. The emotion was overwhelming and hard to cope with. It is the same, even now, like how I felt when I was with Nicholas. I sometimes wish I could get rid of it, even if it means giving up everything forever.

"Everyone lives there," Alex says, rocking forward and reducing the space between them. "Everyone in their own way knows what it's like to hate themselves. Look at all the shit I've done to people over the years . . . how could I not hate myself?"

The rawness of the moment makes me glad I'm here to witness it, even though there's so much pain and anguish carried in it. It reminds me that everyone feels pain and sometimes they try to turn it off because it's easier than feeling it. Ultimately, though, our emotions own us and we have to take the good in with the bad.

Laylen shakes his head, but then releases the woman. She crumbles to the ground and he sinks to his knees with her, sitting in the gravel and dirt. He cradles his head in his hands, brings his knees to his chest and it sounds like he's sobbing.

Alex glances at me and then nods his head at Laylen. "Check on him and I'll see if she's okay."

I nod and sit down beside Laylen while Alex makes sure the woman's all right. I place a hand on Laylen's shoulder and he tenses. "Are you okay?" I ask cautiously.

He sucks in a sharp breath and then leans away from my touch, his fangs retreating back into his mouth. "Don't touch me . . . I think I killed her . . . I could feel her blood running out."

"No, she's okay." Alex walks over and stands behind me. "She's unconscious, but still breathing and has a pulse."

Laylen elevates his head and I instantly notice how watery his eyes are. "It doesn't matter. It's still there." A tear drifts down his cheek and I watch it slide to his jaw.

"What's still there?" I reach forward and wipe the tear away.

"The . . . the hunger and need to feed." He chokes. "God, I can't get it out of my head. It's worse than before . . . something about almost dying changed me." There's so much torture in his voice; my heart aches to take it away from him and bear it myself.

"It's going to be okay," I repeat, rubbing his tear between my thumb and my finger. He may be part Vampire, but I'd like to see Alex or Aislin question his humanity now. His tears are as real a mine—as real as anyone's. "We'll get through this."

He rests his forehead on his knees. "You and me?"

"Of course." I brush my fingers through his hair. "You've always been there for me and now I'm there for you."

It doesn't take much convincing after that. We prop the woman up against the door where someone's sure to find her and then we get back in the car to drive a way. No one speaks the entire drive and I tell myself that everything will be okay. That we got him back and that he didn't kill the woman, although I can't help worrying that he's forever changed. And what if he is? What if the Laylen

I met is gone?

WHEN WE ARRIVE back at the beach house, morning is kissing the land. Laylen goes straight into his room and says he is going to bed. I'm afraid he might leave again, but Alex promises that we'll all take turns watching him. We wake up Aislin and reluctantly fill her in on what's been going on. She's upset, however she still wants to help Laylen. I sit in the living room for about an hour listening to Alex and Aislin argue over what to do while the seashell clock on the living room wall ticks the wasted time away.

"I might know a spell," Aislin says, crossing her legs and leaning back in the chair. She has a tank top on and a pair of pajama bottoms with little pink hearts on them. "One that might help him get in the right state of mind."

"Right state of mind?" I ask, unzipping my hoodie to take it off as the heat of the day gets to me. "You mean out of the Vampire state of mind?"

She narrows her green eyes at me. "Look, he hasn't always been like this. He didn't used to crave blood until you came along.

"Aislin," Alex warns, helping me slip off my jacket. "Don't."

"You know it's true," she says. "I can tell that you think it."

"You can think whatever you want." I get to my feet as the prickle does a nagging dance on the back of my neck and I fill vindictive. "But I've actually talked to him about this long before he even bit me, and he told me the craving is always there."

She gives me a cold, hard stare. "Well, you forced him

to delve into it."

"You know what, you're right." I head around the couch and toward the hallway. "But you've also done a lot of shitty things, too, like help everyone make sure my soul is detached. "

It's a great exit line and I take the opportunity to leave the room. I go to Laylen's room and find him out on the deck with the blood of the woman still on his hands, shirt, and jeans. His arms are resting on the wood railing as he stares out at the ocean waves rolling up against the sandy shore.

I walk up beside him and put my own arms on the railing. I gaze out at the ocean, waiting for him to speak first because I can sense that it's one of those moments. He needs to say what's on his mind first before I can plan what I'm going to say, so it'll be the right words.

"For the last few years," he finally starts with his eyes fixed on the ocean, "I've felt so empty. After I was turned into a Vampire, Alex and Aislin wouldn't have anything to do with me—none of the Keepers would. My parents were already gone, so . . . I was basically all alone." He turns his head to the side and then meets my gaze. "I pretended it was okay. I shut down and it helped, but all that crap I've kept bottled is slipping out and I don't know what else to do other than feed because that's what my instincts are telling me to do."

I place my hand on his arm in a comforting gesture. "Laylen I'm so sorry for making you bite me . . . I didn't realize how bad things would get." I shake my head. "I'm really screwing everything up."

"No, you're not," he says. "I wanted to bite you. It was my fault."

The prickle emerges and suddenly I know I need to say something important. I turn to face him and he moves with me so we're facing each other, my neck angled up to actually look at him. The sun shines from behind him and I blink against the brightness.

"I know you want to take responsibility for this," I say. "But I kind of need to, you know. It's part of learning and I need to learn because I spent so much time in this dark, subdued, hindering place. It makes it hard to know what's right and what's wrong. I need to learn from this and I need you to accept that if I wouldn't have been there to make you do it, then we wouldn't be in this place."

He opens his mouth, but then quickly shuts it when he spots tears forming in my eyes as my guilt becomes too much to keep bottled inside me. He lets out a sad sigh and then wraps his arms around me, tensing just a little before relaxing into me.

"All right, Gemma Lucas," he says, kissing the top of my head. "You can take the blame for this one, but the next thing we screw up together is all on me."

"Deal," I whisper against his chest as hot tears stream down my cheeks. "I'm sure there will be many more. At least on my part." I listen to his heartbeat. "You'll be okay, right?"

It takes him a moment to answer. "Honestly, I'm not sure." He carries doubt, yet I don't anymore. I'll make sure to help him, no matter what sacrifices I have to make. I will make up for what I did to him.

We don't move. We barely breathe as we hold onto each other and stand in the sunlight out on the deck. We stay that way for a long time, just two friends who understand each other. Two people who know what it feels like to have no one. Maybe that is no longer the case, though.

Maybe we have each other.

CHAPTER TWENTY-FIVE

"**I** FEEL LIKE today is the day," I tell Alex as we sit down on the bed, cross-legged, facing each other with the Ira positioned between us on the white comforter.

It's been two days since Laylen's episode and he seems to be feeling better, for the most part. He's talking to me again and I even caught him smiling, which has so much beauty in it that it's almost heart stopping to witness. I in no way think he's completely gotten over it, however. I know it will take time. A lot of time. But I'll make sure to be there for him through it.

Alex crooks an eyebrow as he leans back on his hands. "Wow, someone's really cheerful today."

I skim my fingers across the sparkling, teal glass. "Well, it's about time, right?"

The French doors are agape, letting the sea breeze blow into the room and the white curtains surrounding the canopy bed flap around us.

"I love the spout of confidence," he says. "But can I ask where it's coming from?"

I shrug, putting my hand onto my lap. "Nowhere in particular."

That's actually a lie. The feeling was seeded and started sprouting when I'd gotten done hugging Laylen for hours, then I'd gone back to my room and cried. Cried for him. For me. For my mother. For Alex and Aislin who can't help who they are—or were. I cried for everyone's lives that have been messed up because of this stupid star inside me and the tears were liberating. I woke up feeling everything again; not just the heat of the sun or the touch of the air. I could feel what was inside my heart and who I really was.

A girl with a lot of power.

A girl who is going to save her mom and the world so people like Laylen, who are genuinely good at heart, can have a chance at life.

"You're acting weird," Alex states with curiosity.

I put both of my hands on the Ira and watch the outer shell glow. "As weird as I always am." I stare at my reflection in the glass, my brown hair hanging to my shoulders, my violet eyes radiating the life within them. Most of the cuts and bruises on my face have healed. On the inside of me, though, deep beneath my skin, I still feel torn.

Alex hooks a finger under my chin and tips my face up to his. "Are you sure you're okay? You've been through a lot over the last few weeks and I'm worried you're going to break."

"You know, I should be asking you the same question since a few weeks ago your main concern was that I'd go back to being soulless."

He shakes his head, frowning. "I may have done stuff to make you think that, but only because I thought it was what I was supposed to do. Deep down I was secretly hoping that you'd be stronger than me."

"And what verdict did you reach on that one?" I hold his gaze, waiting for his answer.

"I got exactly what I was hoping for." He slides his finger up my chin and touches my lips as one of the curtains flaps over our heads like a canopy. "Now will you please quit being stubborn and kiss me? You haven't kissed me all day."

The strange thing about all of this is after Laylen's and my talk, things went back to friendly with us. The connection drawing me to him, sexually anyway was broken. I wonder if it's because we finally talked about the problem out loud. If maybe admitting what we did freed us from everything we were trapping inside.

I give Alex what he asks and lean over the Ira to kiss him. Our tongues twine together as I knot my fingers through his hair, pulling him closer while he presses on the small of my back. Our lips spark like firecrackers and drive my body to the edge of wanting more than just a kiss. It feels like it's starved and I realize that it's been forever since he's been inside me. Jesus, I want to feel it again. So damn badly.

He consumes every part of my body with his hands until I can't take it anymore. Finally, I climb on his lap and straddle him. He groans as our bodies conform together and I feel his hardness pressing between my legs. We kiss for an eternity, our bodies and tongues melting together and the spark of electricity combusts with eagerness. It wants to be near him just as much as I do and I moan from the heat and need of my sexually deprived body.

His fingers leisurely stray up the back of my shirt, leaving a searing hot path on my skin. I put my hands on his shoulders, pulling myself closer, and rocking my hips against him, rubbing against his hardness. His touch becomes rougher as his hands travel to the front of my body and his fingers graze my stomach, drifting downwards to my hips. He grips me, pressing his fingertips into my skin as I continue to rock against him. His lips make a fervent path from my mouth to the front of my neck, his teeth gently grazing in an echo of his kisses.

My head willingly falls back as he sucks on my skin and a possessive heat swells through my body, building between my legs. I rock my hips faster and he moves with me perfectly in tune. He groans and bites at my skin while I slip my hands under the top of his shirt and stab my nails into his back.

He responds with a shudder as his skin splits open. "Fuck. . . . Gemma . . . that feels so good . . ."

My body climbs higher and higher into bliss until I feel like I'm on the verge of exploding. I tremble, my skin dampening with sweat as fireworks shower through my entire body and the prickle goes wild on the back of my neck. I'm panting as his hand moves up to my chest, slipping under my bra. He cups my breast, grazing his finger across my nipple, adding more heat to the bursting sensation.

I scream out in utter and complete bliss, clutching onto the nearest thing and I end up making more scratches on his shoulder.

"I want to be inside you so fucking bad," Alex moans against my neck as he grips my hip with one hand and pinches softly on my nipple with his other. He continues feeling me, basking me with kisses and soft nicks until I start to relax and come down from the high he put in my body. He leans back and looks at me with glazed over eyes.

"You're so beautiful," he whispers and moves in for another kiss.

I catch my breath and lean back, breaking the moment as I hurry to climb off his lap

"You're leaving me high and dry after that?" He fakes a sexy pout. "Seriously?"

I hold up my finger as I stare down at the Ira iridescent from the energy radiating off me. "It's for a good reason," I say. He keeps pouting as I place my hands on the glass ball, grasping onto the emotions he instilled in me by kissing me and making me orgasm. Lust, desire, pure and heavenly elation are mixing inside my bloodstream, along with electricity. There's so much power inside me and I let it drain out, heating the glass of the Ira.

"Alex hold onto me," I whisper as the glass begins to glow.

"You're getting smarter by the second. You know that?" He places a hand on my knee, scooting closer. The contact only amplifies the voltage of my emotions and makes the crystal ball glow brighter. "Are you sure you want to do this?"

I nod as a teal glow bursts throughout the room and the curtains float above us. "Yeah, I'm about as sure as the last time you asked me."

He cracks a smile, but it's a nervous one. He's anxious as hell.

I'm nervous as hell as well, and the feeling only magnifies as more energy pours through me. "Do you have the diamond?"

He pats the pocket of his jeans with his free hand. "Yep, it's right here."

"Thank you," I whisper and then I take a deep breath as light and energy expand, consuming every inch of space existing around us. The curtains singe from the blinding glow and scattered ashes fall over the floor while smoke begins to swarm around us in a whirlwind.

Alex tenses as the heat of the Ira raises our own temperature to the point where we start to sweat. "Are you sure you want to keep going?" he questions.

"Yes," I reply with confidence and then close my eyes.

The first thing that appears in my mind is a clear picture of the lake. Panicking, I shove the image out of my mind, not wanting to drop us there. I focus on the tunnel I went in during the vision I entered with Nicholas; dirt walls that leak water, damp air, darkness, and Water Fey. The ground begins to vibrate and I feel the world shift apart, open up, and swallow us whole.

THE TUNNEL IS as dark as I remember. The damp air causes my clothes to cling to my skin while the dirty water seeps from the ceiling to drip down on our heads. If what Nicholas said was true about the Ira, then we're not in vision form, but we'll only know if that's true when we cross paths with someone.

"Do you know which way to go?" Alex asks, wiping some dirty water off his forehead as I tuck the Ira into the side pocket of my denim shorts. "Where we first went in the vision when we arrived?"

I glance left and then right. "No, the only reason I found the cave where the vision took place was because Nicholas was running from a Water Faerie . . ."I head to my left, inspecting the muddy ground and watery walls, hoping something will spark a memory. "I can't remember which way we went . . . I don't even know if we're in the same place."

Alex releases my hand and drags his fingers through his damp hair, leaving it sticking up all over. "Okay, left or right?"

An abrupt scream reverberates from the left side of

the tunnel and the vines growing from the ceiling move with the sound.

"Right," I say quickly and we dash down the right side of the tunnel, leaving the noise behind.

Alex takes my hand again as we hike through the dimly lit tunnel, listening to the horrific screams shooting at us in every direction. His touch brings me a little comfort, though not much. I can't help thinking how I've only been down here for a few minutes and I already feel like leaving while my mom's been down here for years.

God, how does she feel? How broken is she?

I'm telling myself that I have to be strong, that I can do this, when a white, wispy Water Fey appears in the distance. I tense as its hollow eyes lock in our direction

"Alex," I hiss, pointing at it as I continue to walk through the mud.

He puts his finger to his lips, shushing me, and we keep moving, one foot in front of the other. As we get closer to it, my heart thumps, upping my adrenaline and amplifying up the sparks. My legs tremble, my knees knock together, and my breathing becomes erratic and loud.

The Water Faerie doesn't budge, watching us as it floats in the same space it appeared in. When we pass by it, it opens its gaping mouth and lets out a breathless scream that rings loudly inside my ears. The vines above our heads move again and brush the top of my head. I clutch onto Alex's arm as the Water Faerie rotates around and trails after us, the bottom of its fabric body dragging along the ground.

The farther we get into the tunnel, the more the Water Faeries multiply, flying out from every angle and direction. Pieces of their fabric bodies touch our faces and heads as they fly back and forth above us, their boney fingers reaching down in our direction, but never touching.

The longer it goes on, the more afraid I get. The fear only seems to encourage them and they get rowdier by the minute. Then I remember Alex said they feed on fear, so I try to calm down, however it's difficult.

Just when I think that I can't take it anymore, the tunnel opens up to a cave. A rock-shaped throne is in the center, the back coiling up to the ceiling. But the Queen isn't sitting in it like she was when I saw the vision. That's when I realize something about all of this is terribly wrong.

"What is it?" He gives me a quizzical look. "What's wrong?"

"This isn't how it works." I look over my shoulder at the herd of Water Faeries floating behind us, making raspy noises and taunting screams. "We don't come in here by ourselves. We're brought in by some sort of Water Faerie . . . This isn't what I saw in the vision."

Alex's brows furrow. "But how can that be? If you saw it, then it should happen, right?"

Someone—or something—clears their throat from behind us and we spin around. Standing in the cluster of white fabric covered bodies is the Queen. Her frosty hair veils down her back and her eyes are soulless, yet I detect a hint of amusement in her desolate character.

"Well, it looks like I have some unexpected visitors," she says and the Water Faeries begin to swarm around our heads like bees. We hunch over as the Queen steps toward us, holding the bottom of her dress. "Coming here willingly to be tortured in my world? Let the Fey take you and torture you? I have to say, you two are brave souls."

This is all wrong. This is not how I saw it. This is not how it's supposed to go.

Fuck.

If I can't fix it, then Alex, my mom, myself and the world are screwed.

CHAPTER
TWENTY-SIX

D
URING MY FIRST visit to the City of Crystal, Dyvinius had explained to me how visions work. He said if a vision wasn't seen correctly then the world as we knew it could shift. I never considered the depth of what he'd said until now. The vision that I took Nicholas into, the one where we entered The Underworld, never really was finished. Nicholas had flipped out and choked me until I nearly blacked out and took us back. I'm assuming it means I didn't read it clearly, and now I have no idea what's going to happen.

I'm the worst hero of all time. I really am.

"I have to say," says the Queen as she circles around us with her dress dragging in the mud, "It isn't every day that someone voluntarily enters my world. Usually it's with much force and fussing on my Faeries' part. Yet the two of you enter it at your own free will." She stops in front of us with her hands behind her back. "Tell me why."

"We came here to get something," I tell her in a firm voice as I grasp onto Alex's hand.

"Ah, I see." She turns around toward the tunnel. "Come with me."

We follow her down the tunnel in the direction we'd

just come from, the mob of Water Faeries trailing behind us, some daring to touch our heads. The Queen is taller than Alex, her head clips each one of the vines dangling from the ceiling. With the contact, they shrivel and die, the browned pieces fluttering to the ground like ash. In each of their places a new vine regrows. This pattern continues on and on, death and life repeating itself.

We finally enter a room. There's a slender, antique table and an eccentric chandelier made of thorns with vines in it. The chairs around the table have backs that look like thorny rose bushes and the idea of sitting on them makes me cringe.

"Have a seat." The Queen gestures at the chairs, gathering her dress as she sits down at the head of the table.

Alex and I reluctantly sit down, making sure to keep our backs straight so no thorns stab us. The Water Faeries linger in the arched doorway where water cascades down the sides of the wall and floods the floor of the room, making the floor sopping wet.

"So you've come here for something?" The Queen asks, tapping her long, black fingernails on the tabletop.

"*Someone,* actually," Alex tells her, exchanging a glance with me as he holds my hand below the table. "Her name is Jocelyn Lucas."

I can tell she knows who we're talking about by the way her posture briefly stiffens. "Tell me, boy, what is your name?"

"Alex Avery," Alex says with some hesitance as he runs a finger along the back of my hand.

"Ah, you're a Keeper." She continues to thrum her nails against the table, her eyes moving from him to me. I unintentionally cower back and get disciplined for doing so as a thorn enters the center of my back. "And you? What's your name?"

I lean forward, pushing past the pain, too worried to reach around and pluck the thorn out of my back. "Gemma Lucas."

She ceases thrumming her fingers. "So you are, what?" she asks. "The daughter of Jocelyn?"

I nod and then breathe inwardly as Alex reaches around and picks the thorn out of my back. "I am," I say.

"I see." The Queen muses over something. "What did you expect exactly? That you'd come down here and demand I give you my best slave all because you asked really, really nicely?" Her hollow mouth forms a pout and it's unsettling to look at.

Alex reaches for his pocket. "We've brought something to trade for Jocelyn's freedom."

"I can assure you that you have nothing I want," the Queen replies with her gaunt chin tipped up in arrogance.

Alex slips the flawlessly cut sapphire out and drops it down on the table. "Not even for this?"

She looks shocked, but then she starts to chortle and the chandelier above us shakes and flickers along with the puddles on the ground. The Queen finally stops laughing, wiping tears from her eyes, and then her laughter rapidly shifts to anger.

She pounds her fist on the table and a few of the chairs topple over while the Water Faeries flee. "You think that you can come down here and make a bargain with something the Keepers took from me to begin with?" She rises from her chair, towering over us as she swishes her dress behind her. "How dare you insult me? You are just like your father. Taking whatever you want and doing whatever you please."

I want to bang my head against the table. It's ridiculous how Stephan can haunt us when he's not even here.

"I have been waiting for the day when I'd see your

father again." She strides toward us and reaches us in only a few steps. "So I can settle what he started a long time ago."

Alex holds her petrifying gaze. "I understand that you have had some issues with my father, but I can assure you that—"

"Silence." The Queen tips her head back and roars, making the whole room quake. The walls begin to cave in as she pants ravenously and the roof cracks. The power in her is clearly evident and it makes me nervous of what else she can do. "I don't want to hear excuses. I always swore that one day I'd get even with Stephan, whatever it took, and here you are. It's the perfect opportunity. A much smaller version of him." She makes a pinching motion with her boney finger. "However, it'll still do."

"He's not like his father," I interrupt, but then shrink back when the Queen's attention focuses entirely on me. "A-And he only came down here because I asked him to, so if you want to take this out on anyone, take it out on me."

The Queen's face alters from anger to inquisitiveness. She suddenly calms and walks back toward her chair. "You know, Jocelyn never mentioned having a daughter, so I find it peculiar that someone would show up with the son of one of my sworn enemies and claim to be her daughter."

"Well, I am," I assure her in a surprisingly steady voice. "And I want to take her back with me."

"Take her back?" She throws her head back and laughs. "Oh, I'm afraid there's no way I can do that because you yourself are never leaving."

"No, we can leave," I tell her. "I came here through the Ira, and you can't keep us here—there are laws that say you can't."

Her grin deepens and then she swats her hand through the air. I feel a tug on my pocket and the Ira abruptly shoots out and flies across the room, smacking into the wall where it shatters. Shards of teal glass land on the floor and table and I swear I feel pieces of my own heart join them. I leap from my chair, ready to wring her neck and hopefully kill her, but Alex grabs the tail of my shirt and quickly pulls me back down.

"That's bullshit!" I cry, flipping a piece of glass off my arm. "You can't do that!"

"I can do whatever I want." She smiles before motioning her hand around the room. "Now, let me welcome you to your new home."

CHAPTER
TWENTY-SEVEN

I WANT TO get the hell out of here. Run. Flee. However the Ira is gone, destroyed back on the table, and I don't know another way out of The Underworld.

The Queen locks us in a cement chamber that has a single metal-framed bed with a ratty mattress on it. There are bars on the door, which allow light to filter in. We have no water. No food. No toilet. It's basically jail except for there aren't any guards, only crazy Water Fey who feed off torment and fear.

After the Queen leaves, Alex and I lie down on the bed, side by side with our feet up on the wall, waiting for whatever comes next. Torture? Death? Something worse? Surprisingly, we're both pretty calm, but I think we've entered some weird state were we're too shocked to panic.

"Let me welcome you to your new home." I mimic the Queens tone with bitterness in my voice. I kick the side if the wall. "What a bitch."

"I'm really starting to wonder just how long the list of people who my father has pissed off is," Alex says with an exhausted sigh as he stretches out his arms above his head.

"Probably pretty long," I say, yawning. I'm

exhausted—the energy I used to come here took a lot out of me. If it weren't for the screams from outside, I might close my eyes and go to sleep

"We should find a way out." He props up on his arms and looks over at me. His hair is wet from the water drizzling from the ceiling and so is the collar of his shirt

"How?" I motion at the room. "I mean, look at this place. There's no way out except for the door."

He lies back down on the mattress and turns his head toward me. "Do you have any idea why this didn't work out like the vision you saw?"

I massage the sides of my temples and shut my eyes. "Because I didn't finish seeing the vision, at least that's what I think happened. Nicholas forced me to take us back before I saw the whole damn thing play out." A scream echoes from close by and I shudder, opening my eyes. "I'm sorry," I say, crossing my arms over my stomach.

"Sorry for what?"

"For messing this up."

He shakes his head and rotates to his side, supporting his elbow against the mattress and resting his head against his hand. "You didn't mess this up, Gemma. You were simply taking a risk to try to do something that was right and things didn't work out."

"Because I screwed up and didn't plan things well enough."

"Sometimes things are kind of out of our hands."

I turn to my side and face him, my arm tucked under my head. Our faces are mere inches away and it's comforting knowing he's close. "But I do it so often and I've just barely started actually living my life," I say. "Imagine how bad my screw up list is going to be in like five years . . . if I get that far."

"You will," he insists, tucking strands of my hair

behind my ear. "And you'll get better—things will get better. I promise." Once he gets my hair out of the way, he strokes my cheeks with his fingers until I feel like I'm going to doze off.

"What will she do to us?" I murmur tucking my hands under my head.

His fingers briefly stop moving. "I'm not sure." He's lying. I can tell by the unevenness in his voice and the way the current of the electricity speeds up.

"Just tell me." I yawn, forcing my eyes to stay open. "I need to know what I'm in store for."

"You really want to know?" His fingers delicately caress my cheek in soft, consistent patterns. I nod, letting his touch calm me. "Unbearable pain," he says.

I feel strangled, hands wrapping around my neck, suffocating me. Pain? What kind of pain? "Oh."

It gets quiet. Water drips on the mattress and us. Alex keeps touching my face; my chin, my lips, my jawline, as if he's worried he'll never touch me again. I start wondering what death is like, too. Whether it's better than getting tortured. Better than feeling unbearable pain. Better than feeling the burden of my mistakes.

"Look," Alex says unexpectedly, rolling on top of me, his warm body flawlessly settling over mine. "No matter what happens, you try to hold on, okay? Turn it off."

"Turn it off?" I open my eyes to find him passionately staring down at me.

"Yeah, just like you used to," he whispers and tenderly kisses my lips. "Just turn off anything you're feeling. They thrive on fear and the less they get from you the weaker they'll get." He kisses me again and again until I can barely breathe or think straight. Maybe that's what he's trying to do. Distract me from my worry. Or maybe he just loves kissing me.

"And what about you?" I say between his breathless kisses. "What will you do?"

He pauses, offering me a sad smile. "You remember all those times I was around you and I was a douche?"

I roll my eyes. "How could I forget? I hated you because you were an ass, but the damn electricity made it impossible to *actually* hate you for real."

His smile turns to a real one. "That entire time I hated doing that to you. In fact, I swear to God it killed me, but I did it because I had to." He slants closer to me, so we strategically touch in all the right places. "I can control what I feel, Gemma. It's what I've been taught to do. The only exception to this is you."

"Then how can anyone know what you're really feeling?" I question, gripping his lean arms. "If you're shutting it off and saying contradicting things."

He considers what I said then leans down and covers his lips over mine. He kisses me until I'm desperately gasping for air, until my heart's pumping blood at an unhealthy rate.

"Do you feel that?" he whispers against my lips. "Do you feel how *I* make you feel inside?"

I blink dazedly through emotions of yearning, elation, and contentment. "Yeah."

"Well that's exactly how you make me feel inside." He looks me in the eyes and I can almost see my reflection in his overly large pupils.

He could be lying, but he might not be. Maybe I do make him feel the same as I do inside. Maybe he's just as confused as me. Maybe he's erratic on the inside, unstable. Perhaps it's the hardest thing in the world not to be close to me. I choose to believe that he's being genuinely honest because it'd be the perfect ending to my sad story. The one where the guy falls in love with the girl and the girl falls equally in love with the guy. The flaw to this story, however, is that at the moment, there's no prickle on the back of my neck confirming I've felt love before, so in the end it's only a story.

Nothing more.

CHAPTER
TWENTY-EIGHT

"**Y**OU KNOW IT'S *going to happen,*" Stephan *says, propping a hand on each side of my head.*

Alex is gone and I don't know where he is. He left me. No he wouldn't do that.

"You've already felt the evil and you're going to change," Stephan says, his black eyes glinting wickedly.

I try to sit up, but I'm glued to the mattress by an unseen force, my arms kinked to the side and my legs stuck together like melting wax. "I'm not evil! I'm good! I know I am!"

"You about beat Nicholas to death," he reminds. "How does it feel to have blood on your hands?"

"Terrible," I say, but the red and black triangle singes onto my upper arm, revealing the lie. I can smell the scent of burning flesh and feel the good in me dissolving "I hated every second of it."

He leans back and sits down on the mattress, "Now we know that's a lie. You loved it and we both know it."

I shake my head, denying what lies deep inside me; darkness, a shadow opposing the good. "No, I didn't."

He grins as he elevates his hand and a razor-sharp

knife appears in it. "If that's true, then I guess I have no use for you." He moves to swing the knife down.

I scream as it dives for my heart. As it plummets closer, I shut my eyes and picture the blue beach house while I channel my Foreseer power. As the blade grazes my skin, almost splitting my heart open, I blink myself away from this place.

MY EYELIDS SPRING open. "Holy shit!" I gasp. "I know how to get us out of here."

Alex is lying on his side, watching me with his arm draped across my stomach. "How?" he asks and we both sit up on the bed. "Gemma, what are you talking about?"

I catch my breath, wiping the sweat from my forehead. "I can use my power to get us out of here."

He shakes his head, looking lost. "But you don't have a crystal ball."

"But I've gone into visions without them before."

"Yeah, but those are visions, not present time."

"I know that," I say, sitting up. "But I can try. It pretty much works the same way. I just need to feel enough emotion and try to remember things . . . memories seem to get it going pretty well."

He opens his mouth to protest as he sits up. "I don't—" His eyes dodge do the door and he quickly stands to his feet, grabbing my hand and pulling me behind him.

A Water Fey watches us from the open doorway, interweaving through the ceiling vines as it heads toward us. It stops when it's about to reach the bed and seconds later the Queen appears behind it. She's changed into a black, mermaid-shaped dress that has red roses growing on vines, which trim the bottom half. Her frosty hair has been braided up on the top of her head and is woven with black ribbons and her lips are tinted purple.

"It's time," she says and snaps her fingers. "Both of you, follow me."

Alex and I trade a look and then we follow the Queen out of the cell. We quietly walk just behind her as she struts down the tunnel lined with jail doors. Water Fey enclose us, floating in curving paths. I consider shutting my eyes and seeing if I can really pull it off—take us out of this place in the blink of an eye—but I can't just yet, not until I find my mom. As I glance over at Alex, however, guilt begins to rot in my stomach. I drag him into this mess and look where it gets him. Now what's going to happen to us? Will we get tortured until we go insane?

All thoughts of what's right and wrong leave my mind when we reach the end of the tunnel. As I take in the square space only one thought remains inside my mind.

Fear.

It's worse than I'd expected. Water Faeries are everywhere along with what look like ordinary humans, but I'm guessing not all of them are. Each one of the humans is strapped to a wooden plank perched on a steel stand. They're being tortured in different ways, some with knives inserted into their arms, others getting their bodies stretched with ropes attached to a large wooden wheel. Some have Water Fey hovering over them and it looks like they're trying to kiss them, but I think they might be doing something worse.

"Don't look at them," Alex whispers in my ear and I jump, startled. "Focus on turning it off."

I try my best, but it's hard to block out the sounds . . . the cries . . . the anguish and suffering. It's pretty much impossible and I end up being overwhelmed by it.

The Queen leads us to a back room that has dirt walls and a stone floor. The ceiling arches up toward what looks like a skylight, but the glass is frosted so I can't see what's on the other side. A single wooden chair that has straps attached to the arms and legs is perched in the center of the room.

The Queen shuts the door and then turns to face us. "Tell me, Gemma. What are you most afraid of in this world?"

Love. I blink at my mind's declaration. "I don't know," I say, shifting my weight uneasily.

"You don't know?" She taps her lips and a toothless grin spreads across her face. "Well, I think it's time we found out. Don't you agree?" She raises her arms in the air and claps her hands together. "Think about it. Finally discovering the one thing that will make you lose your sanity. Isn't it exciting?"

Two Water Faeries zoom up behind me and wrap their boney fingers around my arms. Alex grabs my hand and holds onto me as tightly as he can, attempting to pull me away from them.

"Let me go first," he says, tugging on my arm. He reaches up and tries to punch one of the Water Fey.

It swerves out of his reach, opens its mouth, and screams so loudly the room rattles and dirt crumbles from the walls.

The Queen shakes her head as she ambles around the chair, tracing her finger along the back. "I have a feeling that forcing you to watch her get tortured is going to provide a very great amount of fear in you."

Two more Water Faeries come flying up behind us and wrap their fingers around Alex's arms. He tries to shove them off, but Water Fey are impressively strong for such boney creatures.

The Water Faeries drag me over to the chair, separating Alex and I from each other. I sink into their hold, and challenged their strength against my dead weight as I plant the heels of my shoes into the ground. But it's a worthless effort.

Once we reach the chair, they shove me down into it and the Queen stands behind me as she snakes an arm around my neck. The Fey secure my legs and wrists to the chair with the straps before the Queen leans over my shoulder, putting her lips near my ear.

"Fear is the most powerful emotion," she whispers, her foul breath startling icy against my cheek. "And the most painful."

That's where she's wrong. Fear is just fear in my eyes and I've experienced it many times. There are so many more emotions that can be so much more painful; sadness, anger, caring for someone that in return can split your heart open and stomp on it.

"Now, which way to go here?" the Queen dithers as she struts around the chair and stands in front of me. "Oh, I know." She sticks out her hand and one of the Water Fey swoops down from the ceiling and drops a sapphire in her hand. "Since you guys were so kind to bring it back to me, I'll let you be the first person I use it on again." She slams her hands down on the armrests and hunches her back as she leans down into my face. "What do you say, Gemma. Shall we torture your soul?"

Laughter slips though my lips. "Torture my soul," I say, inching closer so our foreheads almost touch. "Been there. Done that."

She snarls and forcefully shakes the chair, letting me feel her wrath. "Are you mocking me? Me? The Queen of the Underworld?"

No. I'm just trying to stay calm, but the irony of what

she's going to do is kind of amusing.

"Have you lost your sanity already?" she snaps, the tight grip of her fingers rupturing the wooden armrest of the chair. "Are you worthless?"

"Maybe," I say dryly.

She gapes at me, but then all shock and rage erase from her expression as she holds the sapphire up in front of my face. "How about I take that smirk off your face?"

I try to turn off anything that I'm feeling as the sapphire begins to shimmer and vibrantly glow, but then an image of Alex lying in a pool of his own blood beside the lake presses into my head and fear starts to surface. I shove it down, yet then I see my mom rotting away in this awful place. The Queen's laughter echoes inside my head as I see myself in a room alone, secluded, and detached. Then it shifts to a different room, one where I'm with Alex and he tells me he loves me and I can't say it back.

Fear floods through me as I see myself killing Nicholas, slitting his throat, and liking it. I see the mark on my arm. I see myself standing by Stephan and the Death Walkers. It's too much and I let out a scream wanting to rip my heart out of my chest so I don't have to feel the pain anymore.

The Queen laughs as I scream again when I picture myself burning into ash. The speed of the images only quickens the more time goes by, flipping at such a swift rate they start to muddle together.

Then suddenly it stops; the noise in my head and the ache in my heart. When I open my eyes, the Queen and the sapphire have dropped to the floor.

Seconds later, the Water Fey also drop to the floor in piles that encompass the Queen's slackened body. Time freezes for a moment as Alex and I take in what happened.

We both stare at the heaps of boney bodies and then

Alex rushes toward me.

"What the hell happened?" I ask as he crouches down and unlatches the straps around my ankles.

"I have no idea," he says.

I glance down at my locket. "Did this do it?"

He eyes the violet-stoned pedant. "I'm not sure . . . It could be . . . or it might have something to do with you . . . with your soul." He slips the last buckle loose from my wrist and then pulls me to my feet.

"Because it's broken," I state, massaging my aching chest with my hand. "Maybe it broke her, too."

He looks at me with remorse. "Let's get out of here before they wake up."

I nod and we run past the bodies of the Fey and out the door. The Water Fey in the torture chamber are out cold, too, slumped all over the floor and the tables; even on the humans who are awake and instantly beg us to free them.

"Come on, little girl," one guy with blonde, shaggy hair and sullen eyes purrs from his restraints. "Just undo the straps, okay? I promise I don't bite."

"Gemma." The sound of Alex's voice brings me back to reality as he tugs on my arm. "Let's go. Remember they're here for a reason."

We hurry away from the guy and I sprint to keep up with Alex as he dashes into the tunnel. The vines above our heads are charred and aren't re-growing, bits and pieces are all over the ground, floating in the mud puddles.

"We have to try and find water," Alex says as we race past the cell doors. "They have to get into the lake somehow and, if we can find out how, then maybe we can swim up through it."

"I can't swim, though," I say, my shoes splashing in the puddles.

"I'll help you," he replies, curving us to the right. We round a sharp corner and more doors appear.

"Wait," I skid to a stop, tugging on his arm, forcing him to stop. "We have to find my mom first."

He shakes his head, looking at me sympathetically, but there's stubbornness in him as well. "We have to go," he says. "We don't know how long they'll be out."

"I'm not going without her." I refuse to budge, digging my shoes into the dirt and holding my ground. Alex shakes his head and I quickly add, "Alex, it's my *mom*."

He wavers, his expression softening, and then he grudgingly nods. "All right, but as soon as I hear any sign that they're waking up, we're leaving without her. Got it?"

"Thank you." I stand on my tiptoes to place a kiss on his cheek.

We hastily start to unlatch doors and check inside the cells. Most of them are empty. A few have humans in them, most are sickly looking, scrawny and underweight. A few of them scream at us the instant we open the door while others look comatose.

I'm growing frustrated with each dead-end, wondering where else the Queen would keep my mom. However, then I open the last door on the right side and my frustration turns to anxiousness. My heart drops to my stomach as the door swings open all the way.

Inside the tiny cell is a woman, her back hunched over as she sits on the edge of the bed. She's wearing ratty, torn pants and a shirt. Her brown hair is braided behind her head and her blue irises are fixed on the cement floor in front of her bare feet.

"Mom," I whisper from the doorway. The word feels strange coming out of my mouth, like it doesn't belong there.

She blinks up at me, and then looks back down at the

ground.

"Jocelyn." Alex inches around me and enters the cell. "Are you alright?"

My mother only blinks her eyes, refusing to look up or speak. Tears burn in my eyes as pain and the feeling of being unwanted flood me, but I suck them back. Summoning courage I didn't know I had in me, I step into the room and up to the bed then kneel down in front of her.

"Mom," I say, lowering my face into her line of vision. "It's Gemma . . . your daughter."

She glances at my violet eyes, curiosity and confusion emitting from her own. Then something flickers in her expression and, suddenly, she's *really* looking at me instead of through me. She leaps to her feet and starts to hug me, but then quickly retracts and wraps her arms around herself.

"What are you two doing down here?" Her voice is tight and unwelcoming. "You shouldn't be down here."

"We came here for you." I glance warily at Alex and then back at her. "To save you."

"You never should have come here," she says, rocking back and forth as she hugs herself. "How did you even get down here?"

"With an Ira," I explain, trying not to go into shock over her detached state of mind. *She's been here for a while. She's been through so much.* I ball my hands into fists and stab my fingernails into my palms, shifting the emotional pain inside me to physical.

She frowns up at me. "So you got your father's power." She says it with such hatred.

A thousand questions run through my mind, but I bite them back and grab her arm. "We have to go."

"We need to get to water," Alex tells her, moving up

beside me. "There's supposed to be a place somewhere down here that will take us up through the lake. A water route maybe? Do you know where it is?"

"We can't go anywhere." She shakes her head and shuffles back until the backs of her legs bump into the bed. "The Fey will make us suffer if we try."

"Jocelyn, no one's going to hurt you anymore," Alex says. "We're taking you home."

She laughs and then spins in a circle with her arms out to the side. "You think you can escape here? We're trapped. Forever."

Great. She's crazy.

"What about my Foreseer power?" I ask, reaching out to touch her, but fear of rejection forces me to pull back. "Can it get us out of here?"

"We don't have a crystal," Alex points out. "We need to find water."

My mom stops spinning in circles and chews on a strand of her hair as she assesses me, tapping her foot on the floor. "She might not need one if she's entirely like her father, but if that's also the case, she's doomed."

"Doomed for what?" I ask in horror. "What else could I possibly be doomed for?"

She lets go of the strand of her hair and strides forward, placing her hands on my shoulders. "Evil." Her smile radiates her insanity.

"I-I'm not evil," I stutter, though a voice inside my head laughs at me. I don't know what to say or do. She isn't the person I've seen in the visions. She's cruel, insane and derisive. "And I'm going to show you right now by getting us out of here, which is a good thing."

She only laughs, moving away, but she doesn't argue when I take her hand. "Well, you can try," she says. "I'm not going to stop you."

"Okay," I say determinedly, yet I falter when I realize I only have a vague idea of how to do it. "Now how do I do it? Channel the energy without the crystal and get us to present time."

"Emotion," she says simply. "Your father used to do it all the time by getting really angry." Her gaze skims to Alex. "Or when I would tell him that I love him."

I shift uneasily. "Is that it? Just feel a lot of emotion?"

She shrugs. "That and you need to have the ability to look a split second into the future then drop yourself into the vision a second behind what you saw, so by the time you make us drop, we'll have aligned with present time."

"Huh?" Alex and I say at the same time.

She ruthlessly grins as she swings our arms back and forth between us. "It'll take a lot of skill. Seeing things quicker than the human eye and placing all of us in the right spot. One false move and we'll be stuck in either the future or the past. Maybe forever."

"Sounds pretty simple to me," I say sarcastically.

She shrugs again, as though she doesn't care about anything, and it makes me want to bawl my eyes out. "I told you it was hard." She rubs her hand across her face. "Honestly, we'd be better off here anyways, rotting in our own heads."

"No fucking way. I'd rather die." I summon a deep breath. "I'm going to try it."

"This is a bad idea," Alex says as I lace my fingers through his and tug him closer. "Using your power like this . . . it's too risky and unknown."

A scream rings through the air and we all flinch, glancing at the door in panic.

"It's more risky staying down here." I cup the side of his neck and guide him closer as my mom holds my hand from behind me. "Now kiss me."

His brows furrow as I lean in and crash my lips against his. I channel every emotion he instills in me as I taste him and let his tongue feel mine. I feel a gentle tug, but it's not enough. I need something more powerful—something I've never felt before.

I pull away and Alex opens his eyes when the high-pitched shrieks of the Fey grow louder as they get closer to the cell.

"I need something more," I say, my eyes glued to the doorway, my pulse hammering with fear. I bet the Water Fey can sense it. I bet they're devouring it as they search for us. "I need to feel something new; that's when it's most intense."

Alex rakes his free hand through his hair, leaving his arm on the back of his neck, his elbow bent upward. "What haven't you felt yet?"

"I don't know," I say, ignoring my mother's laughs of hysteria. "I felt so many already."

He swallows hard, his hand falling to the side. The screams of the Water Fey quake around the room and the vines are starting to revive, turning back to a healthy shade of green. They're close and so is the Queen. If I don't get us out of here, then we're doomed just like my mom said.

"How about this." Alex puts a hand on the side of my face and gazes deep into my eyes. His chest rises and falls with his ragged breath and his pulse throbs though his fingertips. "Gemma, I love you."

I'm not sure if he means it, if they're just desperate words or not. The idea of love scares the hell out of me, though.

It's not the reaction I was expecting, but it does the trick. As a new brand of fear emerges in me, one based on something that's potentially good, but also terrifying, the prickle stabs the back of my neck. The electricity devours my soul, fractures it open, and leaves it vulnerable and exposed. Alex leans forward to kiss me, feeding the sensation even more. The longer we kiss, the more energy develops between us; until I feel like I'm going to erupt like a volcano full of liquid hot magma. Then I let my mind see what it needs to.

I picture myself sitting on the bed in the room at the beach house, the ocean right outside. I let myself see it happen, us dropping right into the place, safely in the middle of the room with the sunlight spilling through the windows and open doors.

Then I jump a second back and drop us into the world, praying to God I've got it right.

CHAPTER
TWENTY-NINE

T HIS ISN'T HOW I pictured my reunion with my mom. Maybe it was a delusional thought process, but I'd imagined more hugs and happy tears. Instead I get insane laughter and looks of disdain as well as loathing.

Things only get worse the second I drop us down into the bedroom of the beach house. I land on my ass on the bed and Alex lands across from me still holding my hand.

"Where's my mom," I say, uncrossing my legs and pushing to my feet. I spring off the bed, the ashes of the curtains still scattered all over the comforter and floor, and spot her lifelessly laying just to the side of a large metal trunk. I drop down on my knees beside her. Her eyes are sealed shut, her skin lined with veins that contrast with her pale skin. She's breathing, but barely.

"No . . . no . . . no . . . no . . ." I shake my head in denial. She looks like she's sleeping, even when I lift her head up and place it on my lap.

Alex crouches down beside me and for a second he just looks at me. I wonder if he's thinking about how he said he loved me. Did he mean it? Why did he do it?

"Is she going to be okay?" I ask him, forcing him to

focus on the bigger problem.

Alex picks up my mom's arm, presses two fingers to her wrist, and then relief washes over his face. "She's alive." He sets her arm down over her stomach. "I don't know what's wrong with her, though." He rests his arms on his knees, leaning back on his heels as he glances at the open French doors, the sunlight filtering in.

"Are we even in present time?" he wonders, assessing the room. "Everything looks the same as when we left."

I point over my shoulder at the empty bed. "Except the Ira is gone." I straighten my knees and stand up. "There's one way to find out for sure, though . . . Aislin! Laylen! Can you come in here?"

A few moments later, Aislin and Laylen come running into the bedroom. They screech to a halt when they spot my mom on the floor with Alex and I beside her.

"What happened?" Aislin asks, working to catch her breath as she presses her hand to her heart.

"You can see us?" I ask them and they both nod, looking baffled.

"Good." I sink down to the floor and breathe in relief. "That means I did it."

"We're in the present?" Alex asks hopefully as he straightens his legs and stands to his feet.

I nod, letting a small smile seep through. "Yeah, we made it."

IT'S THE FIRST time I'm thankful for my unique Foreseer ability. Without it, we'd probably still be imprisoned, if not crazy or dead. Alex and Laylen move my unconscious mother to the bed where I cover her up with a blanket and shut the French doors. The four of us quietly sneak out of the room, letting her sleep, hoping she'll wake up and tell us something that will make all this trouble worth it.

In the warped, concealed part of me, I don't want her to wake up. The woman I saw in the visions and memories, the kind and enduring person, doesn't seem to exist in her anymore. It saddens me to the point that I feel like sobbing my heart out. But these thoughts I keep to myself, because I know how wrong they are.

We go into the small kitchen and Aislin makes us coffee while Alex and I fill the two of them in on what happened. All the curtains are shut, blocking out the beach right outside, although I can still hear the ocean crashing against the shore as it carries pieces of sand away.

"So all the Water Faeries just passed out?" Aislin asks, lowering into a chair next to Laylen. "And the Queen?"

I take a gulp of my coffee, the heat of it simmering the inside of my throat, but in a good way. "Yeah, one minute she was trying to torture my soul with that diamond we took down there, and the next moment her and all her Fey were on the ground."

"Was it because they were trying to do something to your . . . soul?" Aislin asks and then hurries and takes a gulp of her coffee, then leaves the mug in front of her mouth to conceal her expression.

"I don't know what happened exactly." I add some milk to my coffee and stir it with a spoon. "It could have been my locket or maybe it was my soul."

"I don't think it was either, honestly," Alex interrupts, pulling a chair out and sitting down beside me. "Now that I think about it, I'm guessing that it was from the overload of fear you shot at them."

"What overload of fear?" I wonder, but I can clearly remember how I felt about everything I saw and how it scared the shit out of me; more than even the Death Walkers.

He chooses his next words carefully as he picks up the coffee pot and pours some coffee into a mug. "I think because your emotions are so new, they sometimes come off a little. . . . strong. Maybe a little too strong for the Fey."

"Strong," I say, scowling at him, insulted. "You say that like it's a bad thing, yet it's what saved us back in the cell . . ." I clear my throat and quickly fill my mouth with coffee before I can bring up any more uncomfortable subjects.

He smashes his lips together, his gaze boring into me. "Yeah . . . it did." He gives a long pause, like he's expecting me to say something. But what? That I love him. Is that what he wants? Because I can't give it to him at the moment. Not when I haven't felt it yet. They'd just be empty words associated with the fractured part of my soul.

"I'm going to go check on my mom," I mutter, scooting the chair away from the table. I get up and put my mug in the sink then leave them in the kitchen, fully aware that Alex's eyes are following me the entire way.

I hurry back to the room, scared and relieved to find that my mom's still passed out in the bed. She looks dead, a corpse in a coffin waiting to be buried. Maybe she kind of is. Maybe The Underworld has practically killed her. Possibly that's why she was so cold toward me.

I inch toward the bed, taking slow steps until I reach the side. "Mom," I whisper, staring down at her. The word still feels strange coming from my lips. I always called Marco and Sophia by their first names and always said them formally. However saying "mom" is different. It means something. "Mom." The prickle traces down my neck. "Mom," I say louder, tears dripping from my eyes. "Mom." I reach up and touch the wet tears, trying to figure out what I'm feeling. Sadness. Pain. Abandonment.

As more gush out, I collapse to the bed on my stomach, bury my face into the pillow, and bawl my eyes out until I fall asleep.

I DON'T DREAM at all. I see nothing except blackness the entire time my eyes are shut. When I wake up, the curtains are open and the French doors are agape. Someone's been in here.

I bolt upright, rubbing my puffy eyes as the pinkish glow of sunset creeps in through the open doors.

"Gemma." The sound of my mom's voice scares me to death, and I fall out of the bed, smacking my elbow on the floor and my head on the side of the nightstand.

"Ow," I rub my elbow as I turn over and get to my feet.

My mom is sitting on the edge of the bed, looking over her shoulder at me like I'm a nut job. "Are you all right?" There's no scorn in her voice, only sincerity.

I nod, get to my feet, and sit down on the bed on the side opposite from her. "Are *you* all right?"

She swallows hard and then starts hacking, covering her mouth with her hand. "I think I need some water," she chokes, leaning over like she's going to vomit on the floor.

"I'll go get you some," I jump to my feet, knowing that what I'm really doing is running away from my problems.

I rush into the kitchen and fill up a glass with water. While I'm shutting off the faucet, I think I hear someone behind me. When I whirl around I come face to face with a tall, blue-eyed, blond-haired Vampire/Keeper.

"Shit, Laylen." I press my hand to my racing heart,

steadying the glass in my hand. "You scared me to death."

"Sorry." He has on a pair of dark jeans and a navy blue t-shirt that brings out the blue in his eyes. "But you are kind of jumpy." He sucks his lip ring into his mouth and nibbles on it, analyzing me over, looking as though he wants to say something more.

"Well, I did just get out of The Underworld." My mouth plunges to a frown. "I think it might have scarred me."

"Is everything okay?" He crosses his arms and relaxes his hip against the edge of the tile countertop. "You seemed kind of distant at the table."

"There's just some stuff going on," I say. "But the good news is, my mom's awake."

He stands up straight, uncrossing his arms, his defined muscles flexing. "Is she okay?"

"I don't know, but I'm about to find out." I wind around him to leave, but I stop at the doorway, glancing back over my shoulder. "Do you want to come with me?"

"Wouldn't you rather take Alex?" he says, sorrow lacing his tone. "I'm sure he has a ton of questions for her."

I turn around and tell him the truth. "Laylen I want you there just as much as I want him there."

He offers me a half smile as he walks toward me. "All right, let's go."

MY MOM HAS wandered out to the deck by the time I make it back to the room. She's standing near the railing, gazing out at the ocean, still wearing her tattered pants and shirt. *I need to get her some clean clothes.*

I carefully approach her with Laylen at my heels, and

the cup of water in my hand. I stop beside her and set the glass of water down on the railing in front of her, accidentally spilling some of the water out.

"Thank you," she says, picking the glass up. She takes a few large swallows and then puts the glass back down on the railing. I wait for her to say something—anything—but all she does is stare out at the ocean.

"Mom," I start. "Are you okay? Is there anything else I can get you? Like maybe something to eat?"

She finally looks at me, sighs, and then her gaze suddenly darts to Laylen. "Laylen, is that you?" she asks, shocked.

He nods, brushing his hair out of his eyes, as he steps away from the doorway and onto the deck. "Yeah, it's me, Jocelyn."

She smiles, however it looks morbidly wrong, like she's working really hard to make the corners of her mouth move upward. "You've grown up so much." She stares at me, her forehead furrowed, her eyes full of desolation. "And you . . ." She abruptly bursts into tears, shaking her head, her lips quivering. "You're—you're still . . ." She trails off, sobbing hysterically into her hands. "You're still you. Oh my God, I thought he'd ruin you . . . turn you into him."

I'm not sure what to say to her; that I'm not the girl she left behind, but someone trying to figure out who she is. I'm afraid if I dare utter those words, she might break apart completely. I let her cry for a moment, feeling awkward.

Finally, the tears cease and she dabs the remaining ones away with the corner of her shirt. "So what's been going on?" She clears her throat and takes another sip of water. "While I've been gone for the last fourteen years."

Jesus, where do I begin? So much has happened,

especially over the last few weeks. I'm not sure what to tell her, and honestly, I don't have all the answers since I can barely remember anything.

I do my best and start at the beginning, though, at least the beginning for me.

I try my best to get all the details right and fill her in on everything that has happened. I tell her about my life-less years with Marco and Sophia and then college. I tell her how the prickle miraculously showed up and freed me from my solitude. I tell her about the Death Walkers and how Stephan is working with them as well as Demetrius, which she knew already. How he can create the Mark of Malefiscus and that he put the mark on Nicholas. I explain my special Foreseer gift and the visions I've seen, at least to an extent, minus the fact that I've seen myself bearing the Mark of Evil. I tell her about how Stephan tried to erase my mind with that stupid rock and how the locket she gave me saved me.

When I'm done, it's nearly dark and most of the beach has cleared. The ocean roars in the distance and a few stars speckle the greying sky.

"I'm so sorry," my mom says after I've given her the rundown. She reaches over and takes my hand with a slight tremor in her grip. I wince, but don't pull away. "I'm incredibly sorry you had to go through all of this. God, it must have been terrible for you"

I swallow hard as I sit down on the railing. "It's not your fault . . . I—I know you tried to protect me."

She shakes her head, freeing my hand, and then sinks down in a chair. "I should have tried harder. I should have tried to run away sooner. I let it go on for too long, know-ing what he was going to do to you . . . We need to stop it—stop him." She glances over at Laylen sitting on the railing near the open French doors. "I need to talk to Alex and Aislin. Could you go get them for me?"

Laylen nods and hops off the railing, his boots scuffing the wood. "Of course." He shoots me a confused look before walking into the house.

"Why do you need to talk to them?" I give her a quizzical look as I slide off the railing and land on my feet.

"Because, I need all of you here," she says, crossing her arms over her stomach like she feels sick. "Because this—all of this—involves all of you. Each of you plays a part in it."

"Plays a part in what?" I ask. "Stephan trying to open the portal? Because I thought he just needed the star."

"Oh, Gemma." She extends her hand toward my face and then brushes some of my hair out of my eyes; her first motherly gesture and I'll admit that it's strange. "There is so much more to Stephan's plan than just you and the star. So much more."

CHAPTER THIRTY

TIME SEEMS TO stop. I'd always assumed it was me, based on what I'd been told. Simply me and the star and the end of the world. I guess I was wrong, though. We all were. Which makes me wonder just how much more we were wrong about.

Laylen returns a few minutes later with a very sleepy-eyed Aislin dressed in pink yoga pants and a fitted white tank top. Tagging along behind her is a very stressed out Alex wearing jeans and a black t-shirt. They each grab a chair and drag them closer so we're all sitting in a circle. Alex avoids eye contact with me, stretching his legs out and staring at his bare feet. The deck light is on as well as the bedroom light and it lights up the night around us.

Aislin fidgets nervously, wringing her fingers in her lap. "Jocelyn, I can't believe you're here . . . It's just really . . . great." She struggles for words she never does quite find.

My mother gives her a tight smile. "Thanks. I'm glad to see all of you . . . you've grown up so much." She talks almost robotically and I wonder if this is what I sounded like back when I was emotionless.

"Laylen says there's something you wanted to tell

us?" Alex asks impatiently, picking at a loose thread on a torn area of his jeans.

My mother nods and finishes the last of her water. "There is." She sets the empty glass down beside her feet and relaxes back in the chair, her shoulders curling inward. "But I need you to tell me what you know first. Gemma's already told me what she knows about your father's plans and what not, however I think you might know a little more than her."

I burn a hole into the side of his head as he presses his lips together with guilt written all over his face. He crosses his arms and shifts his weight while his eyes quickly sweep across the four of us.

"Alex," my mom says and I'm a little shocked at the warmness in her tone. "I understand your initial reaction is to keep things a bottled up. It's what you've been taught to do, but I need to know what you know—it's important."

He tugs on the bottom of his shirt, staring at the floor. "Where do you want me to start?"

"How about from the beginning," she says.

"But where is the beginning?" Alex mumbles, his gaze flicking to mine.

I can tell that even after everything, he still has secrets. Maybe he always will. Perhaps I'll never know him. The raw thought clenches at my heart. I want to know him. Every part of him. Inside and out . . . what does that mean exactly? About me? About us?

"Why don't you start with the day that Gemma's soul was detached," my mom patiently suggests. "Do you remember what happened that day?"

He glances at me and I raise my eyebrows at him as I lean back in the chair, thrumming my fingers against the armrests, implying to go ahead because I'm dying to hear what he has to say about this.

He shuts his eyes, his chest expanding as he breathes in the ocean air. "She and I were hiding out in that little fort in the side of the hill," he says, his eyelids fluttering open. "Because earlier my father told us that Gemma had to go away and I didn't want her to. So I ran away with her, very stupidly thinking that if we did, he wouldn't make her go when he found us."

I touch the palm of my hand and outline the faint scar, remembering the vision I saw. He'd cut my hand and his, saying the words *forem* as we pressed our palms together. What does the damn word mean?

Alex balls up his own hand as if he's trying to hide his scar. "He ended up taking her away from me and I never saw her again . . . Well, until my dad made me enroll in college so I could try to get to the bottom of why her emotions were surfacing again."

"And what happened during all those years when you didn't see Gemma?" my mother asks.

His jaw goes taught and he clenches his hands even tighter, yet his expression is surprisingly stoic. "Basically, my father beat the shit out of me so I'd learn to feel pain over emotion. He said it was an important part of being a Keeper or whatever." He slumps back in the chair and flexes out his fingers. "Who the fuck cares?"

Laylen and I trade an astonished look, seeming equally as surprised, though my mom and Aislin appear rationally calm, like they expected it.

"What about you Aislin?" she asks. "What was your life like?"

Aislin scrapes at her nail polish and tucks a leg underneath her. "I was taught to be a very confident Witch. I didn't go to Wicca school, though. I was trained at home by a Witch named Estella."

"Estella Evernandy?" my mom says sullenly. "Of the

Evernandy Clan."

"Yeah, that's the one," Aislin replies, coiling a strand of her hair around her finger. "But why do you sound so upset?"

"Do you know anything about the Evernandy Clan?" my mom asks, her voice attentive.

Aislin shrugs, putting her foot back onto the floor as she unwinds the hair from her finger. "Yeah, that they come from a very powerful bloodline." She gathers her golden blonde hair and secures it in a messy bun with a rubber band that's on her wrist.

"A black magic bloodline," my mom explains. "Aislin, your father had you taught to learn black magic."

Aislin shakes her head in denial. "No, he wouldn't do that," she insists. "I know it."

"Yes, he would," Alex mutters, staring at his lap with his brows furrowed. "Don't deny things that are clearly possible."

"Shut up." Aislin slumps back in the chair and stomps her foot on the deck. "We don't know her. She might be lying."

"I doubt it." Alex frowns at my mom. "But I really don't get what any of this has to do with the star's power and the end of the world, which is what we should be focusing on; not Aislin and mine's fucked up pasts."

"This stuff has everything to do with it—you two have just as much to do with it as Gemma does," my mother tells him. She rolls up the sleeves of her shirt and crosses her legs, fanning the front of her face with her hand as the heat overwhelms her. "I have one more question and then I'll get to the point." She pauses. "Were you near Gemma the day her emotions first came back to her."

"Why the hell would you think that?" Alex's voice is sharp and rumbles with fury as he sits up straight, slamming his hands down on the handles of the chair. "I wasn't supposed to see her."

"I understand that." My mom's demeanor is professionally calm. "However, I need to know if you went behind Stephan's back and snuck off to see her almost as though it was out of your control."

Alex glances out at the ocean, his eyes pools of black in the moonlight. "It was something I couldn't help . . . going there, I mean. I didn't think anything would happen." He rips his concentration away from the water and rotates in the chair to look at me. "I'm sorry I didn't tell you sooner." There's genuine honesty in his voice.

I gape at him unfathomably. "Why didn't you say something?" I lean in and lower my voice. "After everything we've been through, it doesn't make any sense."

He lets his knee fall to the side and rests it against mine as his back bends and his body moves closer to mine. "At first it was because I thought I couldn't—because I was still my father's puppet. Then . . . well, I had just left you there, crying in the middle of the parking lot surrounded by a ton of strangers. I didn't want to own up to doing that. "

I swallow hard, remembering the day when I fell to my knees and cried for the very first time in the middle of the University of Wyoming's parking lot, my chest feeling like it'd been ripped open. I could barely get up afterward and I had such a hard time dealing with it that when I got home I thought about taking very drastic measures to turn it off—I thought about ending my life.

"I'm sorry," he repeats, lacing our fingers as he takes ahold of my hand. His skin is deliciously warm and is humming with electric sparks that briefly make everything around us—problems and people—vanish. "I wish I could take it back—do things differently—but I can't."

"Okay." It's all I say—all I can say. Not because I'm angry with him, either. I actually feel very sorry for him. Beaten up by his father and taught to be unemotional. No wonder he's so complicated.

I turn to my mother. "What's the point of all of this? I don't understand."

"The point is that all of you are connected," she says. "And that connection is why you've all had such messed up paths."

"What's the connection?" Alex asks, looking at me and not her, as though he's trying to see into my thoughts.

My mom takes a deep breath and glances up at the starry sky. "The star."

CHAPTER
THIRTY-ONE

"THE STAR," ALEX, Aislin, and I say simultaneously while Laylen opts to stay quiet, his eyes locked on the space of deck in front of his feet, his expression undecipherable.

"How does that connect to all of us?" I question. "It's only in me, so . . ." I trail off as a gut-wrenching thought occurs to me. Electricity that flows between two people. Sparks. An irrational, overwhelming, obsession with each other. Always melting into each other's arms. Every time I'm around Alex it's there. I can feel it buzzing right now, a gentle current flowing off his fingers and onto mine as he holds my hand.

"Does . . . Does Alex have a star's power in him, too?" I ask and I feel his fingers tremble.

Alex's head whips in my direction. "Are you crazy?"

"Maybe," I say and then hold my breath as I wait for my mom to answer.

She reluctantly nods. "Not a separate star, but the same one."

Alex shakes his head in refusal of accepting the ugly truth. He tugs his fingers through his hair, forgetting to let go of my hand and my fingers end up going with his hair too. "No . . . There's no way." He stands to his feet and pulls me with him, then sits back down and I fall back into my chair. I think about taking my hand away from him, but I'm worried he might break apart if I do. He looks so defenseless and lost right now. After a lot of heavy breathing and cursing, he collects himself and says, "How?"

"Because what happened with the star wasn't an accident," my mother explains, gesturing at all of us. "None of this was. All of this—all of you—happened for a reason. The star being split up and placed inside you two, Aislin learning black magic, and Laylen turning into a Vampire. None of that was an accident."

My heart thuds in my chest as I remember what Nicholas said in the forest. I glance over Laylen and his head is hung low, his elbows stationed on his knees. He almost looks like a statue cut from marble, created to portray the definition of anguish.

"So what you're saying," Laylen says, looking up, and the lack of emotion on his face is frightening, "is that I was changed into a fucking monster on purpose—that Stephan had me turned?"

Pressing her lips together, my mom nods. "Stephan has been planning for years, ever since he found out the portal could be opened . . . He's been looking for a way to free Malefiscus almost forever because of the mark. No one knew about his mark, though, because his parents cut it off and tried to keep it hidden. I didn't even know he had it until it was too late." She swallows hard. "Stephan is a descendent of Malefiscus, but I'm not sure how it's possible."

"Why have all the Keepers thought the mark died with Malefiscus?" Alex asks.

"Because there are no records saying he had any offspring to pass the mark to," my mother replies gravely.

"Maybe it just appeared on him," I say. "Like it did on Malefiscus. I mean, marks have to start from somewhere."

"No, he has the bloodline," my mother insists. "I heard him talking about it right before he . . . he threw me into the lake."

"Well then, Demetrius is a descendant of him, too," I tell her. "I saw it in a vision."

"I know," she says and I wonder just how much she does know, not to mention how she learned about it. How did she find all this out? "But the question is: how? We need to find out so we know what we're going up against." Her blue eyes momentarily flick to Alex. "And we need to find out how the marks surface without Stephan putting it on them."

Alex slips his hand out of mine and starts anxiously tapping his foot against the floor. "I still don't get it, though. You say all of us play a part in *this,* but play a part in what exactly? Opening the portal?"

My mom nods. "And freeing Malefiscus," she explains. "He's been trapped in the portal since the sentencing."

"But I thought he died." I scoot forward in the chair. "I thought he was hung."

She shakes her head. "Not a lot of people know this, but during Malefiscus's reign, it wasn't just the Death Walkers who were terrorizing people. There were Witches, Vampires, Fey, and even a couple of Foreseers who had joined his reign of terror because Malefiscus has Fey, Witch, Vampire, and Foreseer blood in him," she says, recapping most of what Nicholas has already told me. "When his brother, Hektor, finally captured Malefiscus, the Keepers had to come up with a way to make his followers surrender with him and be free of their Mark of Evil, so they put Malefiscus in a portal and sealed it with the blood of three individuals; a Keeper who also was a

Vampire, a Keeper who was also a Witch, and a Keeper who was also a Faerie. That way the Fey, Witches, and Vampires who followed Malefiscus would be bound to the portal as well, without the Keepers having to track them all down." She gazes up at the luminous moon. "The final step was to seal the portal with the energy of a fallen star."

"So there was another fallen star once?" I ask, glancing at Alex. He meets my eyes and the electricity ignites between us before we can even take our next breath. There's so much power in it—in us—and it frightens me how much I hate it and like it at the same time. "

My mother yanks her attention off of the moon and forces it back onto us. "No. The star's energy you and Alex carry is the same one as the Keepers used those hundreds of years ago. After they sealed the portal, they hid it because no one knew how to destroy it . . . The star was also never supposed to be put in any Keepers." She pauses, considering something. "That's one of the things that I've never have been able to figure out. Why Stephan split the star and put its energy in you two." She lets out a heavy sigh. "But what I do know, is that in order for Stephan to be able to open the portal, he needs his Vampire, his Witch, and his Faerie that also have Keeper blood in them, so he created them—created you two." She looks from Aislin to Laylen. "Then he got his hands on the star, and for some reason he put it in you and Alex."

I feel like I've been run over by a truck, my guts splattered all over the pavement, my body mangled. I'd never realized how easy it was to bear the burden of carrying the star in me, but now Alex, Aislin, and Laylen are carrying their own burdens and I realize that things just got a hell of a lot more complicated.

"So if he opens the portal, then what happens?" I ask, sounding strangled. "Malefiscus is freed, along with a shit load of Death Walkers and the whole damn world turns to ice?"

My mother unenthusiastically nods. "He'll be able to enter our world again. Every Death Walker will come out of hiding and even more will come out of the portal. He controls them because the mark binds them together in blood, which is the same reason why Stephan has control over them." She pauses. "And every Witch, Faerie, and Vampire who are the descendants of his first followers will be under his control, so what you saw in the vision, Gemma—the world ending in ice—is probably at the very end of what's going to happen to the world, after the massacre."

"Massacre," I breathe and then shove the bloody images away from my head. "But there's one thing I'm still confused about, how does Stephan know how to do all of this?"

"Because he was told what to do by a Foreseer," she says with a hint of anger in her tone.

"Is my father that Foreseer?" I ask, shocking her and everyone else, although it's not that ridiculous of a question. She mentioned him back in The Underworld and I could hear the loathing in her tone.

My mother leaps from her chair and it topples to the ground. "No, it's not your father!" she screams, crouching over and savagely moving toward me. "Shut your mouth this instant!"

I hover back in the chair, realizing how temperamental she really is. "I'm sorry."

She glances at all of us and the rage in her eyes diminishes as she tips the chair back up and lowers down in it. "I'm so sorry, Gemma. I have no idea why I yelled at you like that." She smoothes her hands over her hair, trying to comb it back into place, however the braid is slipping loose and strands of her brown hair are sticking up. "I'm so sorry."

"It's fine," I say numbly, shutting myself down by choice because I don't want to feel the pain from knowing that the mother I have now is not the mother I had—she'll probably never be the same. None of us will. There are things in life that happen that change who we are, things that are hard to come back from, and in the end we never really are the same.

Aislin jumps to her feet. "I think I need to go lie down. This is a lot to take in." She's on the verge of crying as she hurries into the house before anyone can say anything.

Laylen sighs and gets to his feet. "I'll go check on her." He follows after her, leaving the door open.

A moment of silence passes between us and all I can hear are the waves and Aislin's sobs from inside the house.

My mother's blue irises drift back and forth between Alex and me. "I really want to understand, why he separated the star and why he detached Gemma's soul and raised you to be unemotional. I know what he told all the other Keepers, but I want to find out the real reason."

"Maybe it's the opposite reason of when we thought he was protecting the world," I suggest with a shrug. "Maybe he needs to preserve the power inside me . . . and Alex so it would be useful for the portal. Maybe if we . . . if we felt too much the star's power would die."

"You might be right," my mom says, her forehead creasing as she deliberates. "But we need to find out for sure." She slumps back in her chair. "We need to find out a lot of things."

"Like why he created Aislin and Laylen," I say, biting my lip as I gaze out at the waves. "Why not just find a Vampire and Witch who are also Keepers?"

"Because their kind are not easy to find," my mother

answers. "I think it was also so he could keep an eye on them and make sure everything turned out the way that he wanted."

Unexpectedly, the electricity surges to a nearly unbearable temperature, putting more power in me than it ever has, to the point that it's suffocating.

"Alex, are you okay?" I lean over in the chair and put a hand on his knee, hoping to calm him down.

He looks at me and I mean really looks at me, with fire in his eyes. Then he stands to his feet, throws the chair over the deck, and storms inside the house, slamming the door behind him. The glass shatters and scatters all over the cracks in the deck.

I start to get up, but then sit back down, not wanting to leave my mom alone just yet.

"I'll be fine," she assures me, motioning at me to go after him. "Now go check on him."

"Are you sure?" I ask hesitantly.

She nods, cracking a smile. "Gemma, I've been surrounded by screams and torture for the last fourteen years. I'd love a little break from the noise and drama. Maybe just a few minutes of peace and quiet."

I nod and leave her alone on the deck, wondering what I'm leaving behind and what I'm about to walk into.

As well as whether or not I can handle any of it.

CHAPTER THIRTY-TWO

I FIND ALEX out on the front steps, the porch light shining down on his back. He doesn't look up at me when I walk out the door, but I know that he knows I'm behind him, thanks to the electricity. The connection feels different now that I know why it's there. It's almost painful, the sparks now feeling more like prickly needles, yet somehow it still feels so damn good.

The salty sea air kisses my cheeks and my hair as I shut the screen door. I sit down on the cement step beside Alex, pull my legs up, and rest my arms on my knees. He rolls his tongue in his mouth as he taps his foot against the step with his arms on his knees. His hair is disheveled, a sign that he's been raking his fingers through it, a stressful habit of his.

"How are you feeling?" I ask and then shake my head at the absurdity of my ridiculous question. "Sorry, dumb question."

His expression softens, his muscles slightly unraveling. "No, it's not a dumb question. I just . . ." He blows out a breath. "I don't know how to answer it because I don't know how I feel. I really don't." He kicks a rock on the step and it shoots across the grass. "I feel like I don't know anything anymore—I never really knew anything."

"It's insane, isn't it?" I say. "How all of us fit into this—how we were all created."

"Gemma." His voice holds uncertainty as he angles his face toward me, staring at me remorsefully. "I'm sorry for everything. I really am."

"It's fine," I tell him, shrugging it off the best that I can. "It's not your fault. Besides," I stare down at my hands. "I think we're past needing to say we're sorry."

He turns to the side to face me, takes my hands, and pulls them to him. "No, we're not," he says in a low, meaningful tone and I look up at him. "I think you're letting me off a little because of the electricity—or the *star* anyway."

"It's fine," I repeat, thinking about how he was beaten by his father. I may have been abused by neglect and demeaning words, but Alex had been physically abused. "I'm not the only one who's suffered." I pause as he grazes the scar on my palm. "Can I ask you something?"

"Yeah, go ahead." There's an edge in his voice.

"What does *Forem* mean?"

He sighs heavy heartedly and looks up from my hand. "I had a feeling you were going to ask that." He pauses, deliberating as he searches my eyes. "You remember how Nicholas told you about the Blood Promise the Fey made to Malefiscus?" he asks, sketching his finger along the scar on my palm.

I nod, shivering from his touch as my skin tingles. "Yeah, I remember, though he never did explain to me what it was."

He slips his hand over mine, presses our palms together and his hand nearly swallows mine. "Remember in the vision how I cut our hands?"

It clicks like a lock unlatching. "Did we make a Blood Promise?"

He nods. "We did."

Forem. "What kind of promise exactly?"

"Forem or . . ." His exhale is shaky, conveying his insecurity. "Forever."

I'm a little lost still. "So Forem means Forever, but I still don't get what exactly a Blood Promises is."

"It's an unbreakable promise," he says quietly. "And it means we're bonded together . . . forever."

Forever. *Forever.* What the hell? How is that even possible? We were . . . were so . . .

"But we were so young," I finally manage to say through my racing thoughts and heart. "Why the hell would we do that?"

He closes his hand around mine, brings my hand to his mouth, and grazes my knuckles with his lips. "Because we were really weird kids," he states amusedly. "And honestly, I didn't really know what I was getting into when I did it. I think I said it more as a lets-be-best friends-forever kind of thing."

I explore his face for what's hidden inside him. Did he mean what he said in The Underworld? Does he really love me? "And what does it mean now to you?"

"I'm not sure yet," he says, staring out at the road.

"Me, neither," I utter softly and then the silence drowns us.

I want to ask him so many things. Like what he's thinking and feeling. Does he think it's the electricity that's pulling us toward each other? Does he really love me?

In the end I keep my lips sealed because I'm afraid to find out the truth. Then I'll have to admit what I'm really feeling and I'm not sure I'm ready for that.

"Gemma, I . . ." he starts, struggling to keep his voice balanced.

I can tell by the way that he looks that he's either going to crush my heart or send me running, so I cut him off, rapidly leaning in and silencing him with my lips.

I gasp from the spark of our lips and then moan at the warmth of his tongue as he urges my lips open and kisses me ardently. I readily liquefy into the kisses, opening up and letting him completely in. He meticulously explores every inch of my mouth as he grips at my waist, his hands just under the hem of my shirt; flesh burning flesh.

At first the kiss is innocent, simply two confused people making out on a porch, however the longer it goes on, the more intense it becomes until something snaps in both of us and the faint sparks blaze into a scorching fire. Before I can even acknowledge what he's doing, he scoops me up in his arms and carries me into the house. Passion and heat take over and we no longer have control, but we never really did anyway. We've both been helpless against our emotions, without them and with them. The drives of our lives and our decisions have solely been based on what we didn't and did feel.

I secure my arms and legs around him as he maneuvers through the screen door and into the living room, his lips staying fastened to mine the entire time. He trips over the threshold and my back slams against the wall as his weight crashes against me. He leaves me pressed up to it for a moment, his tongue slipping deeply into my mouth, and then he moves us away. He manages to find his way to the hall without breaking the kiss and starts to head to the room we've been sleeping in.

"Not in there," I murmur against his lips as I thread my fingers through his soft hair. "My mom's in there."

Groaning, he turns the other way and stumbles into the vacant spare room across the hall. It's smaller than the one we're staying in and doesn't have a view of the ocean, but I could care less at the moment what the hell the room looks like as long as it has a bed.

He continues to kiss me as he moves for the bed and then he turns around at the last second so we collapses onto the mattress with me on top of him. I straddle him as he presses his hands to my back, enfolding me against him. We kiss recklessly through our pain and confusion and the longer our lips remain sealed together, the easier it is to forget that this all might be an deception based on stars and misguided emotions.

Alex ultimately breaks the kiss, but only to remove my shirt. It's tight fitting, though, and has a ribbon up the front that makes it complex to get off. Finally he threads his fingers through the laces and rips the fabric in half. Then he tosses the pieces aside on the floor, his green eyes blazing with uncontrollable hunger as he reaches around my back and unclasps my bra. My breasts spring free as he discards it to the floor beside my ruined shirt, then I reach forward and grab the bottom of his shirt. He helps me take it off him, roughly tugging it over his head, and throwing it aside. I leisurely glide my fingers up his chest and de-fined abs before I groan at the mouthwatering hardness of his lean muscles, his skin making my skin burn. When I reach the top of his chest, I slip my hands around to his shoulders blades while his travel up my back.

Halfway up my back, he presses his hand inward, forcing my back to bow up and my breasts to move closer to him. With neediness in his eyes, he lowers his mouth to devour my nipple, sucking hard while his tongue traces eager circles. I allow my head fall back as I moan in ec-stasy and my thighs tingle as my stomach coils. He keeps sucking and sucking, moving back and forth between my breasts and right when I can't take anymore, my body about to combust from emotional overload, he pulls back.

I start to stammer a protest when he lifts me up with one hand and jerks my shorts and panties off. I fumble to undo the button of his jeans and then he slips them off and kicks them aside. When I sit back down on his lap with a leg on each side of him, his hardness presses between my legs. I wait for him to slip inside me, raggedly breathing in anticipation, but his fingers wind around the back of my neck and he entices my lips to his while his finger slips up between my legs and slides into me.

He starts moving his fingers, harder and harder, feeling me thoroughly and pushing me toward blissful elation. His tongue and fingers move rhythmically and then he sucks my bottom lip into his mouth and grazes his teeth along it. His fingers push me higher until I'm drifting away from reality, lost in the sweltering feelings I barely recognize. I finally scream out, completely letting go as I grasp forcefully onto his shoulders. I'm barely coming back down when he slips his fingers out of me and with one final kiss, he thrusts himself into me.

I cry out again as a thousand different emotions soar through me and speed up my heart rate. My pulse throbs and my body pulsates more erratically with each of his thrusts. I start to move with him, wanting more, needing him to be as close as possible so we're linked together. My skin beads with sweat as he pushes harder, his hips meeting mine as he sinks into me, driving me farther into blissfulness. He grabs my arms, guides them behind my back, and secures my wrists together with one hand, forcing my chest outward. With each penetrating movement of his hips, my chest presses against his and it makes my nipples go hard. His lips find my neck where he kisses and licks a path down to my collarbone while his other hand grips at the flesh on my waist.

He lifts his hips higher as he holds my wrists together

and leaves me vulnerable and trapped in the most insanely good way. I want to hold onto him, dig my nails in and feel his skin split open, letting out some of the overpowering passion inside me. But I can't do anything except let the feeling build as he pushes me closer the edge of reality. I get more lost with each connection of our bodies until I feel like I'm going to explode. I scream out as I lose it completely and it feels like I'm breaking apart on the inside, crumpling, falling into the dark.

Seconds later, Alex movements slow down. He gives one last deep press into me and we both cry out in unison. His fingers press against my wrist to the point where I wonder if they'll bruise and he pulls my waist forward so our bodies align perfectly together.

As we both gradually return to reality, we work to catch our breaths and slow our heart rates. His fingers loosen on my wrists and he finally frees me from his dominating hold. I move my arms forward and lean back, massaging my wrist with my fingers.

Alex falls back against the mattress, his chest sheen with sweat. He places a kiss on my wrist before putting his hand on my cheek. "Are you okay . . . I was a little rough?" he asks, tracing my cheek.

I nod as he searches my eyes. "Yeah, I'm fine . . . Are you okay?"

He nods then removes his hand from my face. Then he lies down and draws me down with him, pressing our foreheads together. "About what I said in The Underworld."

I hold my breath, too afraid to speak. What if he says he didn't mean it? Can I handle it? Can I manage it if he says he loves me? I'm not sure what I'll do, and honestly, I wish he'd just keep his mouth shut so I can bask in the euphoric sensations he put inside me moments ago.

He takes an uneven breath and then releases it,

the warmth hitting my cheeks. "I think I . . . we need to . . . Jesus, Gemma I—"

Someone bangs on the door. "Alex! Gemma!" Aislin cries from the other side of the door. "I need to talk to you."

Shaking his head, Alex leans back and calls out, "Not now, Aislin. Go away."

"But Laylen's missing!" she yells. "We were talking and he was upset and then . . ." she starts to sob, choking on her tears and her voice is muffled. "He took off and I can't find him anywhere. I'm worried about what he's going to do."

"We'll be right there," I call out as fear ascends in me. Laylen was already in the wrong place before, fighting his blood thirst and now he's hurting over his past. The combination is a deadly mix and I'm worried he's either going to hurt himself or someone else.

I instantly climb off Alex's lap and he slips out of me. "Shit, this is bad." I reach for my panties balled up on the floor. "He looked so upset when my mom told him he was created on purpose."

Alex sits on the edge of the bed, watching me put my panties and shorts on. "We were all upset."

I fasten the button on my shorts. "Yeah, but he's been completely alone."

Alex stands to his feet and stretches his arms above his head, like he has no intention of hurrying. "So have you."

I pick up my bra. "Alex, aren't you worried about him?"

He collects his boxers and jeans from the floor. "Apparently not as much as you."

I frown as I hook my bra. "What's that supposed to mean?"

He picks up his boxers and slips them on. "It means you're awfully upset."

"Are you jealous?"

"Maybe." His blunt honesty throws me off a little.

I go to pick up my shirt and realize it's in pieces. "Alex, if you lo . . . care for me at all, then you'll help us find him." I bite my tongue at my stupid blunder.

He slips his jeans on, studying me with an unreadable expression as he does up the button. "Okay, I'll help you find him," he says simply.

I'm not sure what it means exactly, yet it feels like it means something. The prickle is starting to emerge, but it quickly vanishes as Aislin bangs on the door again.

Alex tosses me his shirt. "Here, put this on."

I catch it and tug it over my head, the smell of his cologne mixed with the calming scent of him overwhelming me. There's so much that's unsaid between us; so much that needs to be said. But I think we might be afraid of the truth in ourselves and each other. As he opens the door so we can walk out, I think about asking him how he feels about me, but in the end, fear owns me and my lips end up staying shut.

CHAPTER
THIRTY-THREE

ALEX, AISLIN, AND I split up, Alex heading to town while Aislin and I go out onto the beach. With flashlights in our hands and cell phones in our pockets, Aislin hikes up the left side of the beach and I take the right.

"If you need anything, either scream or call me," she says as she hurries down the shore, sweeping her flashlight across the sand.

I nod and turn away, aiming the flashlight in front of me as the waves rush over my feet. The moon is glistening down on the water, making it look oily and the stars twinkle so brightly they look like diamonds.

I walk swiftly, shouting out Laylen's name as I leave my footprints in the sand. I check behind rocks, in the backyard of nearby houses, and I even stare at the water a few times, fearing that's where he went. Hours go by and dawn arrives, kissing the land with shades of pink and orange, making the ocean blue again.

I'm about to head back to the house when my phone rings. I slip it out of my pocket and answer it.

"Did you find him?" I ask.

"Not yet," Alex says. "But there are a lot of places he

could still be."

"Have you heard from Aislin?"

"No, but I'm going to call her after I get off the phone with you."

"Okay, well, I'll keep looking."

"Come back to the house first," he says as I start to head further up the shore. "I don't like you out alone."

"I'm not going to sit around and do nothing," I tell him. "But I'll come back and check on my mother, then I'm going out again."

"Then you can come look with me," he replies with a silent plea in his voice. "I need you . . . I need you close to me. I can barely concentrate because all I keep thinking about is that something is going to happen to you." He's acting strange and I wonder if something's wrong with him, like maybe he's found Laylen and it's bad.

I'm about to tell him I'll head back, when I hear Aislin call out my name. It sounds like it came from somewhere down the shore behind me so I turn around and head in that direction. "I gotta go. I just heard Aislin call out my name . . ." I scan the shore with my hand shielding my eyes to block the glare of the sunrise. "She might need my help."

"Be careful," he warns as I run up the shore. "And call me back."

"I will." I hang up as I reach an assembly of cliffy rocks that the waves crash into. There's a slender, sandy path that winds between them, disappearing around a corner a ways in.

"Gemma!" Her voice is as clear as day and is coming from inside the rocks. "Gemma, I need your help. I fell off the rocks and I think I might have broken my leg."

I sigh. "All right, I'm coming!" I put my phone in my back pocket along with my flashlight and dash down the path. Sand seeps between my toes and the echo of the waves shatter against the jagged rocks. The farther I get, the narrower the path becomes until I have to maneuver over sections of the rock that are nearly touching.

"Aislin!" I yell as I grab onto a lip on the rock and hop over it onto the path.

"Back here!" she hollers. "Please hurry. It hurts so badly."

"I'm coming!" I split my knee open as I climb over a larger rock and then twist my ankle as I dismount onto the path. I hobble up the rest of the path, clutching onto the rock wall, until I reach a dead end.

I glance around at the empty space. "Aislin, where are you!"

"Right here!" He voice floats over my shoulder and I spin around, with my arms out into front of me.

There's nothing behind me other than rocks and sand. I start to panic, reaching for my pocket and my phone, but something bumps my elbow. The impact lurches me forward and I trip over my feet then stumble to the ground, landing on my hands and knees.

I push up to my feet and quickly turn in a circle with my hands out to the sides of me. "Who's there?"

"Me," Aislin says and her voice sounds like it's everywhere. "I need your help, Gemma."

I need to get the hell out of here. I run toward the path and bend my knees to leap over the rock, but an invisible force rams me in the stomach. I fall back down into the sand and land on my back, my head slamming against the side of the rough sandpaper rock.

My scalp splits open and blood oozes out, drenching my hair. As I blink up at the sky, my ears ring and my thoughts jumble together in incoherent images. There's a glimmer of light from the afterglow of the sun and then

Aislin appears above me. Her green eyes shine like two lustrous emeralds, her smile is cheerful, and her golden brown hair blows in the breeze.

"Hey," she says cheerfully and then her smile plummets to a scowl. There's another flash of light and then her green eyes shift gold and her golden brown hair morphs to sandy blond as it shortens to the top of his head. "Beautiful day, isn't it?" Nicholas says, hovering above me with a shovel in his hand. "Glad to see that damn spell that Witch put on you finally wore off. God, I've missed fucking with your head."

I moan, clutching my head as I roll to my side. "No . . ."

"I bet I know what you're thinking," he says. "Why, oh why did I hit Nicholas over the head with a rain stick." He raises the shovel over his head. "Payback's a bitch."

I open my mouth to scream, but it gets cut off as he slams the shovel against my skull. The vibration of the impact reverberates through my brain. I cry out, but the sound of my voice quickly fades along with the world and my body as I disappear into darkness.

CHAPTER
THIRTY-FOUR

WHEN I OPEN my eyes again, I'm worried I'll be buried alive in the sand. What I see, though, makes me wish I was. I've been to this place before, when Laylen bit me and I passed out. Also in a few of my dreams. I've seen myself trapped in this land with Stephan as he turns me into something evil.

Acres of muddy land stretch as far as my eye can see and are buried beneath piles of twisted and warped metal objects. Some look like junk and others like art and the deep shades of grey in the sky blend well with everything.

I slowly sit up, fighting the excruciating ache inside my skull, and glance around, knowing that something bad is about to happen. I can sense it in the metallic air, feel it in my aching bones, and I've also seen it, way too clearly before.

Black ravens caw above my head and shower black feathers all over like ash. I push to my feet and check my pockets for my phone, but not surprisingly, they're empty. I try to summon the energy inside my body to Foresee my way out of here, but I can't so much as feel a spark. There's *praesidium* nearby; I can feel it hindering my power.

I place my hand on top of my head and wince at the large lump where the shovel hit me. "Damn bastard Faerie."

"Yes, the Fey can be conniving little creatures," Stephan's cold voice rises over my shoulders and I whirl around before instantly stepping back.

He's leaning against a shiny, metallic sphere about the size of a compact car with his arms crossed. He's dressed in a black shirt and slacks, a golden chain hangs around his neck, and his dark eyes match his hair. His scar is also more evident than ever. He's not carrying a weapon, but I doubt he thinks he needs one. I wish he was wrong, however I know I'm nothing but an ordinary girl who has a lot of useless power trapped inside her.

"Gemma Lucas, my star and the girl who's caused me a great amount of trouble over the last few weeks." Stephan's coal eyes study me, his face carrying confusion and intrigue. "You've been a busy girl."

"And you've been a busy villain." I take a step back and my elbow bumps against a stack of crinkled metal boxes. "Creating stars, destroying your children, ruining lives."

He only smiles as he stands up straight, squaring his broad shoulders. "So I see you've discovered some of my secrets." He weaves around a pile of wire and then stations himself in front of it, only a few steps away from me. "Tell me, Gemma," he stuffs his hands into his pockets and his grin widens. "Have the nightmares and power been getting to you?

"What nightmares and power." I play dumb, dodging to the side, but end up smacking into a stack of iron rod spears.

"Smart girl," he says. "A lot smarter than that son of mine." He shuffles closer to me, removing his hands from his pockets and starts unbuttoning the sleeves of his shirt. "I tried and tried to teach him to be more like you, so accepting to being emotionally detached, yet he just couldn't seem to get the hang of it."

"You mean by beating him?" I question daringly, glancing around for an escape route.

He shrugs, rolling up his sleeve. "I had to do it some way, since his damn soul refused to take to Sophia's gift, the *unus quisnam aufero animus*. Such a beautiful thing, watching someone's soul getting detached," he muses. "But I never could figure out why it wouldn't work on Alex," he says as he rolls up his other sleeve. "Other than maybe he was in love with you and too weak to succumb to it."

"That doesn't make him weak. It makes him strong," I say, staring at the mark on his arm. It's strange looking, not quite like Laylen's Mark of Immortality, but similar. The lines are just a little more angled and the black bleeds out on his skin.

He laughs as he turns his other arm over, revealing the black and red triangle inked on his forearm. "We'll see who's really weak here in a few moments, won't we?"

I quickly step back, but crash into the sizeable pile of steel cubes. I skitter out of the way as they clatter down to the ground, then dodge to my left and sprint across the dirt, winding through the loads of metal objects and bolting for the hill. I climb up it and then slide down it before racing off toward a section of antique cars that are wasting away. It's like a maze where every turn leads to another turn until I finally reach a dead end. The ravens are thick and cloud the sky as more feathers rain down.

"Oh, Gemma," Stephan calls out and his voice sounds like it's everywhere; beneath me, above me, behind me. "You and I both know how this is going to end. We've both *seen* how this is going to go."

I swallow hard as I sprint in the other direction toward a mid-sized car with a concaved roof. I pry open the door, then duck inside, lying down on the torn leather bench seat and then maneuver the door shut. The fact that Stephan knows about my nightmares and knows what I've been seeing makes me wonder if Nicholas has been tapping into my future and replaying it to Stephan.

"If you'd just come out, it'd be simpler," Stephan says and I hold my breath at the nearness of his voice. "I'll make it quick. I promise."

My chest heaves as I struggle for air and fight to remain still. Nervous energy is charging through me and my heart is beating so loudly I'm worried Stephan can hear it.

"You know, it could be beneficial," he tells me, his footsteps loudening. "Feeling evil is a lot easier than feeling things like love. Although, I know you don't understand that emotion yet."

I throw my hands over my mouth as I spot him through the window with his back turned toward me. How does he know that I haven't felt love yet?

"You're probably wondering how I know you haven't felt that appalling emotion that only belongs to the weak minded." He angles his neck back and stares up at the ravens in the sky, a halo of black feathers around his head. "How could I possibly know that you haven't been in love with anyone, even my son . . . although, I think he's probably getting there with you." He turns to the right and starts walking toward a small dirt hill rolling in the distance. "See, here's the thing. You two were never meant to be with each other."

I touch the scar on the palm of my hand, telling myself that he's wrong, that he has no idea what he's talking about. *Forem.* We belong together. Forever . . . maybe.

"But just because you weren't meant to be together," he says. "Doesn't mean you weren't going to try. Let me tell you something, though, love is way overrated. It makes humans weak and stupid." He starts to climb up the hill, his voice growing louder as he brings himself higher toward the grey sky. "It makes you do stupid things like go against everything you've been taught. Alex giving you that locket was very wrong of him and made it impossible for me to get to you, at least for a while."

What the hell is he talking about? Impossible to get to me for a while. Why?

"It doesn't mean I couldn't try," he says, standing on the hill with his arms folded. "Although, trusting the Fey to bring you to me might have been a stupid mistake. They always did like to dither around. Keeping you at his house like that; I should have had you here days ago. I knew where you were, but Alex's sacrifice—taking the impact of the *memoria extracto* like that—made it impossible for *me* to get near you."

I have no idea what's going on. Alex's sacrifice kept Stephen away from me. How?

I can't see him anymore and it's making me even more nervous, especially since he's stopped talking. I can't even track his voice. I remain as still as I can, breathing through my nose while trying to stay calm as raven's caw and litter the land with feathers. Then I hear the car door opening, metal bending and cringing, and then a hand grabs my ankle. I scream as I'm jerked out of the car and land heavily on the ground.

Stephan drags me toward the stack of metal boxes, whistling under his breath. I attempt to flip over onto my stomach as I claw at the dirt, but it does no good and the ground ends up tearing a few of my fingernails off. The pain is blinding and for a moment all I see are spots.

Finally, Stephan stops and lets me go. I swiftly roll over and push to my feet to run away, but he slams his foot down onto my back and I fall flat on my face, dirt entering my nose and mouth and I gasp for air.

"You're better off this way," he says as I turn over to my back, coughing to catch my breath. He gives me a kick to the side and I hear a bone crack as the tip of his boot collides with my ribs. He kicks me again and again until my whole body aches and starts to swell and turn black and blue.

I lie in the dirt, tired and heavily sore, gasping to breathe and stay alive. He smiles, pleased at my beaten state, as he reaches into his pocket. Then he crouches down to the side of me, holding up a silvery sharp object with distinct engravings on the sides of it that almost take the shapes of letters but not quite. It looks the like a chunk of metal, but I have a feeling it's more than that.

"You can never love him, you know." He sets the rigid piece of metal down on my stomach, the engravings along the flat sides smoldering neon green. "Every time you two are close to each other, it ignites the power. Once you actually fall in love—in actual, real, genuine, pure, true love—you'll kill the power and yourselves."

I gasp, shaking my head. "You're lying," I choke, wiping blood from my nose.

"Am I?" He raises the piece of metal in front of my face. "Why do you think I've been so dead set on keeping you two unemotional and apart from each other? If you fall in love my star is ruined. It's been told in a vision."

"Then I guess you lose," I hack, clutching my side.

"I never lose," he growls, pricking his finger with the metal and drawing blood, which drips down on me, disgustingly warm and sticky against my skin. "The vision said that it could happen, but that I stop it somehow." He grabs my arm and I struggle to get away as he aims the tip of the metal at my upper arm and then pricks it. "I always win." He drips his blood on my open wound and I gag. "I thought detaching your soul would do it, but apparently not. This way's better anyway. You'll enjoy being evil, Gemma."

"It won't work." I bring my knee up to kick him, but he stomps down on my swollen shin and then strikes me across the head with his arm. I can barely see or feel past the unbearable pain. I just want to die. Fall in love and die. Would it be a good way to go?

"It will work," he assures me and then stabs the piece of scorching metal into the incision on my arm, inserting it straight into a vein. I let out an earsplitting scream as the energy of it violently streams through my blood and singes my skin. "And you want to know why?" He slopes over me, his eyes darkening, showing the evil inside him. "Because you already have evil blood in you, thanks to your father. It's the only way I can put the mark on you."

I open my mouth to protest, but a foul, sinister feeling slithers through my veins and my blood suddenly feels thick like tar. The feeling continues to build, a vile sensation burning feverishly underneath my flesh. It sears into my bones, turns my heart into a pile of ash, and leaves my soul empty.

Empty. My heart keeps beating, my lungs seeking air, but everything else is dead.

When I open my eyes again, Stephan has risen to his feet. I turn my head to the side to see the red and black triangular symbol permanently branded on my skin. It's surprising how easy it is to accept, like it's always belonged there. The more accepting I become to it, the less pain I feel, and I finally just give in and let it own me.

Stephan searches my eyes for life, but there's nothing

in me except a shadow of myself, a rotting corpse, the soulless girl I've become accustom to. "How do you feel?" He asks, tugging his sleeves down.

I search my brain for a response. "Dead."

He grins. "Good." He buttons the bottom of his sleeves back up and steps back from me. "I'm going to need you to stay here for a while, just until I can figure out one more thing; then I'll come back for you."

"Okay," I say simply, staring into the sky at the ravens swooping above me. "But where am I?"

"The Wasteland," he says. "Which ironically enough is a place for broken, discarded, magical objects."

I nod, obeying. "Okay."

"And don't go anywhere," he remarks with a clever smirk. "I know that you can with that power of yours, however I need you to stay here."

"Okay," I agree. "I won't go anywhere. I promise."

"Good girl." He walks off toward a pile of knotted barbed wire and then he disappears, leaving me alone with my new mark.

I remain lying in the dirt, beaten and bruised, watching and listening to the ravens flap their wings as they cry out to each other. Inky black feathers drift down from the sky and surround me in stacks as time aimlessly drifts by. I count the seconds to pass the time, but somewhere I lose track. Everything begins to blend together and the sky becomes lighter then darker as the days change. The ravens grow tired and so do I. Suddenly I'm tired of sitting here and obeying. I don't want to obey. I want to feed the darkness stirring inside me. It's hungry and needs to feed.

Every once in a while I do feel a dim spark flicker inside my heart, begging me to come back, and it briefly warms my chilled core. I know who's causing it and the more it happens, the more frustrated I get.

Finally, I get up and hike across the land, scooping up a saber with a bent blade that's resting in a heap of swords and knives. The ravens fly after me, circling my head as I stride over shallow hills toward the skyline. I stop only when I'm far enough away, then I can open up the box locked inside me. I let the darkness inside me flood out and consume my mind, allowing any trace of my old self to dissipate. Then I shut my eyes and channel my Foreseer energy, fueling it with the evil living beneath my skin.

I picture Alex's sturdy body, dark brown hair, and green eyes as clearly as I can. Once I see him perfectly, I clutch onto him and let my Foreseer power pull me to him, holding onto the saber as I prepare myself to see him soon. Prepare myself to kill him. Kill the electric spark concealed inside my soul, the last speck of good inside me.

Then I'll be nothing other than a shell. A hollow, evil shell.

About the Author

JESSICA SORENSEN IS a *New York Times* and *USA Today* bestselling author that lives in the snowy mountains of Wyoming. When she's not writing, she spends her time reading and hanging out with her family.

Other books by Jessica Sorensen

The Coincidence Series:
The Coincidence of Callie and Kayden
The Redemption of Callie and Kayden
The Destiny of Violet and Luke
The Probability of Violet and Luke
The Certainty of Violet and Luke
The Resolution of Callie and Kayden
Seth & Grayson

The Secret Series:
The Prelude of Ella and Micha
The Secret of Ella and Micha
The Forever of Ella and Micha
The Temptation of Lila and Ethan
The Ever After of Ella and Micha
Lila and Ethan: Forever and Always
Ella and Micha: Infinitely and Always

The Shattered Promises Series:
Shattered Promises
Fractured Souls
Unbroken
Broken Visions
Scattered Ashes

Breaking Nova Series:
Breaking Nova
Saving Quinton
Delilah: The Making of Red
Nova and Quinton: No Regrets
Tristan: Finding Hope
Wreck Me
Ruin Me

The Fallen Star Series (YA):
The Fallen Star
The Underworld
The Vision
The Promise

**The Fallen Souls Series
(spin off from The Fallen Star):**
The Lost Soul
The Evanescence

The Darkness Falls Series:
Darkness Falls
Darkness Breaks
Darkness Fades

The Death Collectors Series (NA and YA):
Ember X and Ember
Cinder X and Cinder
Spark X and Spark

The Sins Series:
Seduction & Temptation
Sins & Secrets
Lies & Betrayal (Coming Soon)

Unbeautiful Series:
Unbeautiful
Untamed

Unraveling You Series:
Unraveling You
Raveling You
Awakening You
Inspiring You (Coming Soon)

Ultraviolet Series:
Ultraviolet

Standalones
The Forgotten Girl
The Illusion of Annabella

Coming Soon

Entranced
Steel & Bones

CONNECT WITH ME ONLINE

jessicasorensen.com
and on
Facebook and Twitter

Made in the USA
San Bernardino, CA
21 January 2016